First published in Great Britain in 2015

by

Ringwood Publishing

7 Kirklee Quadrant, Glasgow G12 0TS

www.ringwoodpublishing.com

e-mail   mail@ringwoodpublishing.com

ISBN 978-1-901514-27-8

British Library Cataloguing-in Publication Data

A catalogue record for this book is available from the British Library

Typeset in Times New Roman 11

Printed and bound in the UK

About the Author

A Fifer by birth, Alan Ness moved to Edinburgh to study and has lived there for most of his adult life. He has made his living as a community worker in one of Scotland's most disadvantaged communities. Alongside this, he has written, recorded and performed music, both solo and in a number of rock bands, including on national radio sessions.

A Man's Game will be his first published novel, though another, also featuring journalist James Donnelly, is waiting in the wings.

Acknowledgements

I'd like to thank Carol Targett for all her support in so many ways, all at Ringwood for the opportunities they offer to new writers, including myself, and Paula O'Connell for help and advice.

Dedication

To Aidan and Cara with love.

Prologue

'Is it possible,' he wondered, *'to have a memory of something which you did not experience? It had been a dream certainly, but it had felt like a memory. Either way, it was almost forensic in its detail:*

The room is large and expensively furnished. Sash windows have been left open to expel an odour like burning rubber, only sweeter.

On one wall, an impressive flat-screen TV is mounted on violet, flower-patterned wallpaper. Another boasts a large, abstract, lavender and yellow screenprint. Bottles and glasses, mostly empty, stand abandoned on walnut table-tops or parquet flooring. It is clear that many people have recently been present.

Nothing can be heard except the low hum of a music system playing no music.

A tall chrome and glass floor lamp illuminates a white-faced man, prone, unconscious, possibly dead. He is wearing a light grey suit and a pink shirt, both stained dark red around his chest. The parquet flooring next to him is also red.

On a pure wool, plum-coloured rug lies a woman. Her blouse is open and she is naked from the waist down. She is unconscious, white-faced and possibly dead. Her limp hand holds a kitchen knife.

Chapter One

Ten years later:

'It went in aff Davie's fat arse. Andy crossed it, a nudged it on and Davie "arsed" it intae an open goal!'

'"Arsed it?" That's no' even a fuckin' word. It was ma knee. A put it in wi' ma knee. Onyway, it was the only goal o' the game so think yirsel lucky a wis there, as usual, in the right place.'

'Well, a'm glad you ate a' the pies 'cause you definitely put it in wi' yir big backside.'

A chorus of 'you fat bastard, you fat bastard,' echoed around the slightly grimy and very steamy lower-league changing room.

*

It was a long journey home from Elgin to Cowdenbeath after the match and Davie Thomson preferred to spend it with his iPod, therefore avoiding further banter. The relative lack of comfort in the coach befitted Cowden United FC's lowly league position and straightened financial circumstances. Davie, however, was used to better things. Tall, big-boned and somewhat awkward, he had always cut an impressive, if not entirely athletic figure. And - with a shock of blonde hair - he was easily noticed on a football field. His strength, however, and natural ability with a football, had allowed him to succeed, despite his ungainly gait, and he had eventually found himself in the Glasgow Athletic first team by the age of twenty-two.

No one really understood what had gone wrong since then. It was true that he'd put on a fair bit of weight, but that had come after he'd slipped out of the team and then down the divisions. He also drank a little too much, but that was hardly remarkable and not, seemingly, out of hand. Pundits had put it down to a change in his attitude. He had apparently, in football parlance: "lost the hunger". He hadn't suffered a bereavement, or been convicted of something sleazy. Nothing manifestly traumatic had happened to him and so it remained a mystery. Though it was a mystery pondered by few.

Davie had gradually adjusted to life in the lower divisions, now a yard slower, a stone heavier and with his blond hair dirtied by the years. His natural talent, however, mitigated against the loss of fitness and the lack of any great desire to win. He was still earning a fair bit more than most of his pals from school and without having to work too hard, so things, he told himself, could be worse.

Unfortunately, they were. He was thirty-two years of age, had never managed to sustain a relationship beyond three or four months, had very few friends and had eventually agreed to move back in with his parents when they realised he was drinking too much.

Davie joined in the football banter as best he could but he didn't have the stomach for it. It wasn't the homophobia, the misogyny or the insults about his weight that bothered him. It was the sheer, unrelenting unpleasantness about … everything, basically. To describe it as negative would be like suggesting there was a minor problem with sectarianism in Scottish football.

There are strategies which can be employed to survive in the changing room jungle. Wit needs to be sharpened, like

3

a stick into a spear. And nothing too lofty – Jim Davidson rather than Eddie Izzard. Learning a few clichéd rejoinders will do, and having them ready as ammunition whenever required. Swear words are important – mainly "fuck" or "fucking" but, imaginative cursing is also encouraged and one needn't fear using words considered especially offensive in other circles. There are no women in the changing room so employing expletives whose original use was as a description of female genitalia need not be avoided. The most important weapon, however, and one that can never be overused, is sarcasm. This is particularly useful as it serves a dual purpose: it gives the appearance of wit without the need for quickness of mind and it avoids demonstrating any genuine emotion except, perhaps, disdain.

Davie could remember when he had enjoyed the camaraderie of the changing room almost as much as he had the actual game, but now he simply went through the motions; did just enough to avoid becoming a victim. As the coach rumbled, causing his stomach to do the same, the darkening landscape rushed by and he tried to lose himself in the consoling chords of the Coldplay album playing through earphones into his head. He found himself thinking about something which had happened nearly ten years before; something which intruded upon his mind whenever there was nothing else demanding attention. Something which made everything else seem hollow and, at times, pointless.

*

Further west, Stuart Robertson lay face down on the physio's couch and enjoyed his after match rub-down. He was still carrying a slight hamstring injury from the Aberdeen game of two weeks before and the club was anxious to keep him fit. They were heading into the last quarter of the season

4

and the league title, and that all-important place in the European Champions League was still up for grabs.

'How does that feel?' asked the physio as he applied a little extra pressure to the injured area.

'No' bad, no' too bad at all. A think it's on the mend. Could you just gi' me a wee rub all over while a'm here?'

'Aye fine, seeing as how you scored, but there's nae extras mind.'

'Fuck off, yah poof, a'm stiff.'

'Aye, well that's what a wis worried aboot!'

'A suppose a asked fur that. Bit ye know whit a mean: a'm an old man now, ye ken?'

'Aye, thirty-two; ye'll be concentrating on yir media career before long. In fact, ye seem tae spend mair time wi' Dougie Vipond than ye do wi' yir wife these days. D'ye sleep over at the Scotsport studio then?'

'Fuck off, a'm jist takin' care o' ma kid's future.'

'Aye and yir next Lamborghini …'

It isn't easy sustaining a career as a top professional footballer. Whilst not as big as some of the European leagues, and much maligned, the Scottish Premier League is still of a reasonable standard and to keep yourself fit and cope with the pressures both on and off the pitch is pretty challenging. This is especially true in the pressure cooker that is Glasgow. Factor the sectarian issue into a situation where there are two very large and historic clubs in a relatively small, working class city and you can guarantee trouble. There are few other places where football carries as much cultural significance as it does in this chaotic conurbation.

5

But Stuart Robertson coped with it all. Of slim build with light brown, copper-tinged hair and naturally chiselled, appealing features, he was once a typical young man around town. Women responded to his "deep, dark" eyes which allowed him to give the impression that he was hanging on their every word. To be fair, he often was. A naturally decent bloke, he was well-suited to the image he had cultivated as the years had gone by; that of a charismatic and well-loved family man. He was the cheeky chappy; the man who coped with all the pressures by never seeming to take them too seriously. The man who had it all.

'Hey, Stu,' was heard a number of times as he made his way through the building. He responded to all with a smile, a wave, and where possible, with use of the caller's first name, when he could remember it. When not, he employed his usual catch-all: "pal". The last call, however, merited more attention:

'Lookin' even lovelier than usual, Dawn,' he offered to the pretty young sales assistant from the club shop. 'Why do those tracksuit bottoms just seem to fit you better than everyone else, eh?'

Dawn blushed happily.

As he left the stadium, he glanced at a plaque on the wall and allowed his mind to pause, briefly, as it often did, on the ex-team-mate for whom that plaque had been erected. Paul Bannerman had been a decent guy, a talented footballer and a good friend. His death, nearly ten years before, had been a heavy blow to Stuart and a cause for mourning throughout the football fraternity and the country as a whole. Stuart still thought about him nearly every day.

*

James Donnelly sat glued to *Sky Sports* in the living room of the comfortable Craigentinny bungalow he shared with his wife and two teenage daughters. He watched intently as each goal came up on the screen from games throughout the United Kingdom.

From time to time, Donnelly supplemented his income as Chief Reporter (East of Scotland) on the *Daily Journal*, with reports of Hearts or Hibs matches. But recently the bias with which this Hearts supporter treated those two teams in his carefully considered pieces had become too pronounced for his employers to countenance, and he had been asked to take a soccer sabbatical.

'That's Kidderminster buggered again,' he murmured to himself, displaying an impressive knowledge of English lower-league football.

His beloved Heart of Midlothian FC had played away to Inverness that afternoon but, as he was still suffering from the after effects of too much drinking at a retiral "do" the night before, he had felt unable to make the journey.

The scores had come in thick and fast in the last ten minutes of the matches and it had been something of a roller coaster ride for Donnelly. Hearts had gone ahead with six minutes to go and their city rivals, Hibs, were one nil down. All was well with the world as far as Donnelly was concerned. Then, in a catastrophic five-minute period, Inverness had equalised with Hearts, and Hibs had put two past Motherwell to win and leapfrog the "Jam Tarts" in the Premier League table.

Donnelly was on his own, his family members well aware that it was best to absent themselves from the living room, if not the whole house, between half past four and five o'clock on a Saturday, assuming Donnelly was not away at a match.

This meant that he was free to swear profusely and he took full advantage of the opportunity.

His wife, Jacqui, however, had only retired upstairs and after Donnelly had thrown the remote control at the skirting board of the opposite wall, she couldn't resist going down and popping her head round the door.

'Did you hear a really loud noise just a moment ago, Jim?' she asked. 'Do you think we've got rats … rats with great big hobnailed boots on?'

Picking up on the sarcastic tone, Donnelly sheepishly replied:

'Eh, the remote control just slipped out of ma hand. I was, you know, just changing the channel.'

'Seriously, I fail to see what pleasure you get out of following football. They never seem to win and when they do, you just start worrying about the next game. Whatever enjoyment you get seems so short-lived.'

'Aye, short-lived but sweet. What you have to understand is this: when you're at a match and your team scores, for about thirty seconds you experience a euphoria so intense, so pleasurable, that it goes beyond anything else that ever happens to you. Except, I suppose, except, well you know ...'

'Yeah, I know James, but that never lasts as long as thirty seconds does it? Anyway,' she continued, 'I take it Hearts got beat?'

'Aye, a'm afraid so.'

Jacqui Davidson – she'd kept her own name on marriage – was a senior psychiatric nurse and enjoyed teasing her husband, particularly with regard to psychological matters on which he took a rather more unsophisticated view than she:

8

'Well can we hurry through the grieving process as quick as possible?' she asked. 'The girls'll be back soon. Come on, I'll help: "Denial" – it must be a mistake, Hearts couldn't possibly lose to Raith Rovers; "Anger" – I hate the manager, the new centre forward, the ball boys; "Bargaining" – perhaps we could ask for a replay because somebody threw a pie at the goalkeeper; "Depression"- I can't cope with being a Hearts supporter, it's not fair; and lastly; "Acceptance" – oh well, what's done is done, time to move on, Ok?'

Donnelly didn't look impressed. He stared at the screen and Jacqui, aware she was fighting a losing battle, headed off to the kitchen in search of a chocolate biscuit.

Donnelly was slumped in an almost prone position on their new, stylish, though restrained, dark beige sofa. He'd wanted something in leather, possibly maroon. The DFS showroom was all out of maroon leather, however, and he had been outvoted as usual by the block female vote. Two daughters and a wife were Donnelly's crosses to bear.

'Too many bloody women in this house!' was his regular cry.

He was dressed for comfort rather than style. His unfailing change from outdoor clothes into jogging-bottoms and "baffies" when arriving home marked the transition from work mode into relaxation.

Donnelly wasn't sure whether to be appalled or delighted by the fact that in his current position his ample belly provided a handy location on which to place a mug of tea. In his mid-fifties his appearance hadn't so much gone to seed as become slightly overgrown: unfashionably long, now greying, brown hair ("it was stylish in the seventies, and a see no reason tae change now") and slightly bloated features made him look like an ex-member of a moderately successful heavy rock band. Or, more possibly, their roadie.

As he scanned the scores and scorers, he absorbed each piece of information and subconsciously checked it against existing data in his football-obsessed brain. He noted league positions, unusual victories, the breaking of an enviable record here, the ending of a goal drought there. Amongst it all he noticed that Davie Thomson had scored for Cowden United and that Stuart Robertson had found the net for Athletic. Without even realising, he connected the two in his mind and for a few seconds touched on the changes in fortunes of those two men who had once been team-mates in the victorious title winning Athletic side of 2001. That, of course, led him to think of the tragic death of Paul Bannerman and the lasting effect it had had on that particular group of players.

*

'Paul Bannerman, Paul Bannerman, that's it. It's brilliant; I can't believe I didn't think of it before.'

Bill Slater, genial, but jaded, editor of the *Daily Journal's* Scottish edition looked up at Donnelly over the top of his less-than-fashionable glasses and screwed up his face.

'What … what … is it a game? Word association? Dead footballers? Jim Baxter … there you go.'

'No, ma series, you know, revisiting celebrated crimes from the past. It's perfect.'

'Are you still wanting to carry on wi' that idea? I mean the last story was a bit of a damp squib, wasn't it. You buried it. We could've gone for the jugular wi' that politician and his dead brother but you came over all Mr. Moral in the end. God knows what got into you. The eventual impact wasn't worth the time you put into it.'

'I know, I know, I lost my nerve on that, I kinda blew it, but this is the best idea I've had for years.'

Slater settled his wiry frame further back into his executive swivel chair. Playing out time until his retiral, and generous pension, he was faintly jealous of the enthusiasm which Donnelly seemed able to muster. It wasn't an emotion he'd felt able to conjure for some time. Donnelly didn't normally get too excited about anything much, to be fair, except maybe Hearts, but, when he did, he was an unstoppable force. Slater surveyed his impressive, if slightly jaded, wood-panelled office and resigned himself to his fate:

'Go on then.'

'Right, well I was thinking about it. You'll remember what happened, I expect, but I'll recap 'cause I know your memory isn't quite what it was.'

'It was 2001; Athletic had already clinched the title wi' three games to go. They were coasting to the end of the season. There was a party at Bannerman's flat after a match. Most of the first team were there and they'd invited some girls back as well – not girlfriends though but lassies with, shall we say, less than impeccable reputations. Anyway, at the end o' the night, everybody'd gone except Bannerman and this one lassie – Avril Gallacher was her name. Obviously, we don't know for sure but it seems that they … did the dirty … and then when he was in bed she'd tried to rob him – cash, some medals, that kind o' thing. Anyway, he heard her, got up and confronted her. She was in his kitchen. He tried to stop her; she grabbed a bread knife and – bang, he's dead.'

'What, was it a special explosive knife - the kind that go bang?'

'All right, not bang then, but what noise does a knife make when it goes into someone's chest? Whoosh? Eh? When the police get there he's dead in a pool of blood and she's unconscious from the alcohol, drugs and God-knows what else. Anyway, the whole thing sends her doolally and it was an open and shut case. She wasn't able to give any defence at all, so she ends up in the mental prison and him in the crematorium.'

'That's pretty much all as I remember it, Jim, but, God knows, it got plenty of coverage at the time. What makes you think you can add anything to the story now?'

'Ah,' Donnelly replied, obviously anxious to deliver his coup de grace. 'What I realised when I thought about it was what happened afterwards. They'd won the title right? And the Scottish Cup. They'd had a pretty good run in Europe. And they were mainly a very young team, full of potential. You would have expected that side to have dominated the Scottish league for the next four or five years, wouldn't you?'

There was no reply from Slater, so Donnelly continued:

'But they didn't, did they? If you look back, most o' that team scattered to the four winds at the end of the season. Only a couple of them remained at Athletic, some dropping into the reserves, others got transferred, ended up going down the leagues. Two or three of them did pretty well – got a move to England, or elsewhere in the Scottish Premier. Out of that whole title-winning side, only one player remained beyond the end of the next season …'

Again, Slater refused to take the bait so Donnelly answered his own, implied, question.

'Robertson, Stuart Robertson. And of course, he's still there yet. Look at the likes o' Davie Thomson. He's slumming it wi' Cowden United these days – gone to seed. A

12

guy wi' his potential – what's that about?'

This time Slater couldn't resist contributing:

'He wouldn't be the first working-class lad to lose the place when faced with the pressures – and rewards – of professional football.'

'Aye, but he's not the only one: Robert Brown, Graham Todd, I could name a few more …'

'Well I dare say that is a reasonably interesting idea, Jim; I suppose the trauma of the murder had an effect on them as a group. It'd make a good psychological study, I'll give you that.'

'Thanks, Bill, and you know, there could be more tae it than that. How do we know that what they say happened really happened? Maybe the lassie's regained some o' her faculties – you never know. Maybe she'll be able tae tell us more about it.'

'Well, be very careful – I'm not wanting a lawsuit for harassment of a mental patient. And, anyway, they'll not let you speak to her.'

'Aye well, Bill, you know me: I've got my ways of getting to the nub of a story – and getting to those that can help me wi' that.'

'Aye, I do know, Jim, but be careful. Go ahead, sure, but this time don't get in any trouble, eh?'

Chapter Two

'There he is, the hero o' the hour, only goal o' the game – can't ask for more than that.' Davie's Dad, Tam, welcomed him home later that evening.

'When Jeff Stelling said you'd scored, we couldnae wait for it to finish.'

'Jeff Stelling mentioned me, eh? A must still be famous. It kind've went in aff ma knee but they a' count, a suppose.'

'It could be the difference between relegation and staying in that league, so you're damn right they all count.'

'D'ye want something tae eat, love?' asked Agnes, Davie's Mum, looking up from her jigsaw.

'Aye, Mum, a'm starvin', a could eat a scabby dug.'

'Well there's nae scabby dugs left but I've some pork chops heating in the oven for you so you can come and get a seat.'

'Thanks, Mum,' Davie replied as he eased himself into a kitchen chair, still sore from his exertions and the few heavy tackles he had taken during the game. Davie towered over both his parents, which had led to a great deal of banter over the years about the accurate identification of his parentage. Blonde headed and thickset, he had been a physically impressive young man but the effort required to keep his weight in check was no longer being applied and he now moved with a lumbering gait.

Agnes fussed over him as he ate his meal. Truth be

told, she enjoyed having one of her boys back home; having someone to look after again. But at the same time she knew that it would be best for him to move on again before too long. Not until they'd helped him get control of his drinking, though. Small, and now a little on the round side, Agnes' features were fine and it could easily be seen that she must once have been slight and pretty, almost petite. She had always moved with a precise delicate manner, but this had been exaggerated by the need to compensate for the loss of fine motor skills caused by her arthritic fingers. She carefully placed Davie's meal in front of him and seemed to take advantage of a suspension in the laws of gravity by pouring his tea unfeasibly slowly.

Tam enjoyed seeing his wife in her domestic element. He was a soft-hearted old man. Grey haired, slight and ever alert, he resembled an ageing whippet. Tam just wanted Davie to be happy, whatever that took, and he was particularly proud of his son's footballing prowess. He had been an amateur player himself and though it had been especially exciting when Davie had played for the mighty Athletic he was almost as happy watching him turn out for Cowden United. There was less travelling for a start.

The family stayed, as they always had, in Dunfermline, conveniently situated just ten miles from the town in which Davie plied his trade. Their semi-detached bungalow was modest, but was still more than they could have afforded from Tam's working days as an electrician's mate and Agnes' occasional shop work. It was Davie who had proudly part-funded the purchase of their home whilst still on Premier League wages. The interior and garden alike were pretty but plain and unshowy.

Dunfermline isn't such a bad place to live as far as small Scottish towns go. It may have its share of less than salubrious housing schemes, but it was once the ancient capital of Scotland, and retains some fine historic buildings and a wonderful leafy extravaganza officially named Pittencrief Park, but known locally as "The Glen".

Davie had spent a great deal of time there as a boy, hanging out with his pals, when he was only an apprentice drinker. He had since become more experienced in that regard.

Agnes and Tam had forsaken their own modest, domestic tippling since Davie had come back to stay. They were happy to settle for an occasional Saturday night binge at the British Legion club in the town. Better, they thought, to have no alcohol at all in the house. After a cagey period of cat and mouse the subject had eventually become fully aired and Davie now knew that they were searching his room when he was out, to find his vodka stash. Of course, this only led to him spending more time in the pub, but they were doing what they could. Since moving home, Davie had hooked up again with a few old school pals who had never left the town.

'Are you going out tonight then?' Tam asked and then avoided his wife's scowl as he immediately realised that his question would be interpreted by her as an encouragement to Davie to drink.

'Aye, a'm meeting some pals at the East Port at nine then we'll probably go tae a club afterwards.'

'D'ye think that lassie'll be there?' Agnes asked.

'Mibbae; she's Robert's girl's best pal so she often is.'

'Well in that case you should try no' tae drink too much. Girls urnie impressed wi' blokes that are always drunk.'

'Well a'm no' always drunk so that's a'right eh?'

'A'm just saying …'

'A know, Mum.'

Agnes carefully settled her full frame into her usual armchair and used the remote control to locate Ant and Dec.

'Lovely young men, those two,' she murmured, 'and talented as well. Which one's which, again?'

*

It was after midnight before Stuart Robertson returned to his prepossessing West End townhouse. His equally prepossessing wife was still up, as was her practice when Stuart had been out on the town. It was easier, she had realised, to scan for the tell-tale indicators of infidelity when fully alert rather than when newly wakened and, literally, in the dark.

Even the best of men are prone to lapses in that department, Jo had told herself many times, and he does get so much temptation offered up to him. He wouldn't be human if he didn't give into it occasionally ...

In just about every other way she felt he was a good man. Well-liked by everyone, he was polite, even to the more demanding fans; he was attentive to her and most importantly, he was a fully involved and loving dad. Brodie was only three years old but obviously doted on his equally doting father. Although Jo was aware, unlike his adoring public, of Stuart's weaknesses and foibles, the overall package was pretty damn good, and she was, by and large, all said and done, pretty much, most of the time, happy.

On this occasion, she could detect nothing untoward and she was in a good mood anyway, with Brodie tucked up in bed and having watched a particularly satisfying rom-com on the TV. She greeted him with a smile and a hug, a hug

17

which led to a kiss which led to a cuddle and then a hand reaching inside the front of Stuart's jeans to find the hardness that was apparent within.

*

Donnelly returned to the office and slowly began to turn it upside down.

'Oh, Christ, what's going on, Jim?' asked Steph, one of his newer colleagues, who was not used to his semi-regular office rearrangements.

'It's like this every time he needs to research a story,' came a voice from behind a computer at the other end of the room.

'I need to find some files; what am I supposed to do?'

'The clue's in the word, Jim: "files!"' replied Steph. 'You're supposed to file stuff so you'll know where it is next time you're looking for it. You know, colour-coding, sticky labels, *filing* cabinets, that kind of thing.'

'Fuckin' hell, sticky labels? Who do you think I am? A'm no' fae Stockbridge, ken? Gorgie Road, born and bred. We don't do sticky labels or colour-coding in Gorgie.'

'Away ye go, you live somewhere in bungalow-land now, with the other middle-class, middle-aged mummies and daddies.'

'I may have moved to more salubrious surroundings, but you can take the boy out of Gorgie …'

Steph was a sturdily-built woman of about thirty-five. Sturdy, but shapely. Her figure was admired by her male colleagues as was her thick dark hair and full-mouthed smile. She thought for a moment whilst she made her way to the kettle. She then prepared to re-enter the fray:

'Here's a revolutionary idea for you, Jim. See these big plastic boxes we have in the office? You know, the ones with the TV screens attached? We call them "computers". All the young folk are using them these days. Why don't you do your research on one of those?'

'She's a match for you, Jim,' came the voice from beyond once more. 'She's got you on the ropes.'

'It's all up here and in there,' Donnelly replied, pointing first to his head and then to the massive pile of paper in front of him. And by the way, "on the ropes"? I don't believe women should be allowed to box; it's not ladylike. Or maybe it's wrestling you're thinking about. In which case I may be prepared to take her on – topless of course.'

'Aye, that'll be right,' Steph replied, "I'm no' going topless wi' you. With the size o' *your* breasts, you'd show me up.'

'Oh! She's definitely ahead on points now.'

'Fuck off, Norman, she's a lassie, you know I don't fight lassies at full-strength. It wouldn't be fair.'

'"Full-strength!" exclaimed Steph. 'The only thing full-strength about you is those sailor's cigarettes you smoke!'

'He's down … and out!' came the voice from behind the computer.

*

'That fucking light, it's driving me mad,' Donnelly railed against the strip light that both flickered and buzzed. 'And as fur Steph, it's no' fair,' he complained to Norman. 'It's like you're fighting wi' one hand behind your back when

19

you argue wi' women. There's certain words you cannae use, certain things you cannae say. I mean, she can make jokes about me having breasts but if I commented on the size of her bazongas she could have me up on a charge of sexual harassment before you could say "Dave McLaughlin".'

'What? Who?' Norman looked confused.

'You know, that guy on the sports desk that lost his job just for complimentin' one of the typing lassies?'

'Oh yeah, I remember, but I'm not sure that telling her that her arse was so tight you could bounce pennies off it was quite the sort of compliment she would have wanted.'

'Aye, and a dare-say he shouldn't have tried to prove it either, but you know what I mean?'

They shared a conspiratorial laugh and considered, with disdain, the curse of political correctness.

Steph returned and, feeling sorry for the older man, enquired as to the reason for his research.

'I've got this great idea for a story, you know, for my revisiting celebrated crimes series?'

'Oh, it's a series is it? I've only seen one story, and it was buried on page twelve.'

"Aye, well a series has to start somewhere, doesn't it? And this'll be much bigger, just you wait and see.'

Steph felt guilty again:

'Sorry, Jim, go on, tell me all about it.'

'Don't patronise me,' Donnelly complained.

'No, go on, Jim, spill the beans,' said Norman.

Donnelly relaxed into his swivel chair and began to

recount the story of the death of Paul Bannerman and what he saw as the inconsistencies therein. He spoke at length, and with some passion, about the effect that the event had had on those who were involved at the time. By the time he had finished, two other colleagues had joined the group and Donnelly was rewarded for his storytelling skills with a round of applause.

'Bravo, Jim,' was the response from his equally venerable sports colleague, Donald Johnston. 'If you could write as well as you talk you could probably get a job as a journalist.'

This brought laughter from around the room and provided the catalyst for people to slowly drift back to their desks.

Norman Campbell lowered himself gingerly into a chair near Donnelly, his arthritic hips giving him much pain, as usual. Tall, and moustachioed, Norman wore a grey suit which matched both his hair and his pallor.

'You sound pretty passionate about this story, Jim, why does it mean so much to you?'

'No special reason,' Donnelly replied, but with Norman looking unconvinced he felt impelled to give a little more:

'Don't you think there's something incredibly poignant about wasted opportunity? Most footballers would never make a lot of money if it wasn't for the game, would they? It's their one chance to escape their surroundings and build a better life. It used to be boxing, now it's football. Quite a few of those lads; the ones in that Athletic team, have gone right back down again – back tae where they started. Now you'd expect that of one or two – getting into drink, drugs, whatever, but so many? I mean Davie Thomson's a perfect example. He cuts a pretty sad figure these days whereas once he had the world at his feet.' Donnelly immediately regretted the cliché and endeavoured to rescue the metaphor by continuing:

'And he probably would have dribbled it past two defenders, rounded the goalie and slotted it home for the winning goal in a cup-final. Rags to riches then back again. Why have so many of them struggled since? Does it no' get your journalistic nose twitching?'

Silence.

'No?'

Chapter Three

'Here he is, the big man - the goal-scoring hero.' Robert Gellatly announced Davie's arrival to his friends at the bar of Johnson's Nightclub in down-town Dunfermline.

'Whit ye drinkin', Davie?'

Davie had been frequenting this place, on and off, since he was still at school. Always tall for his age, he was able to get in with older pals when just sixteen. He would sit in one seat for the whole evening getting through as many beers as his limited finances would allow, whilst lusting quietly over the glamorous, untouchable older women of eighteen or nineteen.

Now he was back, and though he hadn't quite formulated the thought yet, on one level he already found this profoundly depressing. However, it was good of Robert to invite him out with his group of pals, most of whom Davie didn't know that well. And of course, the potential presence of Melanie Ryan was reason enough to brave the nightclub war-zone.

Johnson's, like any other small-town club, or any night club at all, really, had a superficial, lighting-induced glamour. Like monosodium glutamate in sweet and sour chicken or peroxide blonde hair on a wannabe WAG, well-placed and sensitively deployed lighting can offer a spurious attraction to something otherwise very dull. You just knew it would look rather less glamorous in the cold light of day.

Robert Gellatly was Davie's only genuine remaining friend from the old days in Dunfermline. Davie knew it was partly his fault. He hadn't come home that often when he was playing football, in Glasgow, for Athletic. It was understandable, perhaps, that some of his old school friends began to feel that he'd left them behind. But he felt that it worked both ways. They hadn't tried so hard either. And when he did meet up with them, there was always discomfort. Everyone knew he was making a fortune, so should he buy all the drinks so no-one thought he was tight? Or would that make him seem too flash; like he was showing off? Davie remembered an interview in the paper with Billy Connolly where he said that just his presence in a room would make old friends feel like they were not successful; that they had not achieved. Davie understood this and could feel the resentment coming towards him. The vicious circle was completed when he gave up meeting with them altogether.

Robert, or Rab, as he was universally known, was different. He didn't care about Davie's fame. He didn't, it was commonly believed, care about very much at all. Rab just wanted to get through his week at the GPO depot with as many laughs and as little hassle as possible; go to the football on a Saturday and get blind drunk on Friday *and* Saturday night. *Every* Friday and Saturday night.

Somehow, he had managed to conjure up a girlfriend along the way, and a nice girl at that. Susan may not have been the most ambitious of local girls but she was kind-hearted, moderately pretty and seemed genuinely fond of Rab. His friends felt that he had lucked out with Susan, big time.

'Pint of Special please, Rab, thanks.'

Davie surveyed the group; no girls present so far, he noted with disappointment. And of the men, he recognised them all and could remember the names of most. He wasn't sure that they all looked especially happy to see him, though.

There were one or two, he felt sure, who seemed to resent his recent attempts to join their group.

'A heard it wis a fluke; yir goal a mean; went in aff yir hip or yir bum or somethin,' shouted Calum Williamson, stony faced, over the noise of some particularly repetitive dance track.

'It went in aff ma knee but who gives a fuck? It's ma job tae score goals and that's what a did. Anyway, a nivir said it wis a great goal. A nivir even said a'd scored a goal; it wis Rab that brought it up.'

'Well you showed the mighty Elgin City anyway,' replied Calum. 'So, d'ye think Cowden'll qualify for the Champions league this season?'

'Maist o' them wouldnae qualify fur a bath,' was the nonsensical contribution from Paul Macintyre, to raucous laughter from those who had heard him, and amused smiles from those who couldn't but assumed that he'd said something that they would have found funny had they been able to do so.

Davie couldn't be sure if his companions' mocking comments were aimed at him and his reduced circumstances or were just run of the mill insults which Dunfermline supporters felt obliged to make about their local rivals. Truth be told, Cowden United weren't really much in the way of "rivals" to Dunfermline who had, literally, been in a different league from their neighbours for a great many years. Dunfermline supporters still enjoyed putting them down whenever possible, though.

'Ye nivir know, we could lift the Fife Cup this year if wir lucky. We've got Burntisland Shipyard in the semis.' Best to go with it, Davie thought.

As the large group fragmented into two or three smaller ones, Davie found the opportunity to ask Rab if Susan was meeting him later.

'Like you care if Susan's comin'. A know who you want tae see,' Rab laughed. 'Aye, she'll be here in aboot half an oor and aye, she's bringin' Melanie.'

'Rumbled,' replied Davie.

'Y'know, a think yiv got a chance thair. Susan says that Mel disnae find ye completely repulsive. That's probably the best thing a lassie's ivir said aboot ye'.'

'Fuck off; a've had ma moments with the ladees!'

'Aye, when ye were a Premier League superstar, but Davie Dodds probably did a' right fur burds when he wis playin' and look at the pus on him!'

'Naw, mind at school. A went oot wi Sharon Jones 'n' she wis the best lookin' lassie in third year.'

'Aye, right enough,' replied Rab, with a squint smile, 'naebody did understand that wan.'

Rab, Davie and Rab's best friend, Neil Grant, spent the next half hour or so downing bottles of beer at the bar and concentrating on watching the girls dance on a raised area in front of them. Perfectly placed to have the best view of long legs in short skirts, they were happy not to attempt too much in the way of conversation. When they did try to chat they generally found the effort of shouting above the noise of the music too great for them to consider it worth it.

Eventually, though, Susan and Melanie did show up with a posse of four or five other girls, some of whom were attached to some of the men in Rab's group. Two, in fact, were married to guys present but had started the evening apart, preferring to spend some time with their female friends.

'So, Davie, how're ye doin? I heard ye scored today?' asked Mel after Davie had bought drinks for the new arrivals.

'A'm fine, thanks,' Davie replied. 'That's ma eighth o' the season.'

'Great,' replied Mel, already regretting bringing the subject of football up.

'A'm playin' mainly wide right at the moment. The manager thinks a can dae mair damage that way.'

Melanie looked blank and Susan quickly stepped into the breach:

'D'you remember me and Mel at school, Davie; we were two years below ye?'

'Whit? A mean, pardon?' Davie yelled over a mildly euphoric Swedish House Mafia tune.

'A said, "we were two years below ye at school".'

'Really,' Davie replied, 'a didnae know yis went tae Woodmill, a thought ye wir at Queen Anne.'

'So the answer's "no" then,' Melanie joined in. 'Ye didnae even know we existed whilst we wir worshiping you from afar.'

Davie reddened and searched fruitlessly for a reply.

Susan rescued him again:

'She's havin' ye on ya pillock. We do remember ye though. D'ye no' mind that school trip to the battlefields of the First World War. We were the ones that were always singing in the back o' the bus.'

'Christ, were you part o' that crowd? Fuck, a can remember yis now. Yis were wee brats. No' so wee now, though.' Davie coloured again after his last comment. 'A jist mean, yiv grown up, yiv developed; no, a mean; och ye ken what a mean?'

Rab, Susan and Melanie looked at each other and enjoyed a laugh at Davie's expense.

Davie continued:

'A left school at the end o' that year so a suppose that's why a nivir got tae know ye. Anyway, this calls for another drink; whit ye's havin'?'

Davie collected their orders and headed for the bar only to be pursued by Rab. 'No fur you though, Davie, yiv hud three or four a'ready. Yir Mum made me promise tae stop ye getting blootered.'

Their conversation was interrupted by a ruckus from the far side of the room, near the door. The suited and, fully booted, bouncers had reacted quickly to an altercation involving some High Valleyfield lads who were making their presence felt.

'Fuckin' bouncers in here, worse than the punters, jist lookin' fur a fight.'

'Aye, yir no wrong, Rab, and, by the way, you telling me no' tae drink is like Oliver Reed being appointed as the designated driver. A went on tae the non-alcoholic lager after the first two. A really dinnae want tae blow it wi' Mel, ye ken? But a dinnae want ony o' the lads tae know, that's why a'm getting so many rounds.'

'Well done, neebur,' Rab replied, 'this one's on me then.'

*

Jim Donnelly arrived home to chaos in the Donnelly-Davidson household. Ironing, cooking and showering were all taking place simultaneously with varying degrees of panic.

When Donnelly's work colleagues had found out that Jacqui, a senior nurse at the Royal Edinburgh Psychiatric Hospital, had kept own surname after marriage, they had ribbed him mercilessly.

'Big Jim Donnelly marrying a feminist, who'd a thought it?'

This had led to their fourteen year-old twins, Fiona and Katy being saddled with a double-barrelled surname. Usually a marker of the upper-middle class, her children's posh-sounding names made Jacqui almost as uncomfortable as it did her husband. However, it seemed like the best solution at the time and they had told the kids that they could choose to drop one of the names when they were older if they wanted to. This had been Donnelly's suggestion as he realised that on marriage they could gather one, or even, two more names, and so on till somewhere down the line one of his great-grandchildren wouldn't have room to fit their name on the back of their Scotland shirt. Quietly, he had let his daughters know how unhappy he would be if they chose to drop "Donnelly".

He soon discovered that it was Fiona who was bathing, Jacqui who was ironing and Katy who, if not exactly cooking, was watching guard over whatever was bubbling away on the hob.

Twins, Fiona and Katy shared almost identical facial features (small and pretty) and shape (tall and slim). Other than that though, they were different in every way. Like angelic and devilish versions of the one prototype fifteen

29

year-old girl, they had both accentuated their appearance, but in opposite directions. Fiona had 'helped' her naturally dark blonde hair to become light blonde and was very much a "pretty-in-pink" sort of girl. Katy, in contrast, had chosen a darker route and her hair and dress code very much betrayed an interest in some of the more angst-ridden bands of the day.

'Hi, Jim,' Jacqui began, 'sorry, there's no food on for you, I thought we were meeting you at Katy's show. You were going to get something to eat on the way, remember?'

Donnelly did have a vague recollection of such an arrangement though, in fact, the school talent show had completely slipped his mind. He found it difficult enough to know where he should be during his working hours, and he didn't keep a diary outwith work, preferring to think of Jacqui as his social secretary as well as his spouse.

'Somethin' smells, Mum,' came a voice from the kitchen. 'Somethin's burning.'

'Well you're the one *in* the kitchen, Katy, how can't *you* tell what it is? Look in the oven, eh?'

There was a pause before Jacqui suddenly thought and began to shout: 'Remember to use …'

'Aaagh,' screamed Katy.

'… the oven gloves …' Jacqui tailed off, aware she had been too slow. 'Run your hand under cold water, love … for at least ten minutes. I'll get some arnica.'

'Yeah, then I'll do some chanting and present an offering tae Wicca,' said Donnelly, unconvinced of the efficacy of homeopathic-type remedies.

'Shut up, Jim, you're not helping,' replied Jacqui. 'I've

30

only been in for twenty minutes and I'm having tae cook a meal and get everyone ready before we leave in another twenty-five. The least you can do is help, not hinder.'

'Sorry, love, what can I do? Will I take over the cooking?'

'Yeah, that would be good.' Jacqui calmed a little before suddenly grimacing and running through to the kitchen. 'Oh my God,' she screamed to Katy, 'I just remembered … your concert … which hand have you burned? Can you play the guitar?'

'Yeah, Mum; don't panic, it's my wrist. I'll still kick ass at the gig!'

'Katy, you know I don't like that kind of talk,' Jacqui replied whilst Donnelly winked at his daughter then made the devil horns sign with his hands and simultaneously stuck his tongue out wide. Katy understood the universal symbol of rock 'n' roll but failed to grasp the significance of the outstretched tongue, this being a reference to the rock band Kiss who, he forgot, were popular long before her time.

The Donnelly-Davidson family were more used to going out to watch their other daughter perform. Fiona was a promising ballet dancer, already working towards her Grade Six exam. The family had sat through countless, interminable ballet shows just about sustained through two or more hours by the promise of two or three minutes of stage-time by their daughter. Katy had never found this equation acceptable and so had long since given up attending the shows. She was pleasantly surprised then when her sister readily agreed to come to see her debut performance playing bass guitar for the Goth-Rock band, Dark Feelings. She, at this point, had not realised that Fiona had a crush on David Anderson, who was due on-stage shortly before Katy, to perform "We're all in this Together" from *High School Musical*. She wouldn't have been able to conceive of the possibility of anyone fancying anyone singing anything from such a movie.

The next twenty minutes were a blur for Donnelly as he coped with rescuing the burnt remainders of his family's meal; choking on the combination of steam and perfume left behind by Fiona in the bathroom; and spluttering at Katy's transformation from a pretty teenager into a black-clad, deathly made-up "creature of the night".

Meanwhile, taking advantage of the diversion caused by her sister's appearance, Fiona had slipped out and into the car wearing a skirt at least three inches shorter than that which Donnelly would have found acceptable.

As he was about to get into the second-hand *Espace*, Donnelly noticed and yelled:

'Fiona, get back in and change that skirt. No way are you going …'

'No time, Jim,' Jacqui replied.

'Please, Dad, a can't be late,' Katy pleaded.

Donnelly swallowed his anger and Fiona beamed in the back.

Chapter Four

'Yeah, Bella Como; it's in Partick … Dundonald Street, just round the corner from Adamson Crescent; it's wee, discreet,' Stuart Robertson explained to the man on the other end of the phone.

'Fuckin' hell, Stuart, ye'd think we wur organising a drugs deal; is thir a password or anythin'? A jist thought we might get together fur a pizza,' replied John McDougal, ex Glasgow Athletic team-mate.

'This is no' Arbroath ye know,' replied Stuart, referring to the other man's current posting in the north-east with Arbroath FC. 'We're in the goldfish bowl in Glasgow. If a go oot during the week, someone lets the press know and before long thirs a reporter fae the Record splashing ma coupon all over the papers wi' a pint in ma hand and the headline: "StuRob breaks team rules – drunk on a Tuesday!"'

'A remember, ye ken,' replied McDougal, weary of Stuart's regular, thoughtless slights, 'a played two seasons fur Athletic, mind?'

'Of course a mind, John.' Stuart softened his tone, 'could ye jist indulge me though, eh?'

'Aye, of course; nae problem, pal. By the way, I'm gonnae bring Mark, is that a'right?'

'Mark? Mark who?'

'Mark Sinclair, ya stupid cunt, who d'ye think?'

Stuart's face creased as he realised who McDougal was talking about.

'Oh, that Mark, right, aye, a suppose so; whit's he up tae these days then?'

'No' much, a'm afraid,' McDougal replied, picking up on Stuarts lack of enthusiasm. 'On the dole, eh? But ye ken, we could cheer 'im up a bit; gie'm a good night.'

'Aye, a dare say. See you there at seven-thirty then, John.'

'Smashin', Stuart, see you then.'

Stuart sat in silence for a few minutes, pondering the phone call, before making his way through from his beautiful wood-panelled hall to his beautiful shiny red and chrome kitchen.

'Fuck, Jo, that new coffee machine may look good but it disnae half make a lot of noise.'

He glared at the gleaming Italian design classic.

'Aye but wait till you taste the cappuccino, darlin', ye'll not be complaining then.'

'A'd be happy wi' Maxwell House and nae racket tae be honest.'

'Oh, Stu, what's up?'

'Ach, it's nuthin'. Dinnae you worry.'

'A'm not worried; just wondering what's the matter. That's what I'm here for y'know?'

'It's jist; a said a'd go for an Italian wi' John McDougal but he's bringing Mark Sinclair wi' him.'

'Yiv never liked that guy have ye? What's that about?'

'Nah, it's no' that a dinnae like him. It's jist … he's a bit of a loose cannon and well, he makes me uncomfortable. It's hard tae explain.'

Jo knew Stuart to be an unusually carefree sort of person and when he did get quiet or pensive, it was usually connected to one thing. Or rather, one person.

'Paul Bannerman,' Jo replied. 'Is this about him, love?'

'Aye, a suppose. Being wi' these guys brings it up fur me. But also, a feel uncomfortable about how things have gone since; kinda guilty.'

'You know you've got nothing to feel guilty about, love. You've made the best of things. And that's about strength of character as much as skill on the park. You deserve everything you've got. It's not your fault if others don't have as much about them as you.'

'A know, darlin', a really do,' Stuart replied and succumbed to a warm hug from a sympathetic Jo.

*

'That's another boy who gave up the game; this is even worse than I thought,' said Donnelly to no-one in particular. Steph was the only one within earshot who was inexperienced enough not to realise the importance of avoiding eye contact with her older colleague. Still fairly new to the office, she didn't appreciate how easy it was to get sucked into Donnelly World and find yourself doing his work for him, rather than your own.

In Donnelly World, one could – or at least Donnelly could – completely avoid responding to conversation, requests for help and the like, from anyone else in the room, dominate the space by pulling out reams of files without regard to the comfort or personal safety of others, and comment, indiscriminately, but usually abusively, about anyone else's manner, opinions or language, without expectation of

35

recourse. Also, in Donnelly World, one could - or at least Donnelly could - expect help, sympathy, approval and constant refreshments from anyone unpractised enough not to avoid his searching eye.

In a leaving speech, a previous editor had described him thus:

'Somehow he manages to combine the lack of empathy of an Asperger's sufferer with the outbursts of somebody with Tourettes. Throw in the sociopath's lack of moral responsibility with the manipulative characteristics of Borderline Personality Disorder and you have the unique mix that is our Donnelly.'

Strangely though, almost everyone, grudgingly, found him likeable.

'Graham Todd,' Donnelly continued, 'once a tenacious and talented left back, works for his Dad now, cleaning cars. He left Athletic at the end of that season, lasted a year with Montrose then left the game. Jim Forrester, hard man defender/bouncer in a pub on Lothian Road. Got a bad injury right enough but why did he no' come back fae it? Robert Brown, nippy winger, runs a bar in Bradford or Salford or somewhere – wait a minute – Castleford, that's it – I knew it was somewhere northern English wi' "ford" at the end. He went down to play for Halifax Town – lasted a few seasons but didnae set the heather on fire; ended up wi' enough to buy a bar right enough.'

'Jim, I do believe you've been following my advice and using the internet for a bit of research,' Steph replied, eyes wide.

'Ye ken fine well, I'm perfectly capable o' skatin' the 'net when I need to, but no, on this occasion I didn't need to.'

Steph stifled a giggle and instantly decided to resist the temptation to correct her colleague, preferring to leave him ignorant and vulnerable to future humiliation.

'Enlighten me then, how did you carry out this extensive research?'

Donnelly smiled smugly then replied:

'Simple, I asked the new temp tae do it for me, the lassie wi' the long legs.'

'That'll be Helen then – it'd be nice for you to remember her name at least if she's gonna do your donkey work for you.'

'Why keep a dug and bark yirsel', that's what I always say,' replied Donnelly, replacing her equine metaphor with his canine effort.

'You've a lovely turn of phrase, Jim, and not at all insulting to women.'

'Aye and inaccurate too, if I'm honest, she's a doll no' a dug, that's for sure.'

Steph rolled her eyes, made a "pfhh" sound and used her disgust as fuel with which to travel, metaphorically, out of Donnelly World and back to her own research.

Donnelly continued to read through the results of Helen Lockhart's work, the information which he found, at times, enlightening but more often confirming, what he already knew. He learned that Brian Ferguson was back in Paisley, unemployed; that Derek Ramsay was player/coach at Stenhousemuir and that Andy Stevenson, goalkeeper at the time, had apparently lost his nerve and now worked in IT in Newcastle. He knew, of course, that Ally James was still in the Scottish Premier League with Dundee United and that

Steve Darling was still scoring the odd goal for Ayr.

Helen had, foolishly, lumbered herself with even more work when she had asked Donnelly if these findings were really so remarkable. Perhaps most good teams would yield a similar range of successful and not-so-successful players ten years on, she had suggested. It wasn't the case though. Having carried out what she described as "control" experiments it could easily be seen that this particular group of colleagues had fared particularly badly. For so many to have gone, so quickly, from such success to "nowhere" seemed pretty much unique. Donnelly felt vindicated that his well-honed "hunch" instinct was still in such fine fettle and he celebrated with a lunchtime visit to the pub.

*

McDougal and Sinclair were in situ when Stuart arrived, just five minutes late. On mentioning Stuart's name they were taken to a good table, in a booth, towards the back of the small restaurant. Bella Como yielded to no other establishment in its determination to leave no Italian restaurant cliché unexploited: candles in round wine bottles – check; fake greenery on netting coming from the ceiling – check; red, white and green plastered everywhere – but of course. It was out of the way, though; the food was great and the manager discreet.

'*Buon Giorno,* Signor Robertson,' Stuart was greeted by the portly proprietor of Bella Como. Antonio Pessotto spoke fluent Glaswegian when off-duty, having lived in the city since he was nine years old. However, professionally, he affected an almost parodic Italian accent as he felt this was part of the restaurant experience for his customers and hence, good for business.

'Your friends are ina the back booth, Signor, *benvenuti*!'

Manly hugs were offered and exchanged between the three old colleagues as Stuart eased his way to the back seat of the booth.

'Lookin' good, you two,' he began, though, in truth it was obvious that Sinclair did not.

'And you, man; great to see you,' offered Sinclair with a genuine smile. He was of medium height but was painfully thin with mousy hair and a wispy beard which looked as though it had taken all of its owner's energy to almost achieve.

'You look, eh; well you look jist like you do on TV. A see mair o' you than ma girlfriend these days, the amount o' time yir on the box,' McDougal began. As befits a serving professional player, he was fit-looking, tall, slim and full of nervous energy. He kept his dark hair short and wore a more-than-reasonable amount of tasteless "bling".

The three exchanged a good five minutes of mildly uncomfortable and banal pleasantries before settling on a conversational diet of shared memories and general football chat. Stuart became aware of the occasional head peeking furtively into the booth and he correctly assumed that word had got round of the presence of an Athletic football player in the establishment. This was not good news, it wasn't just the potential paparazzi attendance that frightened Stuart; there was also the possibility of aggro from supporters of Athletic's "great" rivals: Glasgow Rovers.

The word "rivals" is wholly inadequate to convey the depth and complexity of the relationship between these two venerable football clubs. It completely fails to encompass the hatred, the differing - and largely opposing - cultural traditions; the historical baggage and, of course, the hatred (well worth mentioning twice).

Stuart was, therefore, a little distracted as the conversation moved on to what everyone was currently up to. The others both knew all about Stuart's successes and it was when they took their turns that Stuart betrayed his less-than-close attention. This riled them both, particularly Sinclair. He had, understandably, been feeling self-conscious about his current employment status but had hoped for at least some attention to his plight, rather than this apparent disinterest.

He decided to up the ante and dropped the bombshell.

'A'm hooked, man.'

This got Stuart's attention:

'Aw fuck, what on?'

'Smack, what'd'ye think?'

'A don't know,' replied Stuart, 'a wis jist askin'.'

'Aye a ken; that got yir attention though, eh?'

'A'm sorry; it's jist, folk have noticed a'm here; a'm just waitin' fur trouble, noo.'

'Fuck, Stu,' McDougal interjected, 'it's no' aw aboot you.'

'Christ, John, a know; it's jist, well it's got worse since you played here. And wi me on the telly and everythin'. Anyway, back tae you, Mark, whit are we gonnae dae aboot it?'

This was what Sinclair was hoping for. 'Thanks, Stu. A hate tae say it but a'm needin' some dough. A'm practically down an' out.'

'A don't know if that's a good idea, Mark. Yir gonnae spend it on gear aren't ye?'

'Nah, man, a'm tryin' tae get ma shit thi gither; will ye help me or no'?'

'A'm no' so sure, pal; a'm jist no' sure.'

Sinclair shifted uncomfortably. Avoiding either of his companion's eyes, he began again:

'It wisnae this back then, wis it? Ye ken, when "it" happened. It wis a' fur wan an' wan fur a' – fuckin' musketeers, man. We'll all stick thi gither. That wis you back then. Changed yir tune noo.'

'It's no' that, Mark. A'm thinkin' o' you; what's best fur you.'

Sinclair's eyes narrowed:

'Whit's best fur you though, eh, Stu. Whit aboot that? Wi millions in the bank and the dolly-bird wife.'

'Whit are ye inferrin', Mark?'

'Nuthin', Stu, jist talkin' aboot mates stickin' the gither, that's a'.'

Stuart balked slightly at the use of the word "mates" but made a quick decision nonetheless:

'Tomorrow,' he murmured, reluctantly. 'One o'clock at the Royal Bank on Argyle Street. Just this one time though, then get yirsel' thi gither, eh?'

'Aye, thanks, pal, a wisnae meanin' anythin', like.'

'Whit's that noise?' McDougal asked.

Before anyone could answer Toni Pessotto had appeared.

'Oot the back boys, right noo. Thirs guys wi cameras and

41

a crowd wi' Rovers' scarves! Fuckin' hell! It's chaos oot there. A presume ye parked in the usual place?'

'Aye Tony, and thanks, as ever. A'll square up wi ye in the next few days – wi' a bit extra, of course.'

'Nae problem, Signor Robertson,' Pessotto called as they exited. '*Arrivederci!*'

Chapter Five

'Right, in ye go ya bender, we're a' finished,' Andy Parks shouted to a tired and humiliated young footballer as he left the communal showers and went into the team dressing room.

'Dis he really need tae wait fur us a' tae finish before he gits in?' asked Jim Davies, a newly established full-back in the Cowden United team.

'Aye, he does; he's a fuckin' poof and he's no' getting' tae share the showers wi real men. A'm no' havin' 'im staring at ma package while a'm tryin' tae git clean.'

'He says he's no' a poof; what's wrong wi' jist believin' the guy?'

'Listen, a'm captain so dae whit yir telt, right? A'm no riskin' it. A cannae understand why the gaffer brought 'im in. He's got a rep' and a've got it on good authority fae Craigsy at Albion Rovers thit he used tae git a hard-on in the shower when he wis thair. Whit are you, 'is bum-chum?'

'Naw, naw, course no'; a wis jist feelin' a bit sorry fur the lad, that's aw.'

'Well stop it or you'll get a rep' tae.'

'*You* ken whit a'm sayin', Davie, eh?' asked Parks.

Davie had been concentrating on tying his shoelaces and avoiding eye contact during the conversation. As a senior player, Parks often looked to him for back-up when he needed to assert his authority in the dressing room.

43

'Aye,' Davie replied, 'a mean, if he's a poof, it's probably best, a suppose; ye wouldnae want …' He tailed off as Brian McDermott, the young man in question, sidled into the room, covered with a towel, and made his way to a seat in the corner.

Davie glanced at the boy's horrified features, his skin still blotchy from teenage acne, his eyes red and raw.

'A' right neebur,' he said, 'nae offence, like, bit ye can see Andy's point, eh?'

McDermott looked disconsolate. He fought back the tears and said, quietly:

'A've goat a girlfriend.'

There was a momentary silence before a voice from elsewhere in the steam of the dressing room replied:

'Is that whit ye call 'im? Dae ye's take turn aboot?' To the accompaniment of raucous laughter, he continued:

'Ur you the giver, like, or dae ye take it as weel?'

McDermott turned away towards the wall to hide the few tears that had forced their way out. He finished changing as quickly as possible and left without another word.

The dressing room was quiet after that, each player making small talk with those in close proximity.

'That wis a tough session, like,' began Parks. 'A've definitely earned a pint … or three. You comin' tae the pub, Davie?'

'Eh, naw, a cannae thi night; a've got somethin' on,' he responded, hesitantly.

'Oh,' replied Parks, affecting a posh accent, 'I'm sorry, gentlemen, it appears that Mr Thomson cannot join us for a refreshment in the local hostelry this evening as he has a prior engagement. Pray tell, Mr Thomson, do you intend to get yir end away this evening?'

The atmosphere in the room warmed again.

'There's nae lassie'd go near im,' came another voice. 'It's either a prossie or he's jist go'n hame tae watch some porn.'

'Naw,' replied, Jim Drylaw, 'thir's probably still one or two *old* birds thit can remember when he played fur Athletic an' might think he's worth a shag. They'll think he could introduce them tae Stuart Robertson or someone.'

'Some chance, eh?' Parks replied, 'a bet StuRob hasnae stayed in touch wi' the likes o' Davie. You been hobnobbin' wi' him and 'is beautiful wife recently, Davie? Canapés at the Ubiquitous Chip, eh?'

'A'll have you know, a do see Stu fae time tae time. His number's in ma phone as a matter o' fact. A nivir call 'im though 'cause he's a wanker. He's Mr Palsy Walsy on the telly bit 'es a bit up 'imsel' in real life, like.'

'So is it a burd, then? The night?' Drylaw asked.

'Aye … well, kinda.'

'Aw, Christ,' Parks replied, 'this is worse than a thought, is she pre-op or post-op?'

Davie had to wait for the laughter to die down before replying:

'Fuck off; she's definitely a lassie. A jist don't know if it's actually, ye ken, a date, like. It was a' arranged through ma mate, and 'is girl.'

Davie wondered how he'd allowed himself to get dragged

45

into a conversation about his private life. He was aware that he'd forgotten the rules; short, sharp, funny and preferably disgusting replies to all questions about women. Why hadn't he just said he was on a promise with a hottie and left it at that?

Parks began again in almost avuncular style:

'Yir goin' oot tae eat or fur a drink, right?'

'Aye.'

'She's a lassie, and you're a guy - more or less, anyway.'

'Aye.'

'Well it's a fuckin' date then. Make sure ye git a shag oota 'ir, eh?'

'Aye,' said Davie, recovering his composure, 'a'll get a shag all right, dinnae you worry. A'll nail 'er before we even leave thi restaurant!'

Davie left the room to general cheers of assent.

As he drove home to Dunfermline on the route known locally as the Cuddy Road, he turned on the radio, tuned to Radio Scotland and heard a familiar voice:

'Of course, none of us who played with him will ever forget him; Paul was not only an outstanding footballer but he was a gentleman as well. I very much welcome this idea. I think bringing all the boys together for another testimonial, after ten years, will be a great way to keep his memory alive. And if we can raise a substantial amount of money for the hospice then that's even better.'

'Have you kept in touch with your team mates from that time, Stuart?' asked the Radio Scotland interviewer.

'Oh yes, great guys; I see them quite a lot; I just saw

John McDougal and Mark Sinclair the other night – real characters. Brian Ferguson, Ally James, Davie Thomson – all brilliant.'

*

Davie started at the mention of his name and was suddenly filled with more emotion than he knew how to handle. Tears ran down his face as he thought of how his life had changed since then; about the booze, the money, the loss of all that adulation, which had felt like love, and the tragic and terrible events of that evening in a Glasgow flat.

'A'm brilliant a'm a? How wid you know? Wi' yir fancy wife and yir fancy car. Ye havnae spoke tae me fur months.'

Davie drove on autopilot as he ranted:

'Whit we went through! Whit a went through! Whit a did! It's mibbae jist a sad memory for you pal, bit fur me, naw, it's what a live wi' every day.'

'Fuck you, Robertson, fuck you!'

He struggled to see through the tears and the drizzle, the windscreen wipers helping with one but powerless to affect the other.

*

'Fuck you, Robertson,' Donnelly muttered towards the direction of the office radio as he listened to Stuart's interview, sitting alone with his papers, everyone else having left for the evening. 'Another testimonial,' he thought, 'the whole country's gonnae be talkin' about this again. Somebody else is gonnae come up wi' ma bloody idea. There'll be documentaries all over the bloody place. Fuck … fuck!'

47

'Bloody hell, Donnelly, if no-one else is around you actually argue with the radio! That's too good to be true.'

'Where did you come from, Steph? I thought I was on my own.'

'Evidently, though it seems that that doesn't stop you getting into a fight. I'd only popped out for a smoke. Anyway, what's your beef? What's getting you so worked up?'

'Ach, I've just heard that they're having another testimonial for Paul Bannerman – ten years on. The media'll be flooded wi' articles and retrospectives. Ma wee story'll get lost. I can't believe it. Well, I can – it was obvious really – that there'd be some stuff - but this!'

'Tell you what,' Steph replied with a small smile, 'how about you buy me a bite to eat and I'll let you bore me a bit more about this story and how it's all gonnae go belly-up?'

'I'm no' needin' an agony-aunt,' Donnelly replied, though the prospect of some face-to-face time with Steph did, admittedly, appeal.

'Aye, I know, but I could do with a free meal, so it sounded like a good excuse.'

'Are they not paying you well enough here, Steph?'

'As a matter of fact, not really. This is a second career for me. I've taken a drop in pay to come here; following my dream, I suppose. And now that I'm on my own again …'

She paused, and Donnelly imagined that this was said with a knowing look.

'… I suppose I'm kind of skint.'

'Right, you're on,' Donnelly replied, 'get your stuff, yir pulled!'

As he got himself ready, Donnelly thought about Steph and realised that he had been doing that quite a lot over the few months since she had joined the team at *The Journal*. He liked a woman who would take him on – that was, of course, one of the things that attracted him to Jacqui, he realised, with a pang of guilt. Why guilt, he thought? He was simply going for a business dinner with a colleague. An attractive female colleague, though. And one who was maybe hinting about her availability?

He'd long since lost what little ability he may once have had to gauge any interest in him from a member of the opposite sex but he had a feeling that there was something there. 'Why?' he asked himself. Failing to think of a single reason, he left that train of thought behind and moved on.

Donnelly liked to think that he and his wife had a kind of "open" relationship. This was based on an alcohol-inspired conversation twenty-five years earlier during which they had agreed that they should be allowed to see other people in order to avoid their marriage ever becoming a prison. It had never been mentioned since, and if he was honest, Donnelly would have to admit that Jacqui had almost certainly forgotten the conversation by the next morning. However, it allowed him to indulge himself in situations like these, convincing himself that he was doing nothing wrong, though never having the courage to actually follow through.

The two made an unlikely couple as they left the office and walked down the road towards their eating place of choice: he, unkempt and hopelessly anachronistic, was dressed with comfort in mind whilst she, with her full figure packed into a tight skirt and blouse combo, was clearly "dressed to impress".

The street was busy with the after work office crowds

who fill Edinburgh's bars from Friday late-afternoon onwards. Mixed groups moved noisily from pub to pub, the men with ties removed or loosened and five o'clock shadows now worsened by seven. The women having refreshed their hair and make-up but with their eyes betraying an already considerable alcohol intake.

Within a few minutes they had arrived at The Tun, a multi-purpose building including offices, bars and restaurants. Built to exploit the possibilities afforded by the nearby siting of the Scottish Parliament, the subsequent arrival of a new home for *The Scotsman* newspaper and the influx of other businesses, it was a very popular venue.

Donnelly had been unsure of going there, popular as it was with other journos, and expensive to boot. However, he reminded himself of the innocent status of their assignation and decided to thole the expense.

As Steph ordered her meal, Donnelly noted how she charmed the waiter with her warm, open and confident manner. In the low and coloured restaurant lights her sharp features were softened and her thin, yet very red, lips seemed to offer an invitation. To what? He couldn't be sure.

'Fuck,' Donnelly thought to himself, 'I'm like a love-struck teenager. Fuck. Pull yourself together, man.'

'Really, Jim,' Steph offered as they waited for their first course, 'this could work to your advantage. You've got a head start on the story. It could make a much bigger splash as long as you …' she tailed off.

'As long as I what?'

'Well, the thing is, you need to uncover something. And that's what you do, yeah? If you can come up with an angle – something new, then the public interest in the whole thing could mean that you make a really big impact. That's *if* you come up with something.'

'What; and you think I won't?'

'No, I think you will – if there's something to be found.'

'Well I'm sure there is. There is such a thing as a hunch you know. I really believe that. And if anyone's hunch gland is well-developed then mine is.'

'I think that's enough about your well developed glands Jim!'

'God, you're worse than the men, Steph.'

Steph's trout with tagliatelle, mussels and saffron cream arrived just before Donnelly's steak and chips and there was a lull in the conversation whilst they organised themselves and began to eat. It was Steph who began again with a question for Donnelly:

'So, Jim, using your legendary "hunch gland", what do you think is going to be the key to this story?'

'Good question, lass,' Jim replied, immediately regretting his patronising tone which he feared emphasised the gulf in ages between the two.

'Thanks very much, lad,' Steph could not resist replying.

Slightly flustered, Donnelly continued:

'… and one to which I have an answer, the girl – she can unlock it all. If I can get tae her, I can get tae the nub o' the story.'

'Yeah, get to her in more ways than one. Is she not in a mental home? You'd have to get to her, physically and then, you know, *get* to her in another sense.'

51

'I know,' Donnelly replied, his excitement causing him to make the elementary date mistake of talking with his mouth full. But it's not a date, he reminded himself. Either way, he was sure he saw Steph flinch slightly at the sight of the half-chewed mouthful of steak briefly on display.

'But this is what I do,' he continued, 'get to stories, get to people – I've got a plan.'

'Pray tell.'

'Nah, I'll tell you after. Suffice to say, I know a man ...'

'Aye, I bet you know a lot of men 'round Edinburgh.'

Donnelly wasn't quite sure how to take that, so he continued:

'If I can get her tae make some sense then I'll bet she's got a story tae tell; a story that might be different from that of Stuart Robertson and his cronies.'

'You think they're lying then?' Steph asked with some force, incredulity evident in her tone.

'I'm no' sayin' that,' he replied, 'no' yet anyway. You know, sometimes there's more than one truth, more than one version o' it anyway. I just feel there's another story to be told.'

'And you're the one to tell it, eh, Jim. James Donnelly: fearless fighter for truth!'

Donnelly smiled at her joke and admired the way her tongue momentarily flashed across one side of her mouth before she delicately wiped her lips with her napkin.

'So, talking of uncovering the truth, what's your story?' Donnelly asked. 'Divorced?'

'Just come to the point, why don't you? No - long term

relationship, never got married, but just as good as – or as bad. Messy breaking up of house and so on. Gave me the impetus to change things around though – get out of teaching and try my hand at journalism.'

'English teacher?'

'Aye.'

'Where?'

'Broughton High School. It's a good enough school, no complaints there. A comprehensive in the real sense – kids right across the social spectrum, from Stockbridge to Pilton. But, you get burned out teaching; I've no idea how people can do it their whole life.'

'Are you happy you've made the change?'

'Yeah, I am, definitely.'

'And,' Donnelly looked at his drink, 'is there another man around now?'

'Nah, I'm definitely not one of those women who always needs to be with a man, that's for sure. Pathetic creatures. I don't need a man,' she continued, 'but that's not to say I don't want one.' She smiled, with another brief flash of tongue.

'And you?' she asked, 'happily married, two kids, wife too good for you – that's what I hear.'

'Fuck,' thought Donnelly and despite himself, he couldn't manage to disagree:

'Yeah, married; been together nearly thirty years. Two daughters, Fiona and Katy, great lassies …' and with that he launched into a full and obviously very affectionate description of their characters, qualities and triumphs, thereby, he assumed, ruining any remote possibility of a tryst with the lovely, feisty Steph.

After a good ten minutes, Steph was allowed another opportunity to re-enter the conversation and found herself admitting:

'I hate to say it but I'm not sure I'll ever really want to have children. I know that for a woman, that's like admitting to being a secret axe murderer but, there it is; I don't think I want to have kids.'

*

'I'd love to have kids of my own – one day, not for a while though,' Melanie Ryan quickly added as she toyed with an onion bhaji at a quiet table in the Viceroy Indian restaurant in Dunfermline. If the de rigueur décor did not quite manage to live up to the promise of the aristocratic name, it was a perfectly decent local "Indian" and Davie had been happy to agree when Mel had suggested it.

He was not sure how the conversation had got round to the subject of children but what he did know was that he had started to feel remarkably comfortable in the company of this very pretty young woman. Feeling comfortable in the presence of attractive women was a new experience for him and one that he found extremely agreeable. This was despite him having had only one alcoholic drink (having made a point of picking Mel up in his car to provide an excuse for not drinking).

The evening had not started quite so comfortably, Davie having pressed the intercom outside Mel's flat and announced that he was here to pick up Davie. To the sound of her flatmates giggling he had then explained that he, in fact, *was* Davie, and that he had come to pick up Melanie.

She'd come down right away rather than invite him up and subject him to more potential humiliation at the hands of her already tipsy flatmates. There then followed an uncomfortable drive to the restaurant, neither of them wishing to use up any potentially rich topics of conversation in the car on just a five minute journey.

Davie had dressed very smartly, in a suit with no tie, and was very pleased to see that Mel had made considerable effort with her appearance. Her richly coloured short, but not too revealing, dress, high heels and hair worn up, made him begin to, tentatively, believe that this actually was a date. Both Rab and Susan had kept the status of the evening deliberately vague, perhaps at Mel's request, allowing her a get-out clause if it turned out to be a disappointing occasion.

Not only had the restaurant been her choice, Davie noted that the evening, the time, and all the other arrangements had been also. He was more than happy to go along with all her suggestions though, grateful as he was for the opportunity. On the verge of being described anti-depressants from his doctor, this evening represented a major upturn in his fortunes. He'd have let her order for him if she'd wanted to.

The awkwardness had lasted as far as getting into the restaurant and ordering their meals. Davie had got halfway through a joke about a particular menu item and its propensity to bring about flatulence before realising its inappropriateness and backtracking in such a way that the joke lacked a punch line, or a point. He was thrilled, however, to notice Melanie displaying some unexpected nervousness of her own as she bumped into the waiter's arm almost causing him to spill the wine he was pouring.

Once the conversation got going though, it hardly seemed to stop. They covered school, she'd done much better;

friends in common, quite a few as it turned out. Football: he played, she didn't much care. Her work, she explained, he didn't really understand, and then family:

'A have got a brother, actually, but a don't see much o' 'im.' Davie hesitated for a second before thinking, 'what the hell' and continuing, 'he's in Saughton, a'm afraid. Breakin' and enterin' … again and again and again. He's no' a bad lad really, ye ken? A mean he's no violent, like. Well, no really. It's jist … well things've no' gone right for 'im.'

'You don't have tae make excuses, Davie. He's your brother, of course you see the good in 'im. And I'm sure there's plenty o' good.'

Davie smiled, relieved:

'Well, no' that much mibbae. Anyway, ma Mum and Dad are great, they've always looked after me, whatever happened …' He tailed off; concerned about the suggestion he had given of difficulties in his life.

Mel was not concerned though:

'Aye, well we all have our ups and downs and thirs nothing like your Mum and Dad when yir in a scrape, eh?'

'Aye, that's fur sure. Anyway, they were childhood sweethearts and thir still lovey duvey noo. It's a bit gross though, ye ken?'

'Aye, a know what you mean – not that my parents show a lot of affection to each other. They're good tae me though, which is great. A've got a brother and two sisters, and a grand total of five nieces and nephews. A sometimes feel like a'm a full-time professional auntie. A do love them all though and it's no' put me off. I'd love to have kids of my own – one day, not for a while though …'

56

In the softened light of the Viceroy restaurant, Davie felt that Mel looked even prettier than usual. She could not be described as beautiful but her small stature and slight frame combined with slightly sharp but fine features and clear skin led her to being universally described, by male and female alike, as "cute".

Over a shared mango kulfi, Davie felt confident enough to tackle the subject of Mel's employment once more:

'What wis it again, radiographer, eh? So yir no' a nurse or a doctor?'

'That's right; you can train just for that. A wis always good at science and I went tae uni not sure what a wanted tae do. Anyway, a found out about it at a careers fair and eh, a just thought it was fascinating and a went for it.'

'So you do X rays and ...'

'And ultrasound, CT scans, MRIs ...'

'You must be so brainy ... God knows what you see in me. Aw fuck ... aw sorry, a didnae mean tae swear ... a didnae mean that you see anythin' in me ... a mean, why wid ye ... it wis jist, ye ken, 'cause we wir out thi gither ... a know it's no' really a date ... it's jist ...'

'How come it's no' really a date?' Mel smiled, indulgently, 'A thought it was a date. Going pretty well, too a was thinking.'

'And now a've blown it.'

'And why would ye think that? Yir such a sweet guy, Davie; A've had such a good time. Do you want tae do this again?'

Davie couldn't believe his luck:

'Yeah, absolutely … a think … well a just think you're brilliant.'

*

'Well thanks for the meal – and the company,' Steph said as they walked up Holyrood Road in search of a taxi. It was ten thirty on a Friday night and the streets were starting to get busier as those who had been home to eat came out to play and joined those who had hit the pub straight from work.

Just too late, Donnelly spotted a crowd of revellers whom he recognised as being some of *The Journal's* younger staff, coming out of a nearby pub along The Cowgate, presumably in search of an establishment with a little more "edge".

'Hey, Donnelly,' came a high pitched, clearly drunk voice.

'Is that you, Steph?' came another.

'Ooohh!' was the chorus from the rowdy crowd, obviously referring to having caught the older man and younger woman out alone on a Friday night.

'Hi, guys, working late on a story,' Donnelly shouted, trying hard to adopt a neutral tone. 'Just walking Steph, here, to a taxi. No rest for the wicked, eh?'

'Wicked, eh?' someone called out to much laughter, as they moved on, leaving Donnelly flustered and Steph non-plussed.

'What was that about, Jim? You feeling guilty about something?'

'No, of course not, it's just – well you know how tongues wag?' He recovered his composure:

'Young woman seen out with devilishly attractive older man? It'll probably do your reputation a bit o' good, I suppose.'

'Or your libido, you sad old bastard.'

Beaten again, Donnelly said little as he saw Steph into a taxi. Before she entered, they shared an awkward, botched attempt at a chaste kiss before she left him to walk further up the road in search of a taxi of his own.

Donnelly's cab had to park behind an expensive looking people-carrier outside his respectable, if non-descript, Craigentinny bungalow. Katy popped out of the vehicle and Donnelly thought he saw her lean back in to quickly kiss the other occupant of the back seat.

Her girlish skip up the garden path to the house was at odds with the rather darker and more mature mode of dress which she had chosen for the evening. She was predominantly black clad, with the occasional splash of deep purple. She wore patterned tights, a tight skirt, a leather-look bodice (he knew that as a committed vegetarian she would not wear real leather), and a lacy blouse. Her hair was teased out and she wore inky black make-up on a tippex-white face. Her guitar completed the look and gave the clue as to where she had just been. Donnelly knew that Katy's band had their second gig (at an under-eighteens club in the city centre) tonight but was appalled that she would dare to go out dressed like that.

Katy, for her part, had hoped to open the door and skip quickly up the stairs, avoiding any parental scrutiny. She was horrified to hear her father's loud and, obviously angry voice from behind her on the garden path:

'What the hell are you wearing, young lady? And who was that in the back of that car?'

'Aw, Dad,' she cried out.

The commotion alerted Jacqui who quickly came to her daughter's aid:

'Calm down, Jim, it's not that bad – her skirt's not too short, she's just a bit … black.'

'Black? Black!' Donnelly was almost speechless. But not quite:

'She's like a cross between an undertaker and a Halloween witch. And, and, and no … she might no' have a short skirt but it's tight – and all that lace, it's … it's … He tailed off, not wishing to describe the fabric as "sexy" for fear of revealing something about himself. 'And as for the make-up!'

'It was for her gig, Jim, it's stage make-up – just like being in a play.'

Donnelly didn't quite buy this but couldn't think of a response so moved on to his other grouse:

'And who was that in the back of the car? A'm sure a saw her kissing someone.'

'Oooh,' said Fiona, who had joined the throng in the hall. 'You've finally got your hands on Ray then.'

Donnelly was horrified to see Katy nod and his wife smile a warm, indulgent, smile.

'Really?' Jacqui said, 'well he's a good-looking boy, that's for sure.'

Donnelly was almost apoplectic:

'Good looking? Is that all you've got to say? She's only just fifteen.'

'Yes, which is surely old enough to kiss a boy. For heaven's sake, Jim.'

'No' in my opinion it's not. And this'll be the end o' it. Yer no' seein' him again.'

Where previously this would have drawn tears from his daughter, Katy was now of the age to respond with anger:

'Ye cannae stop me,' she shouted back at her Dad, 'yiv got no right.'

'I'll not have you seeing boys at your age.'

There was a blaze in Katy's eyes.

'What about your age then, Dad?'

'What?' asked Donnelly and Jacqui in near unison.

'You're obviously old enough tae see girls, then?'

Everyone looked confused as Katy continued, still spitting mad:

'I saw you – tonight – with a woman – we were passing in the car. You snogged her and she got into a taxi.'

Katy looked slightly horrified at the amazed expressions worn by each and every one of her family in response to her blurted accusation.

Nothing more was said. By anyone.

Chapter Six

Norman Campbell nearly choked on his morning bagel when Donnelly appeared in the office at nine-thirty on a Saturday morning. To see him at all on a Saturday was rare – unless on football related business. But this early?

'Were you chucked out of bed this morning then, Jim?' he asked.

This brought forth a mumble from Donnelly and a wry smile briefly crossed his lips.

'Go on then', Campbell demanded; 'what's the story?'

'Aw nuthin', jist work tae do, that's all.'

'You're a stinking liar, James Donnelly. Somethin's up. Tell me.'

'I said it's nothing. I went for a wee bite tae eat with Steph last night to discuss ma story …'

Norman's eyebrows raised, much to Donnelly's chagrin:

'What? What's wi' the raised eyebrows? It wis totally innocent.'

'On ye go …'

'Well anyway, one o' ma daughters saw her giving me a peck on the cheek as she got into her taxi … and she told her Mum.'

Campbell truly wanted to be sympathetic but this was too good:

'Christ … all … mighty – you're really in the shit, eh?'

'Aye, well kindae. I convinced her it wis innocent but she still wisnae happy. I know she's gonnae want me on a short leash for a while.'

'Stupid question like, but I presume it was innocent? I mean there's surely no way that lovely, fragrant creature could be interested in you?'

'"Fragrant", eh? D'you think this is a Jane Austen novel? Of course it was innocent; I'm happily married. I dunno though - I think I'd maybe have a chance if I wanted tae.'

'Aye, maybe *in* a Jane Austen novel. Or a Woody Allen film, more like. Meanwhile, back in the real world, did you come in here to get out of the way?'

'Yeah, sort of. I couldn't face the potential for pained silence over breakfast. And anyway, I need tae do a wee bit research; a'm having lunch wi' John McDougal.'

'And who's he when he's at home?'

'You know … the footballer … plays for Arbroath, ex-Athletic.'

'Oh aye, this'll be yir big story again: "Dead Footballers Society," isn't it? You're not going all the way up to Arbroath just to see him are you?'

Donnelly smiled, slightly sheepishly.

'No,' he replied, 'I'm paying for him to come down to me. Arbroath are out of the Challenge Cup so he's no' got a match. I'm having to pay his and his wife's fares – she's down for the shopping.'

'So what does an Arbroath WAG look like then?' Campbell asked. 'I don't suppose they need to use the fake tan up there – the "weather-beaten look" achieves the same effect.'

Campbell was on a roll:

'And no need for Chanel No 5, a faint whiff o' smokies does the trick, I'm sure.'

Campbell laughed at his own jokes whilst Donnelly feigned disapproval.

'She's quite a decent looking lassie is Lorna McDougal – stuck with him since his Athletic days. Even though he's a bit of a radge. And they don't actually live in Arbroath. No, they're currently domiciled in sunny Aberdeen.'

'So, where does one entertain the cream of North East society whilst they're visiting the capital then?'

'I thought a Chinese buffet might be good, not too much on the expense account but lots of grub for all. So, anywhere with two Chinese related words repeated in the title will be fine: China China; Wok Wok; Peking Peking; Chopstick … eh … Express. Well you get the idea?'

The two smiled and allowed the conversation to die out as the office began to fill up. Donnelly had laid claim to the office stereo, however, and the bland, nondescript environment was being roughened by the sounds of seventies rock and soul from a compilation CD that he had brought in. Music was important to Donnelly; he wasn't a snob with regard to genre, the most important thing being that almost nothing contemporary should be countenanced. He believed that if something was good enough to last for at least ten years it might be worthy of his, tentative, attention. He had, consequently, just discovered Teenage Fanclub and felt himself to be quite "hip". His car radio was tuned to a local radio station whose slogan: "The best of the sixties, seventies and more," coincided happily with his own taste. He did at times wonder, however, exactly what does that not include?

As Donnelly prepared to leave the office, he overheard one of his younger colleagues expressing admiration for the latest tune wafting across the room:

'Great voice that,' the young man exclaimed. 'It's Paolo Nutini, eh?'

Donnelly nearly collapsed with disgust. 'Paolo who?' he bellowed. 'That's Otis Redding's son – Otis Fucking Redding!'

*

Donnelly was not entirely surprised to see Lorna McDougal arrive at the restaurant along with her husband, Robert. 'They've been living in Aberdeen,' he thought, 'they'll not pass up a free meal if it's on offer.' As a journalist he tended to think using clichés and view the world through stereotypes. He had, in fact, chosen this particular restaurant, on Nicholson Street, precisely because it was a little further away from the city centre and therefore less likely to attract John's wife away from the more popular shopping areas.

'No matter,' he thought, 'we'll feed her quickly and get rid of her.'

The restaurant was a celebrated venue, less for its cuisine and more for its location. In a previous guise it had been the establishment in which JK Rowling was said to have written the bulk of the first Harry Potter book. There was even a plaque in place to that effect. Many's a young person must have partaken of oriental cuisine in order to sit in that hallowed room and dream of wizards.

Donnelly welcomed the pair and reminded them to eat well, the bill being on his newspaper. After ordering drinks, Lorna headed towards the buffet tables and Donnelly took the opportunity to ask McDougal if he minded if Lorna didn't stay too long so they could get on with the interview.

'Naw,' McDougal replied, 'A do mind – a want Lorna tae be here - tae make sure a dinnae say anythin' stupid.'

Donnelly smiled:

'Aye, a can see what ye mean, John, but the thing is a'm gonnae have tae ask ye aboot some quite near the knuckle stuff, man-talk, ken? The sort of thing that boys get up to when they're young, free and single; maybe no' the sort o' stuff you want yir lovely wife to hear aboot.'

'Ma "lovely wife", as you put it, has been around a bit ye ken? She's a woman o' the world.'

'Ok, your choice, A'm just giving you the heads-up, man to man, ye ken – your call.'

Donnelly could see McDougal processing that information and the skinny, but muscular, man finally responded:

'Well maybe we'll stay fur a wee drink after the grub and get tae the nitty gritty then. How big's your expense account?'

'Big enough,' Donnelly smiled and headed off in search of prawn toast.

Conversation was kept fairly general as they ate, punctuated by regular trips to restock, whilst silent, smiling waiters and waitresses scurried around removing plates almost before their contents were consumed. Donnelly got the impression that Lorna was a decent lass who, despite her clichéd appearance: dyed blonde hair, fake tan, etc, was a genuine soul who really cared for her husband. All three spoke of Paul Bannerman with warmth and genuine regard and discussed the upcoming testimonial rematch. Once again, Liverpool FC were to be the opponents, just as they had been ten years before.

Eventually, McDougal had convinced his wife that he was genuinely happy to be left alone with the big bad journalist and that she should hit the shops whilst he enjoyed a few more – free – beers.

Lorna had barely left the room when the tone of Donnelly's questions changed and the subsequent atmosphere at the table became distinctly chillier:

'So, Avril Gallagher – was she a prossie or just, you know, a groupie?'

John McDougal lost interest in his pineapple fritter.

'Hold on – nobody ever said she wis …'

'Oh, come on, John, she wis left alone – wi' a whole football team; everyone else gone home; much drink consumed; drugs? She was hardly a Sunday-school teacher wis she?'

It was a matter of context; on a football pitch, McDougal could have destroyed Donnelly, exposing him as old, slow and hopelessly unfit. In this verbal competition however, Donnelly could use his considerably more developed skills to put his opponent off balance and achieve his goal: information.

'No, she definitely wisnae a prossie.'

'But she was known to you, though, one of those girls who were regulars on the scene – a sure thing as it were?'

'Aye, well, a suppose – she wis a nice enough girl though … she wisnae wan o' the worst … she wisnae, ye ken … a …'

'She wisnae a "chicken head" then?'

McDougal almost blushed at the use of a term he had only ever heard within closed circles, and after plenty of drinks.

'Naw, jist a girl that liked a good time.'

'How many of you did she have sex wi' then?'

'Look, Mr Donnelly, there's no way that you're quoting me aboot this sort o' stuff.'

'No, no, of course no, John – a told you on the phone, this is for background information, no quotes at all, unless approved by you. And, can I remind you, you're gettin' well paid.'

'Aye a ken – go on.'

Donnelly was temporarily distracted by a large piece of something in between two of McDougal's dark yellow incisors:

'Chicken?' he thought, 'or pork, perhaps?'

He suddenly realised he was staring and began again:

'So, how many of you did she have sex with?'

'Wur no' animals, ye ken? It wisnae like an orgy wi' everywan layin' intae the same burd. It wis a party. By and large, folk'll tak a lassie hame tae fuck hir – if they're single. Or a hotel room, or a pal's place. Aw right, occasionally folk wid disappear inta a bedroom, bit nae wan wis keepin' count.'

'So what? Avril played a couple of games o' scrabble, maybe a round of charades, had a few glasses o' orange squash then sunk a bread knife intae Bannerman's chest?'

McDougal winced and Donnelly realised he'd gone too far:

'A'm sorry, a don't mean to be callous – a'm just trying tae get tae the bottom o' it.'

'A jist don't know the answer tae yir question, Mister Donnelly. Who she fucked wis none o' ma business; a jist know it wisnae me. Anyway, yir sayin' she wis left alone wi' a football team and a' that, bit she wisnae. She wis left alone wi' Paul. Everyone started tae leave and she'd been snoggin' 'im earlier on, like, so it wis kind o' understood that she wis gonnae stay.'

'Ok, so no random fucking, but …'

'Excuse me, Sir – I take plate?'

'Yes … yes, thanks.' Donnelly looked relieved as the waitress seemed not to have heard or was discreetly ignoring his profanity.

'Ok,' he began again, 'we really should have started this story from the beginning. Tell me how the whole thing came together.'

As the two gradually moved their heads closer together and reduced the volume of their voices, McDougal explained how the evening had come about and how it had, as far as he knew, ended.

Donnelly had heard it all before, the same story, from each of the players at the time. The same order of events, the same speculation, all, more or less, identical in every detail.

McDougal told of an impromptu gathering in Bannerman's flat; a successful cup tie; a posh meal; a few drinks, a few phone calls; and a few of the usual lassies. He conceded that no regular girl friends (or either of two possible wives) had been invited and that Bannerman's flat was the usual venue for parties of that kind. Bannerman had no girlfriend and had invested wisely in the fanciest, most central apartment.

When a girl entered there she could imagine herself entering a glamorous film-set and she might just be tempted to behave in the manner of many a sophisticated looking actress on such a set.

It was established, then, that sex was likely, alcohol was obvious and that, off the record, drugs were inevitable.

'What was the atmosphere like?' he asked.

'What d'ye mean – it wis a party.'

'Aye a know. But it was a party that ended in tragedy. A'm just trying to establish if there was anything around that night that made sense afterwards, wi' hindsight, given what happened?'

'Nah, no' at a'. You ken whit happened. Everything was fine when we left. As far as a know, they got it the gither, she tried tae rob 'im, he tried tae stop 'ir and she stuck the knife in 'im.'

'A thought you said she wis a nice lassie, and you know, she came from a pretty good background – why would she try tae rob him?'

McDougal already had his reply prepared before Donnelly had finished his sentence:

'One word: "drugs". She wis an addict. A nice lassie, aye, bit an addict a' the same. It's a shame, bit there ye go.'

There was a slight twitch, or perhaps a twinge somewhere in Donnelly's imagination. He asked:

'You seem to feel sorry for her? Even, kind've like her. How come? She killed your pal. It was all her fault.'

'Aye, a ken,' he replied, his tone noticeably changing:

'A nivir said a liked 'ir, and a dinnae feel sorry for 'ir. A'll nivir forgive the bitch.'

'But you said it was a shame.'

'Naw a didnae … well mibbae a did, but a meant it wis a shame for him, fur Paul'

'What – just a "shame"?'

'Yir twistin' ma words.'

'No, John,' Donnelly replied, 'I'm just repeating them.'

The awkward silence was broken by a waiter asking if they wanted further drinks, though with a tone which suggested that he would rather have the table back, if possible.

Donnelly was happy to use the opportunity to bring the meeting to a close. He hadn't learned a lot but somewhere, deep down, a hint, a suggestion of a theory, was beginning to form.

Chapter Seven

Jo Robertson relaxed into the deep red, sleek sofa which she so loved and let her shoes fall from her feet. She'd already had a hard day before having to wrestle with another new security system on the way in and now she felt she deserved a rest.

Having grabbed hold of a rather large remote control device before sitting, she proceeded to lower the lighting, raise the heating and fill the room with the gentle sounds of a chill-out compilation album, all within a few seconds.

Jo enjoyed the trappings of success, most of it purchased through the efforts of her talented husband, but she also enjoyed the fact that she was no clichéd WAG accessory.

The daughter of a research scientist and a university lecturer, Jo had lived in the West End of Glasgow all of her life. She had resisted her husband's temptation to move to one of the wealthy suburbs or nearby small villages in order to spread themselves out in a large, ostentatious manner. Instead, she'd found this tasteful, though still very impressive, townhouse near where she worked and liked to play, and furnished it with the best in contemporary Scandinavian and Italian design. The security issues were a small price to pay.

Her parents had initially been sceptical about her relationship with a famous footballer, rarely out of the papers or off the evening news. They couldn't see what a well-educated, trainee lawyer could see in such a man. That was before they met him. His easy charm, and sharp, though not cruel, wit had won them over by the end of the first meal they had shared. Jo's mum could also understand another reason for Jo's attraction. He was, she had to admit, extremely handsome.

Other than his occasional inability to resist following his penis into trouble, he was a decent and committed husband, and a loving and enthusiastic father. And now, with Brodie full-time in a rather exclusive nursery and she, well-established in a respectable and reputable law firm, all seemed pretty well with the world.

Jo was just about to pour herself a small glass of Premier Cru when she heard Stuart arrive and she felt pleased to be able to welcome him with a rather larger glass of the same.

'Wow, great service in this establishment,' Stuart laughed as he took the glass in one hand and his lovely wife in the other.

'Well we aim to please, sir.'

'And you always succeed,' Stuart winked.

Stuart considered his luck as he drank in the sight of Jo: teenage-slim with small but round breasts and a lovely firm bottom. She was blonde, of course, though more or less natural, and with a cute, small nose and large brown eyes.

'You look great tonight, darlin', that's a dead sexy top,' he smiled, his hands moving over her body and settling on her curvy jean-clad bottom. 'Anyone would think you'd had someone 'round when a wis out.'

Sensing where this might go and feeling in the mood, Jo decided to indulge Stuart with one of his favourite scenarios:

'Ok, you're right, I have to admit it, that girl was here; you know the model from the launch of the new Scotland strip the other day. We got chatting and I invited her over for a few glasses of wine and, well, one thing led to another and before long we were kissing and, well, you can guess the rest.'

'I don't want tae guess it,' Stuart replied, already slipping the tight, silky top over Jo's head and demonstrating his expert bra-clasp releasing skills. 'Please, tell me more ...'

Jo took down the zip on Stuart's jeans and slipped her hand inside both those and his boxers to gently caress his already considerably erect penis.

'She was a great kisser and her skin was so soft. I put my tongue right into her mouth and felt her sucking gently on it and I couldn't resist running my hands over her breasts and then undoing the buttons on her blouse.'

The cool touch of Jo's hand made Stuart groan very quietly and the words she spoke encouraged him to full erection. He quickly pulled his jeans and boxers off and knelt down before Jo to undo the button on her jeans and slowly pull down the zip. As he slipped the jeans over her bottom she continued her story:

'She took my top off – I was wearing no bra and I realised that my nipples were hard and my tits were firmer than ever. Hers were bigger than mine – not quite so pert maybe but plenty for me to get hold off – and I just had to lick and suck on her beautiful large nipples.'

Stuart had taken Jo's panties down by now and, ever attentive, was already pleasing her with his tongue. She moved backwards towards the sofa and slowly descended onto it trying not to allow his tongue to lose contact and interrupt the intense feeling she was already thoroughly enjoying.

'More, more,' he murmured, breathing hotly over the whole of her vagina.

'Yeah, that goes for you too,' she laughed and continued, 'we quickly stripped each other completely. She had a marvellous … big … round … ahh … arse and oh, that's nice – keep doing that – I ran my hands all – oh my God, yeah – over her bum and then we got into a sixty-nine and both started licking each other and ahh, yeah, yeah that's nice, yeah … ahh … ahh …'

Jo slipped off the sofa, moved on top of Stuart and quickly put her tongue into his mouth whilst grasping hold of his very eager penis. She stopped kissing him and whilst moving her hand up and down the shaft more and more quickly, she began again:

'I licked up and down her cunt; her hot, wet cunt, whilst she sucked and licked my clit and we both got closer and closer to coming …'

'Yeah, yeah,' shouted Stuart, getting pretty close himself.

'Then I couldn't resist any longer and we both …'

'Ahh, yeah, yeah, yeah …' Stuart came.

'Put our clothes on and went out shopping …'

They both laughed and held each other close.

'That was bloody brilliant,' Stuart enthused, 'you're dead good at that.'

'Yeah,' Jo agreed, 'I am aren't I?'

They lay on top of the bed, breathing heavily from their efforts and both satisfied.

For a few minutes, no words were required, then Jo propped herself up on one elbow and asked:

'So, how was training then?'

'Yeah, fine, thanks. Same as usual I suppose.'

'Do you never get bored, doing the same routines every day, week in, week out?'

'A bit, maybe, but it's all worth it, come the weekend. Out there in the "theatre o' dreams", wi' all those people. It's the best feeling in the world.'

'You know you tell me that so often I do worry a bit about how you'll cope when it's all over.'

Stuart considered this for a moment:

'In some ways the adrenalin of the TV studio gives me a similar buzz, so I think I'll be all right. To be honest, the thing I'll miss most is the camaraderie. Being wi' your mates; the laughs, the mucking about and then working together and overcoming obstacles. Nothing could replace that. I can only imagine it must be a bit like going into battle with your unit in a war. Nothing's more important than your team mates … well, present company excepted, obviously, but you know, loyalty to them, "all for one" and all that – it means more than almost anything I can think of.'

'"Present company excepted",' thought Jo, 'I'm not so sure.'

Stuart sank into the pillow with an almost imperceptible sigh. Not quiet enough to elude Jo, however.

'What's up, love? Is something the matter?'

'Och, nothing, nothing tae worry about, darlin' '

'Go on,' Jo prompted with a little indignance, 'let me know what's bothering you.'

Stuart's tone changed:

76

'I said nothin' … nothin' right?'

Jo was far from satisfied but wisely felt it best not to push it at this moment. 'Never mind,' she thought, 'he always tells me eventually.'

*

'So, wis it a date, son?'

Though he would have preferred not to have discussed his love life with his parents, Davie's apprehension about the previous evening's events had left him unable to avoid confiding in someone so he had reluctantly discussed potential strategies with his father, Tam. Now he had no choice but to provide him with some feedback on his performance.

'Aye, Dad, it wis,' was his succinct reply.

'Aw brilliant. And did it go well?'

'Aye, Dad, it did.'

'And?'

'And what?'

'And what happened?'

'Aw come on, this is no' an away game against East Fife. A'm no gonnae gie ye a blow by blow account.'

'A'm no' wantin' a blow by blow account, for God's sake – jist the edited highlights. Like on Scotsport.'

Davie laughed.

'It went really well, Dad. A didnae make a total arse o' masel' and, believe it or no', she wants tae see me again.'

'Whit's that; a missed it all?' Agnes asked as she entered the room. 'How did yir date go, son?'

'Naw … no' you too,' Davie looked exasperated as he beat the retreat and headed out of the lounge in the direction of his own room.

'You can tell 'er, Dad,' he called back, from the hall.

*

Stuart's mood had improved again by the next evening.

'Your supper's ready,' Jo called from the kitchen, it having been her turn to microwave the posh ready-made meals from Peckham's delicatessen.

'How many times?' Stuart asked. 'Supper is what you have later on in the evening – toast and cheese at nine o'clock or somethin'. This is tea-time.'

'Not again,' Jo smiled, indulgently. 'It's nearly seven o'clock. Surely tea-time is earlier?'

'Maybe, bit that's jist 'cause we're late home fae work. It disnae matter what time it comes, ma evening meal is ma tea. And by the way, this is a bit late, what's kept ye.'

Having been brought up in a working class Scottish household, Stuart had been used to eating when his Dad got home from work from the factory, anytime from five onwards. Jo, however, ate to a more middle-class timetable, usually at about seven, or later. Their vocabulary betrayed the differences in their backgrounds providing some confusion earlier in their relationship and much amusement now.

'You're such a pleb you know,' Jo remarked, 'I married beneath myself.'

'And you're such a middle-class snob – born with a silver spoon …'

'Yeah, and you had to get up at three in the morning,

78

work a twenty hour shift down t' pit and your Dad would thrash you to sleep wi' his belt, eh?'

Stuart appreciated the Monty Python reference and laughed as he wolfed down his Haddock Mornay.

Their conversation continued pleasantly and by the time they were finishing their pudding, Jo reckoned she could get away with another attempt at getting to the bottom of what was bothering her husband:

'Go on, give us a clue?' she asked.

'What?' he replied.

'I hate it when you won't tell me what's wrong. You should never shut me out – we're partners ... in everything.'

'I should have known you wouldn't give up. It's nothin' really, no biggie.'

'Well, in that case, spill!'

Stuart shifted uncomfortably and began:

'It's just this business about Paul Bannerman and the reunion match. Thirs a journalist sniffing about. Donnelly – he's a bit of a wanker; a Hearts fan; not a sports journalist but does a few football reports – hopelessly biased towards the Jam Tarts. Anyway, he's been interviewing some o' the boys ... from the team o' that time; asking questions about what happened that night; who was there, what the girl was like, that sort o' thing, diggin' for dirt.'

'But there is no dirt, darling, so why worry about him?'

'Aye, a know, but it's no' pleasant ye know. And these guys twist things; make innocent things look sordid ...'

'Like what?' Jo looked perplexed.

'Like nothing.' Stuart's brows were furrowing and his

lips started to tighten. 'What is this, the French inquisition?'

'Eh, that'll be Spanish, Stuart.'

'What'll be Spanish?'

'The inquis … oh, it doesn't matter. Just remember, always let me know when something's wrong. That's what I'm here for.'

'A know, love, a know.'

Now it was Jo's turn to be quiet.

*

Evening training is the unfortunate lot of the part-time footballer, usually after a hard day's shift at their other means of earning a living. Davie was lucky in that regard. Still relatively well-off from his glory days with Athletic and not spending a lot living with his parents, he chose, for the time being, not to supplement his part-time wage from the football club. On the downside, this gave him far too much time to brood on his misfortunes and far too much opportunity to drink.

On this occasion, he had started the day with no reason to brood. Still basking in the glow of last night's successful encounter with Melanie, he had spent a little time watching rubbish on daytime TV and had dragged out a couple of his favourite feel-good albums, even finding himself pogoing, slightly self-consciously in case his Mum came in, to a few Kaiser Chiefs' tracks.

That was all before Agnes had remembered to tell him about the telephone message left for him during the evening before:

'It was a man from a paper,' she had said. 'Somebody Donnelly - wanted to talk to you about Paul Bannerman. A told 'im that ye'd no' want tae, bit he was quite insistent; asked me tae gie ye 'is number.'

That quickly spoiled his mood.

The debate about summer football has raged long and hard with many unsure why the football community persist in playing their game at a time of year when the pitches are either bog-like, sodden marshes or treacherous frost-bitten ice-rinks. Factor in a side serving of horizontal rain or a wind-chill factor off the chart and you have a recipe for misery – for players and fans alike. Yet they persist, "tradition" being the argument that can't be beat.

Davie considered this debate as he arrived at the training ground. 'It's just about bearable on a Saturday afternoon,' he thought, 'wi' the crowd tae get you through the ninety minutes. But at seven o clock on a dark winter's night when yir biggest opponent is the sleet falling from the fucking Fife sky, you almost wish you worked in Rosyth Dockyard. 'Almost,' he thought, 'but no' quite.'

The Cowden United squad got through a training session of sorts, though in the conditions, one hardly liable to promote playing with the intricate, poetic skills of the average South American amateur side.

After two dismal hours fighting the sleet and each other, the Cowden United coaches finally decided that their squad had suffered enough and twenty wretched individuals made their way towards the blessed warmth of the showers.

The steam from those showers had rendered the changing rooms more opaque than the interior of the "smoking shelters" outside the council depot just up the road.

As Brian McDermott waited, patiently, outside the showers for the "real men" to finish, he heard the banter from inside:

81

'So, Davie, did ye nail 'er? Last night. Did ye nail that burd?'

Davie had learned his lesson:

'Too right a did. Too fuckin' right!'

*

As a keen student of psychology, Jo had often wondered about male sexuality. She had been with her fair share of men and couldn't think of one who had not had some "special interest" beyond just enjoying her sexy body. They always found that enough for the first few months but then there'd invariably be that slightly uncomfortable conversation, always in bed, under cover of darkness, when they'd bring up a little something they'd been thinking about.

There was Neil, her first proper boyfriend, who'd wanted her to spank him; Gavin, at college, who badgered her about a threesome – with another girl, of course; Tim, also at college, also wanted spanked; Rob, at her first law firm, had a thing about rubber and leather; Don, whom she'd met at a party seemed to be especially interested in her feet, and now she thought about it, wanted to be spanked as well. Jo had, she realised, with a wry smile, smacked a lot of hairy male buttocks in her time.

Stuart, thankfully, didn't require to be chastised as part of sexual foreplay. He did, however, like Jo to dress as if she were considerably younger than her actual years. Her attitude to this had fluctuated over time. By and large, she felt that a bit of role-play was fine, and the school-girl outfit he'd got her from Anne Summers was quite flattering, she had to admit. There were times, however, when he'd said things as he was near to climax – things about daddies and little girls – that had made her feel distinctly uncomfortable.

'However,' she thought, 'show me a man and I'll show you a fetish.'

It was one of those nights to indulge him a little. That was what she was thinking as she put on a pair of white cotton panties, slipped into the matching, white ankle socks and looked out her two-sizes-too small Minnie Mouse pyjamas. She paused in front of her dressing table and decided that she couldn't quite bring herself to put the bunches in her hair.

Stuart was taken aback when he came through to the bedroom to find his lithe young wife wriggling seductively on their bed, in his favourite get-up. His crotch fought a losing battle with his growing headache before he turned off the light and murmured:

'Thanks, darlin' but I'm no' really in the mood the night; goodnight.'

This was practically unprecedented and Jo lay silent, half humiliated and half concerned. Something was obviously, seriously, up.

*

It was hard to predict when Davie would succumb to temptation as regards the booze. Sometimes it could be when he'd got bad news or when things weren't going well; or at times it was when he was feeling so good he wanted to celebrate and felt that one night down the pub wouldn't be such a terrible thing; sometimes it was just a spur of the moment, "what-the-heck" kind of decision.

On this occasion it may have been any or all of these factors which led him to joining his team mates in the Central Bar for six or seven glasses of beer.

Whatever the reason, Agnes Thomson knew as soon as

she saw her inebriated son that a large reverse movement had taken place in the constant one-step-forwards, two-steps-backwards scenario that Davie had been playing out over the last few years.

Having first simply collapsed, fully clothed, onto his bed and fallen immediately asleep, Agnes had woken him and employed her usual strategy in this situation, she had threatened to undress him herself if he didn't get his act together and get ready for bed.

This had worked but it was with little satisfaction that she sat down in the living room to discuss the latest setback with Tam:

'A thought things were goin' well fur 'im, his teams doin' awright and he's goin' oot wi' that lassie …'

Tam looked ruefully at her and shook his head:

'Aw, Agnes, it's pretty obvious isn't it? You shouldnae have passed on that journalist's number tae 'im. You know that any mention o' the whole Paul Bannerman thing upsets 'im.'

'Aw aye, jist blame me – it's always me.'

'It's no' always you – it's jist, well you know thirs somethin' funny thair. Somethin' aboot that night that's no' right.'

'A don't know whit yir on aboot; aye somethin's no' right, a suppose. One o' 'is pals got killed; is that no' enough?'

'Aye, that's plenty a suppose; it's jist … jist … anyway, whatever. A think it's tae dae wi' that.'

Agnes looked chastened:

'Yeah, yir probably right. Tomorrow – we'll tell him

tae throw that number away – hae nothin' tae dae wi' that journalist.'

'Aye, quite right,' Tam nodded, 'that's whit we'll dae.'

Chapter Eight

'Hello, Mrs Gallacher, it's Mary Donaldson here, from The State Hospital; d'you have a minute to talk?'

Lorna Gallacher listened to the words "State Hospital," but heard something entirely different. She heard just one word "Strathgyte". Shorthand in the Scottish national psyche for "mental and dangerous," it held further, more personal and more traumatic connotations for Lorna. It was in fact the institution into which her daughter, Avril, had been incarcerated after admitting to the murder of that football player, Paul Bannerman.

'What is it … what's the matter?' she asked, whilst attempting to swallow the shot of fear which she felt every time there was an unannounced call from that awful place.

'Nothing to worry about, Mrs Gallacher, I just wanted to ask you a wee question?'

'Aye, go ahead then.'

'We've had a request for a visit … from a David Sutherland. We understand him to be Avril's uncle, your … brother, I presume?'

'Aye, that's Avril's uncle all right, but what on earth is he wantin' tae visit hir fur?'

'Well, we've no idea, Mrs Gallacher, but Avril's given her permission and as you know, for her protection, we need yours as well?'

'A've no' spoken tae him in years; we dinnae get on. Why

would he want tae go and see hir?'

'Well, as I say, I really don't know, but medical staff here are of the opinion that more visits would be good for Avril so unless you think there's any reason to be concerned about your brother visiting, then it's probably not a bad thing.'

Silence.

'So is there any reason, Mrs Gallacher? Any reason to be concerned?'

'Eh … a don't suppose so. No, a cannae think why no' .'

'That's fine then, Mrs Gallacher, I'll get that approved then … thanks for your time.'

*

Donnelly was pleased with himself when he got the call back from Strathgyte. It hadn't been hard to find out about Avril's extended family and when a little bit of digging revealed an estranged uncle he knew he was home and dry. At least till he got to the hospital that is. The question he asked himself was whether or not Avril would be compos mentis enough to realise that he wasn't David Sutherland. 'Ach, a'll deal wi' that when a get tae it,' he thought and finished the second half of his bacon roll in one big bite.

'You really have no scruples at all, do you?' Steph's incredulous question interrupted Donnelly's chewing. 'And no morality.'

'And you'll get nowhere in this business with that attitude, young lady,' was Donnelly's reply.

It was mid-morning and the low winter sunlight from the ceiling to floor windows lit up the dust in the air and assaulted Donnelly's eyes as he turned to look at his colleague at the next desk. He manoeuvred his swivel chair so that Steph blocked out the sun and this had the effect of surrounding her with a kind of halo. Flyaway strands of her long wavy hair caught the incoming light creating a gossamer effect, which combined with her finely sculpted features created a vision which almost took his breath away. 'Either that,' he thought, 'or it must be the smoking.'

'Do you want to take a picture or something?' Steph asked and Donnelly realised that he had been staring.

'Naw, dinnae flatter yirsel', it's jist the light in ma eye, that's all.'

'Yeah, whatever, anyway. I intend to make my way without stooping to lying or cheating.'

'Well, you'll be making your way back to teaching in that case. And anyway, it's not so much lying or cheating – well, okay, it's lying, but it's no' cheating. You have to define the rules first before you can establish what breaks them. And I set my own rules.'

Donnelly was aware that he had sounded like an actor in a Hollywood drama – Clint Eastwood, perhaps, just before promising to clean up the town. He had the good grace to look sheepish though this was partly in an attempt to pre-empt Steph's ridicule.

She may have felt inclined to go easy on him, but Norman Campbell was made of sterner stuff. In mock movie-voiceover tones he began:

'He lived outside the law; women loved him and men feared him; he set his own rules: Big Jim Donnelly, maverick reporter.'

Laughter rippled across the large open plan office before people lowered their eyes to their work to avoid those of

Donnelly which were wide and challenging.

'I hate to say it but he's right though, hen,' Campbell began again, in his own voice this time. 'Scruples are like manners, they're to be aspired to, but can be set-aside in particular circumstances. And morality isn't fixed, it's relative, and subject to cultural parameters. And in this culture, telling the odd porky for the greater good of uncovering the truth is well within journalistic parameters.'

'"The greater good"; "uncovering the truth"; that's your excuse for everything,' Steph replied. 'What you always fail to do is establish that you *are* uncovering the real truth and when you do, that it really *is* for the greater good. I mean, the truth is a relative concept as well, isn't it?'

'Hold on,' Donnelly replied, 'there's two arguments there – at least. One at a time, the truth is always good, and, yes, it's relative but that just proves Norman's point, it all depends on cultural parameters.'

'Wait a minute,' Steph was quick to respond, 'so you're saying that uncovering the truth is always good but that *you* get to decide what it actually is. *Ipso facto*, whatever you uncover is for the greater good!'

'Eh, yeah, more or less. Well, actually, no, we don't decide what the truth is, but we do work to a set of guidelines which are relevant, and set by our profession and we have as much right as anyone else to define the truth.'

Again, Steph was eager to reply:

'But the journalistic tenets by which you work allow you to break rules whenever required, including those tenets, themselves.'

'Now,' Campbell replied, wearily, 'now you're just

disappearing up your own, admittedly rather shapely, backside.'

Steph was looking fed up now. 'Yeah, that's another concept which you don't seem to believe applies within "journalistic parameters" … "sexism". You're both sexist old buggers.'

'Sorry, hen,' Campbell replied, sheepishly, rather undermining the apology with his patronising term of endearment. 'There's no need for that language though …'

'Aye, whatever,' Steph replied, turning her head back to her work.

Donnelly and Campbell exchanged furtive grins like those of naughty schoolboys behind their teacher's back.

*

Katy hesitated when she heard what she considered to be the very bland tones of some or other dodgy boy band escaping from under the door of Fiona's bedroom. She made it a point of principle not to be able to tell one group of wholesome looking young men from another. She was into darker, more profound music; music that spoke to her burgeoning teenage angst, that had something to say about the human condition.

She also avoided going into her sister's room whenever possible, believing that the "Pink Palace" somehow sapped her independent strength.

She must have really needed to talk, then, early on that Thursday evening, when she tentatively knocked on her twin sister's door.

Perhaps it was her innate musicality which led to her,

inadvertently, tapping the door in time with the music coming from within. This, combined with the tentative nature of the knocking, meant that Fiona was unaware of her sister's attempts to attract her attention.

Two louder attempts also went unheard till eventually she gave up and entered, unannounced, as far as her sister knew.

Fiona was practising a dance routine, copied from the video of the band in question and was none too pleased at being caught watching her own moves in front of the mirror.

That this potential flash-point was smoothed over by a rare apology from Katy immediately alerted Fiona to the potential seriousness of her sister's approach.

'So, what's on your mind, Sis? An apology, on my home turf? Must be something wrong.'

'Well if you're just gonnae be sarcastic, then it disnae matter,' Katy replied, with a harsher tone to her voice.

'No, no,' said Fiona, 'sit down; what's wrong?'

'It's … well I just keep thinking about Dad and that woman. D'ye think he's, you know, havin' an affair?'

'No,' replied Fiona, in confident tones. 'Seriously, Dad disnae have the pulling power. What did you say she looked like again?'

'Well she was at least ten years younger than him for a start. She wisnae slim, but she was, you know, shapely; well dressed, not cool or anything, but for a woman of her age, she looked all right.'

'And you seriously think she'd be interested in Dad? The man that time forgot?'

Katy considered her sister's opinion before beginning again:

'That's the thing, I got the idea that maybe he was more interested than her.'

'Bloody hell, Katy, how much could you tell? Did you video it?'

'No, it's really weird, but it's all, like, etched on to my memory, like in slow motion. I've been thinking about that, why did I see it so well? Does this mean it was important? Was I meant to see it?'

'Stop talking crap. You saw what you saw, end of story. So, what d'ye mean, he was more interested than her?'

Katy's face was a study in concentration as she tried to remember the events and shut out the refrain coming from Fiona's iPod docking station:

'I was crazy to believe, girl, that this love could ever last …'

She surveyed the girly surroundings she found herself in. It would appear that the manufacturers of most of what was to be found in her sister's room, worked from the following premise: "If it can be made, it can be made in pink". The relentlessness of that dreaded colour was broken only by posters of boys; many, many boys, none over the age of twenty and none, it seemed, without some variation of a floppy fringe.

She began to recall:

'They were walking; they stopped; he looked at her face, her eyes I think; she looked down; he put his hand towards the side of her head then leaned in towards her face, to kiss her; she turned her head and he ended up kissing the side of her face.' Katy giggled. 'Her ear, really …'

'Ok,' Fiona began, her voice projecting authority, 'it's

straightforward, there's no affair, but he fancies her. Men always fancy younger women; I've been getting asked out by fourth year's all term.'

'Yeah, but that's 'cause you dress like a slut.'

'Fuck off, Katy; I'm just trying tae explain.'

'Yeah, but our Dad shouldn't be going after other women – he's betraying Mum.'

'What you've got to understand, Katy, is that he canny help it; men canny help it; they're programmed that way; they're like animals.'

'That's as may be, but it's no excuse, that'd be like saying that they can do whatever they like … you know, like rape and that. They can control themselves surely?'

'Yeah, well, maybe sometimes, but we've established, no affair; just a weak man with a mid-life crisis.'

'I suppose so,' Katy replied, 'but it's no excuse – I'm not going tae forgive him.'

The conversation tailed off and they both became aware of the saccharine melody and the words:

'I said, once more, then I'm walking out that door …'

The two girls shared a rare moment before the mood was broken by the sound of their mother's voice from below:

'Your Dad's due home soon. Who wants to go out for tea before he gets here?'

*

Donnelly entered the house with a mixture of hope and fear, he hoped that it would all have blown over but feared they may want him to suffer some more. The latter was confirmed when he read the note:

'We've gone out to eat. Make yourself a sandwich. Jacqui'

'No "love",' he thought, 'and "a sandwich." Crap.'

It wasn't long before he settled down on the sofa with cheese on toast (and *Branston Pickle*), a large whisky and Pink Floyd's *Wish You Were Here*. He felt unsettled and melancholy, but to be honest, melancholy suited him. He was like a "pig in shit".

Chapter Nine

'Of course it wis his fuckin' idea. Who else wants the publicity more than he needs the money?'

John McDougal explained his theory to ex-colleague Graham Todd after they had exchanged a fist bump and a few pleasantries on meeting in the car park of Glasgow Athletic's impressive training facility.

'A had a meal wi' 'im recently,' McDougal continued, 'he's totally up 'is own arse, like. Thinks the world revolves around 'im.'

'A hate tae say it,' replied Todd, 'but a'm no' sae sure it disnae.'

Both laughed and their breath turned to steam in the crisp, bright winter afternoon that had been scheduled for one brief training session ahead of the big testimonial later in the week. Matches of this kind were not meant to be taken too seriously as regards the actual football. Both sets of players and the referee would conspire to produce an entertaining spectacle with a veneer of competition. The ex-Athletic players had felt the need for this training session though. Given that they were playing against a side mainly composed of current English Premiership players, this ragbag squad of current pros, bar managers and bouncers felt the need to at least come up with a few tactical ideas to avoid potential humiliation.

'It's a' very well fur him,' Todd continued, 'wi' 'is Lamborghinis and 'is media career, but whit di we git oot o' this? Is this mair money goin' tae Paul's family by the way?'

'Naw, tae be fair, they werenae wantin' ony mair. Thi money's goin' tae some education project aboot knife crime or somethin', and a hospice a think.'

'Aye, well whitever,' Todd looked mildly disgusted, 'a'll tell ye what, a'm needin' it mair than them. Thirs no a lot o' money in the car washing business these days, in a credit crunch.'

'A suppose Stu means well enough, though,' McDougal suggested as they approached the front door of the building.

'Aye, a suppose so; he's a decent enough bloke, jist a bit full o' 'imsel', that's a'.'

The two paused to sign in at the desk in the plush entrance hall.

'D'ye sign in at Arbroath training then, John?' Todd asked, aware that the answer would be in the negative.

'Naw,' McDougal replied, 'the valet parking guy does it fur me after he parks ma Porsche.'

As they approached the changing room, McDougal turned to his pal:

'Ach, it'll be a laugh,' he said.

Todd looked doubtful. 'A dinnae ken aboot that. After whit happened, a dinnae really want tae get the gither wi' this squad o' players. A'm only here 'cause it wid look bad if a wisnae.'

McDougal opened the door of the changing room to be greeted with the distinctive smell of linament and a sarcastic cheer from the occupants.

'We're a' right now, no need tae worry aboot where the goals are gonnae come from', came a voice from the far side of the room: 'Super John McDougal's here.'

'And Scotland's finest retired wing-back,' another voice added.

'Wing-back?' Todd replied. 'In ma day thir wis nae such thing. A'm a full back, a'll have ye know, and that's where a'll be stayin'. A've nivir crossed the half-way line in ma life and a dinnae intend tae start now.'

Amid laughter, the two settled into the room and, just as easily, into the banter. McDougal quickly noticed that the atmosphere was particularly jocular. Everyone appeared to be trying too hard. He had an uneasy feeling about the day, only accentuated by looking around at the unusually plush, if clinical surroundings. He found himself agreeing with Graham Todd's sentiments as he thought:

'A'm no' sure a want tae be here.'

Davie Thomson laced up his boots and realised that he was actually feeling surprisingly all right, back here, in this company. The level of abuse wasn't quite as brutal as he had become used to and there was, after all, a bond between this group of people, even if one formed by tragedy rather than success. The training session should, at least, be fairly enjoyable. The evening meal that they planned to share might not be quite so much fun.

*

'They *can* control themselves,' Jacqui explained to her daughters over ice cream in St Andrews Italian restaurant on Portobello High Street. This was their favourite place for a treat, and the atmosphere, combined with the circumstances, had encouraged Jacqui to speak to the girls a little more freely than she normally would. She had, of course, assured them not to worry – she and their Dad were fine, and this was just a tiny bump on the long road of marital bliss. 'Ok,' she had admitted, when challenged, 'maybe not bliss, but marital ok-ness sounds pretty rubbish.' The conversation had moved on from Donnelly to men in general, a subject upon which she felt both personally and professionally, well qualified to expound.

'They *can* control themselves; it's just that some o' them choose not to. I think there's little doubt that there are differences between men and women. The vast majority develop as a result of social conditioning – the way they're brought up, in other words. You know; girls are encouraged to be caring, boys to be brave, that sort of thing. But biologically, like it or not, men are programmed to, well, to impregnate …'

Both girls giggled, not so much at the word but at their mother's reluctance to use it, as though it was some sort of naughty word.

'… to impregnate, well, as often as possible really. Women, on the other hand, are programmed to look for a man who'll stick around and protect them so they can have children.'

'A don't need a man tae protect me,' Katy replied with some force.

'No, of course you don't, love. But I'm talking about how we've been programmed since cave-man days.'

'Or "cave women days," Mum,' Fiona added, picking up on the feminist vibe.

'Yes, of course,' Jacqui laughed. 'So,' she continued, 'there's some excuse for men's desire to be promiscuous.' She paused. 'On the other hand, society has moved on quite a bit since those days and men don't hit women over the head with a club any more and drag them back to their cave – if they ever did. What I mean is: in the twenty-first century, there's no excuse for men to behave like they did twenty thousand years ago, so no man can use the excuse of not being able to control himself for forcing himself on a woman.'

Katy looked appalled:

'I never said he was forcing himself on her, Mum!'

'No, of course you didn't, darling – I'm just talking about men and their libidos, and I was thinking about those men who use that as an excuse for attacking women. Your Dad, on the other hand, like most men, *can* control himself but maybe on this occasion, he just didn't choose to completely resist the lure of a younger woman. He wouldn't really have followed it through though.'

'So what are you gonnae do, Mum?' Fiona asked.

'Oh, nothing really, love; his punishment's already taking place. Just a little cold-shoulder for a few days; a wee taste of what it would be like without my love and support. He'll soon have learnt his lesson.'

*

The football club had agreed to cover the cost of a private room and four course meal in one of the more discreet city-centre restaurants. The waiters had all been promised a hefty tip should they manage to resist the temptation to leak the whereabouts of this news-worthy event to the press, or to punters on the street.

The evening, on the face of it, went very well but there were so many elephants in the room that there might as well have been sawdust on the floor and bars on the windows. Successful players didn't want to discuss their good fortune with less fortunate individuals; the drug or alcohol habits of some were not to be mentioned, to their faces anyway; and although stories of Paul Bannerman were long and legion, the circumstances surrounding his death were studiously avoided.

Davie found himself seated next to Stuart Robertson and they exchanged similar banalities to those being swapped throughout the room. Memories were shared along with insults for various other Scottish football players and one or two suggestions as to what either would like to do to the extremely pretty young waitress who was making a point of paying particular attention to Stuart.

Alcohol lowers inhibitions however, and for Davie more than most - given that he had fallen off the wagon yet again. He began to move the conversation round to the events of the evening of Bannerman's death. Just as he was steering it closer, Stuart was continually taking it further away, until, Davie, finding this increasingly annoying, couldn't help himself and asked:

'D'ye ever think aboot the lassie, Stu? Rottin' away in that mental prison. D'ye ever hae any doubts?'

There was a moment's silence whilst Stuart composed himself:

'No, Davie, a don't. She's doolally. Whatever happened – she's in the right place.'

'Bit, it jist ...'

'"Jist" nothin', Davie. You and me. You and me more than anyone. We share somethin'. It's harder fur us than the rest. I'm here fur ye. Jist try an' keep it the gether. Eh, pal?'

A comforting hand on Davie's shoulder ended the exchange.

Throughout the room, ties were being loosened along with tongues. The volume was rising, with laughter emanating from some areas and angry voices from others. Waitresses were venturing in less often, having prevailed upon their male colleagues to take the strain in order to avoid lewd comments and wandering hands. Similar conversations to Davie's and Stuart's were beginning to break out across the room and some of the senior players began to feel that perhaps it was time for a few more formal words to be spoken on behalf of their much missed friend: Paul Bannerman.

Although Stuart Robertson was the defacto leader of that group of players, the captain at the time had been the more established Derek Ramsay, now player/coach at lowly Stenhousemuir. He had been a natural leader of men on the field, but had surprised many by his relative lack of success as a coach subsequently. However, he saw it as his duty to show leadership and take control of the situation.

After some vigorous glass clinking by Stuart, Ramsay rose and began to speak:

'I just want to say a few words about our team-mate and friend: Paul Bannerman.'

Initial laughter turned to silence as those around the table realised that this was a serious speech.

'Banns wis obviously a great football player – a midfielder wi' talent and tenacity – but more important than that he was a great bloke, so he wis – one o' the best. I think we all feel privileged tae have known him and tae have played with 'im and I know none of us will ever forget 'im.'

Ramsay paused to allow his words to sink in before

continuing, very slowly, and with great deliberation:

'The circumstances of Banns' death were … obviously … no' very … eh, pleasant, but I think it's important that we all remember that night and remember the promise that we made tae each other. Paul wis a team player and he would want us to remain a team, now and forever. That goes for on the pitch, on Wednesday night, and off it as well. Let's honour Bann's memory by sticking by each other, just as he always did.'

Ramsay looked round at a mixture of expressions from supportive to concerned, and felt it was best he rounded up.

'So, gentlemen, please raise your glasses tae a great footballer, a true gentleman and an exceptional team mate … tae Paul!'

With a myriad of emotions, and varying amounts of gusto, all present repeated those last two words:

'Tae Paul!'

*

When Jacqui, Fiona and Katy returned home to the house from their meal, they were still in high spirits. All were infused with the warm feelings which came from sharing confidences. The house was in darkness and they assumed that Donnelly had decided that the pub was his best option, for sustenance of various kinds.

It was Katy who first entered the living room to find her Dad, fast asleep on the sofa, in the dark, with an empty half-bottle of malt whisky at his side. He had headphones on but Pink Floyd had long packed up and gone home.

Katy called her mum and sister through to see the sorry

sight which caused much amusement. It was Fiona who said what they were all thinking:

'I think he's been punished enough, Mum.'

Chapter Ten

Davie woke mid-morning, head splitting, and totally unaware of where he was. He could see that he was in a large, comfortable bed and the surroundings were considerably more stylish and expensive than he was used to. Looking round the room he took in abstract paintings on the walls, smooth maple furniture and colourful glass ornaments.

'This is one posh hotel,' he thought, 'Christ, a hope a'm no' payin' fur it.'

A gentle knock on the door and a soft female voice confused him even more:

'Morning, Davie; are you decent?'

'Eh, aye,' he replied, and when the pretty face with brown eyes and long blonde hair peeked round the door, he recognised it to be that of Jo Robertson, wife of his old team-mate, Stuart.

'Hi, Davie, Stuart asked me to wake you both at eleven; I hope that's all right. On the plus side, breakfast's nearly ready. D'ye fancy kippers?'

'Eh, no, that's fine – to wake me a mean, and yeah, thanks very much tae the kippers – if it's no' too much trouble.'

'No trouble at all, Davie, I'm sure you two had a hard day so you deserve it.' She smiled, then continued:

'I mean the training, of course, not the drinking.'

Davie smiled, sheepishly, as she went on:

'There's a dressing gown on the back of the door – the door leads to the ensuite. Breakfast in five.'

She could see that Davie was blushing and she smiled, indulgently, at him before leaving the room. Jo wasn't stupid; she knew the effect she had on men, particularly those who were naked, and in bed. She enjoyed the feeling of power this gave her.

Davie, for his part, found his hand slipping down beneath the covers. 'A could wake up tae that every mornin', nae problem,' he thought and he knew that there was something he had to deal with before getting out of bed.

*

Stuart was already at the table, finishing a bowl of cereal, when Davie arrived. Davie had felt a little too self-conscious to go for breakfast in the dressing gown so had put the shirt and trousers on from the night before.

'The invitation didn't say "formal" Davie,' Jo smiled when Davie appeared.

He found himself blushing again and mumbled:

'Eh, aye, it's jist, well a've got tae go quite soon, like.'

'She's just teasing you, Davie,' Stuart replied, looking up from his breakfast. 'She likes teasing,' he added, with a slight scowl in Jo's direction.

'So, did you sleep alright then?' Jo quickly changed the subject.

'Aye, a wis out for the count. No' feelin' that great this mornin' though.'

'Well you'll feel better after your kippers; you get stuck in.'

With that Jo left the men to finish their breakfast and discuss the events of the night before.

'Davie?' Stuart began tentatively, 'I know that a get a lot o' slagging for ma TV career and my supposedly glamorous life and all that …'

'"Supposedly glamorous?"' Davie asked, glancing around the kitchen at the expensive units and the American fridge which was almost as big as his whole kitchen.

'Ok, well maybe it is a wee bit glamorous but what I was tryin' tae say is that I care about everyone that was in that room last night; and on that training pitch. Obviously I want what's best for maself, but believe me, I also, really do want what's best for everyone else as well. Obviously a'm closer tae some guys than others – that's only natural. But we've all got a bond and a know this'll sound corny but a think of us all as brothers, kind of. What's good for one of us is good for us all.'

He paused and bared his teeth as he looked towards Davie. Davie was taken aback till he realised that Stuart was simply removing some kipper bones from between two of his front incisors.

Davie had nothing to say so Stuart continued:

'Have you had a call from a journalist, Davie? A sleazy guy from *The Standard;* Donnelly's 'is name.'

'Eh, no,' Davie lied, unsure whether to give anything away.

'Well, you probably will; he's been in touch with quite a few o' the boys already.'

'What fur?'

'He's digging around tryin' to find out more about the night Paul died …'

106

There was silence as Stuart allowed this to sink in.

The silence almost caught Jo out, behind the slightly opened door. She knew there was more to the story than she had been told and although she understood that those men had suffered a tragedy together and might, understandably, want to keep the details only to themselves, she couldn't resist wanting to know more. Perhaps because of Stuart's infidelities, Jo hated when he kept anything from her and she had become quite adept at coming up with ways to find things out.

'Well a'm certainly no' gonnae tell 'im anythin', Davie replied.

'A know,' said Stuart, 'and a also know that none of us should be ashamed o' what happened that night. D'ye understand that, Davie?'

Davie stared into the middle distance having forgotten his food and allowed his coffee to go cold. His eyes had reddened by the time he replied:

'No, Stu, a don't understand that, and a don't agree wi' it either.'

Jo gasped silently as she realised that there might be more to this than just emotionally stunted men keeping an awful experience to themselves. 'It's about sex,' she thought. 'With men, it's always about sex. Some sort of sex game gone wrong, maybe?'

'Nobody,' Stuart spoke slowly, carefully choosing his words, 'did anything that was not … an appropriate thing tae do, in the circumstances. And if Donnelly gets even a smell o' anythin' to the contrary he'll twist it into something else and God knows where that'll lead.'

'A'm no stupid, Stu; a understand the significance.'

'A know ye do, Davie, but the best thing tae do is jist tae have nothin' tae do wi' the man. That way there's no problems.'

'Naw, thirs problems, Stu; thirs problems in ma mind.'

'A'm sorry about that, Davie, and a'm sure it's the case for all of us, but to be blunt, keep them there, eh?'

Jo realised that the conversation had come to an uncomfortable conclusion and returned to the kitchen, adopting a breezy tone:

'Hey, you guys; how come no-one's eating my kippers?'

*

Davie found himself wandering through Kelvingrove Park after he left Stuart's luxurious home. The experience had been one of sensory overload in so many ways and he had plenty to think about. He remembered having been shown round the park by a girlfriend when he had lived in Glasgow and it felt like it would be a good place for him to think.

He stared blankly into the fast flowing waters of the River Kelvin and without realising, he weighed up his pros and cons: he was drinking again, too much and too often. He knew, in fact, that any amount was too much but at least, if he limited it … But there was Mel – lovely, caring Mel. He had only been seeing her for a few weeks but already she had made him start to feel like life was worth something again.

He knew he could, and should, be playing football at a higher level, that he wasn't doing his talent justice. Cowdenbeath depressed him; not so much the place, though it wasn't exactly Paris; not even the football club, though it wasn't exactly Barcelona. No, it was the players, or at least some of them: their pettiness, jealousy and general unpleasantness. But, then again, that wasn't unique to Cowden United by any means. And there was Mel. Nothing seemed so bad with Mel in his life.

More than anything else, however, there was the death of Paul Bannerman. Ten years on and the events of that night still infused his life like a sulphurous odour.

And now, with all of this, bringing it all up again, forcing him to deal with it … well, he just wasn't sure he could.

But there was Mel.

'No,' he thought, 'even Mel can't make this alright.'

Davie walked up past the Kelvingrove Art Gallery and remembered the famous story that the girl had told him as he had walked past there years before. It was an apocryphal tale about the architect who had designed the magnificent Victorian structure. The story goes that he had meant for the front of the building to face onto the road but that, in his absence, it had been constructed the other way round, with the front facing into the park. In his grief at what he saw as the spoiling of his greatest work, he had thrown himself from the tallest tower and ended his ruined life.

Davie further considered unfulfilled promise as he headed out of the park and down the street towards the city centre. Quickly coming upon Sauchiehall Street, he made a common mistake of those not familiar with that part of town, he assumed that he was almost at the centre, aware that Sauchiehall Street was one of its most prominent thoroughfares. What he didn't realise was that it took one and a half miles to eventually turn into the familiar shopping street.

Davie was exhausted in more ways than one when he

finally boarded the train headed for home. And he was also no closer to deciding whether or not he would speak to James Donnelly.

*

Jo had been left uneasy by the morning's events and she felt that it was time for a little digging. Whilst Stuart showered, she quickly located his mobile phone and searched for any significant text messages. He had long since become used to deleting anything incriminating either from or to another female, but this was not, on this occasion, what Jo was looking for.

She was right in believing that he would not have thought to get rid of messages which weren't connected to women and it wasn't long before she found something:

'Ta, Derek, main thing 2 make sure no-one tlks to Dnlly and if they do say 0.'

Next stop for Jo was Stuart's desk and the locked drawer in which he kept what he thought were secrets. She had long since had a spare key cut for the lock and had always resisted confronting him directly about evidence she had found there. Better to use what she found as a prompt to further investigation and allow him to continue to believe he had a secret place.

Jo was aware that the shower had stopped running and knew she should really wait till later when she might have a better opportunity. She couldn't resist though, and quickly opened the drawer and sifted through the contents. She reached below the familiar porn magazines with titles such as "Barely Legal" and finding nothing else, took a look through the savings books for various bank accounts.

Stuart wasn't aware that she even knew he had private accounts and she kept him in blissful ignorance. In the past, cheques written to florists or jewellers without a forthcoming present to herself would lead her to conclusions of infidelity. More recently it had been credit card statements which had betrayed him. In these circumstances she had gathered further evidence before eventually confronting him. He was currently on his very last warning and nothing had been found within the last year or so.

All looked well in the first one but she was quickly scanning the second when she heard a shout:

'Hey, Jo! Where are you?'

Her eyes quickly landed on one very recent bank transfer, into the account of one Mark Sinclair – for two thousand pounds.

'I'm here, love,' she called out after quickly putting the statement below the porn, locking the door, and moving into the hall.

'Nice bath?'

*

Davie was grateful for his Mum's home-cooked casserole when he finally got home and he was even happy enough to answer their questions about the training session in Glasgow, the night-out and the current marital status of all his old team-mates. It wasn't until he was polishing off his rhubarb crumble that the atmosphere was spoiled a little:

'A see that number's still lying there fur that bloke fae the newspaper. A thought you were goin' tae throw it away?' Tam asked his son.

'A nivir said that,' Davie replied. 'A'll think aboot it.'

'A don't know exactly what it is aboot that night that bothers you so much – 'cause you won't tell me,' Agnes said, pointedly, 'but a do know thit talking aboot it really upsets you, so a don't see the point o' being interviewed by a muck-rakin' journalist. Here, I'll jist throw it away fur ye, son, ok?'

'No, it's no' ok. A'll decide whit a dae aboot it. Would you two leave me alone; stop trying tae run ma life. Ye know what, a think it's aboot time a moved oot again.'

And with that he banged the door and headed for his room.

Chapter Eleven

The State Hospital at Strathgyte appears to have been placed strategically within the Scottish landscape, almost equidistant between the country's two great cities, but south in a no-man's land, not quite in the Borders yet not in the central belt. A place on the map where nothing else seems to exist.

It occupies a special resonance in the emotional landscape of the country as well, the very word "Strathgyte" is shorthand for the worst place you can think of. "That one'll end up in Strathgyte," people would say about a cruel child. Being both a mental hospital and a prison, one could imagine that it housed the very worst and most dangerous of society's undesirable elements.

Donnelly had been there before, more than once. His profession led him towards the extremes of society. Very few newspaper stories inform us about the average. "Average weather has no effect on the country's transport system" is not a headline you'd expect to see. Or "Scottish golfer plays an average round to finish halfway down the field." No, we're interested in the great or the terrible – mainly the terrible.

Nevertheless, he was struck again by the eerily appropriate bleakness of the surrounding landscape as he approached in his car. 'You have to have a sense of humour to build a high security mental institution in the middle of a moor,' thought Donnelly as the building came within sight. '"Gothic" doesn't begin to describe this setting,' he mused whilst gazing on the sixteen foot high perimeter fence.

Donnelly's contemplation was disturbed by an incredibly loud and frightening thirty second shrill blast of sound.

'Fuck,' he shouted out loud and almost swerved the car off the road. 'What the fuck was that?' His response was almost as bad when it happened again though he was more prepared for the third and final blast.

'Just my luck to come on the one day in the month when they test the siren,' he thought as he remembered this routine after coming to his senses. Based on a World War II air raid siren, the alarm exists to let local people know about any unlikely escapes from the institution. It had most famously sounded thirty four years before when a pair of psychopathic lovers had absconded, killing a nurse, a patient and a policeman as they went.

Of course, once inside, one can see that the hospital is no longer the bleak and frightening institution of yore. Now under an enlightened twenty-first century regime, the interior is bright and welcoming and the staff friendly and helpful.

They were certainly helpful in facilitating the visit of David Sutherland to his troubled niece, Avril Gallacher. They had, of course, ensured that Avril was in agreement with the visit and had confirmed with her parents that she did indeed have an uncle of that name and that there was no need to be suspicious. That the supposed uncle was in fact a prominent Scottish journalist was a fact of which they were entirely unaware.

Donnelly was therefore treated with warmth and respect as he completed the airport-like security checks and was taken along a number of corridors to a visiting room where he knew from previous experience that he would be observed but not overheard.

At a bare wooden table he saw a small bird-like girl staring blankly, straight ahead. Donnelly could see immediately that she had once been attractive. Her hair was black, dank, and shoulder length; her eyes were large and her features fine. With some flesh on those bones, she might once have been the kind of girl who was invited back to footballers' plush city-centre apartments. But now, he thought, she looked ... empty.

'Hello, Avril, how are you doing?'

'You're no' ma uncle. Who the fuck are you?'

Donnelly was a little shocked at the strength of reaction, so quickly. Although expert at scheming, lying, and generally manipulating situations to get his own way, he was not so good at planning ahead or preparing for all eventualities. As his brain scanned the available information and attempted to quickly form a plan, he realised that Avril being much more "with-it" than he'd expected was actually, in fact, a good thing. This meant that she was much more likely to be able to assist him with his story and to help him with the breakthrough he needed. But in the short-term he had to deal with the possibility that she would immediately have him thrown out and that this could quite possibly lead to a criminal prosecution.

With so little time to think, Donnelly resorted to the very last resort of the hardened investigative journo, his own most rarely used weapon, he told the truth.

'Eh, aye, that's right, I'm actually a journalist, but your mother said I could come.'

Well, almost the truth.

He could see Avril absorbing this information and he didn't like what he could see in her eyes. The signs weren't good so he quickly spoke again before she had a chance to respond:

115

'The reason your Mum said it was ok is that she thinks a can help you.'

The unease he had detected was getting worse and was spreading like a small earthquake through her body. She began to rock backwards and forwards, not too violently but enough, Donnelly knew, to potentially alert the unseen eyes which were almost certainly watching what was going on.

'A journalist - whit would a journalist help me wi'? You jist want tae tell folk a' aboot how a killed that football player, make mair stories oot o' it. Well ye can fuck off.'

With this she looked towards the door and Donnelly knew she was just about to call for a member of staff when he tried one last time:

'I want to help you get out ... get out of this place and home to yir mum ...'

As this last statement hung in the air Donnelly had enough time to think a little about what he had just said. There wasn't a lot he wouldn't do to help him get to the nub of a story. There weren't many depths he hadn't already plumbed to this end. Even he knew, however, that he had crossed some sort of moral line when he had offered false hope to the poor creature sitting in front of him.

'A want to tell your story so that everyone'll know what really happened that night and they'll, eh, mibbae look again at your sentence.'

Donnelly remembered how surprisingly easy it was to cross those moral lines – when you're very well-practised that is.

'A stuck a knife in a famous football player an' a wis so high on crack thit a cannae even remember doin' it. A'm no' the sort o' person that gets let oot early. Oh aye, an' a'm aff ma heid as well – don't forget that.'

'You're no' off yir heid, Avril. A can tell that already just being with you for a few minutes. Is that what they tell ye'?'

'No, that's no' whit they tell me. They tell me a'm a' right and that a'm gettin' better but it's no' true. It's jist a trick. A trick tae make me behave. They know what a'm capable o', ye see. And a know whit I'm capable o'. A'm here 'cause a'm the sort o' person who can stab someone 'cause they'll no' let me rob them. A'm dangerous. A dinnae deserve tae get oot o' here.'

The rocking was getting no better and Avril had also started to cry. Donnelly assumed that he was only still there because whoever should be watching the room had eaten something that disagreed with him the night before and had abandoned his post in favour of a more urgent need to attend the hospital's toilets.

'Hey, Avril, try to calm down. A don't want tae upset you. A'll just go in a minute if you want me too. A came to help, honestly and if a'm not helping a'll jist go.'

There was a silence during which Avril appeared to calm herself slightly before replying:

'What are you waiting for then?'

'Do you get many visitors, Avril?' Donnelly tried changing tack.

'No.'

'D'you not want a wee chat then?

'No.'

'Someone different to pass the time o' day with? What kind of music do you like, for instance? A've got two daughters, one of them likes all these Goth bands, "Emo" music, they call it, apparently. The other one likes whatever's in the pop charts: Lady Dada and the like.'

'Gaga,' replied Avril.

'Yeah, it's all gaga isn't it?' Donnelly replied. '"All we hear is Radio Gaga," eh?'

Donnelly detected the hint of a smile from Avril as she replied:

'Lady *Gaga*, it's Lady *Gaga* fur fuck's sake.'

'Aw ... right,' Donnelly smiled, both at his own mistake and the fortuitous result it had brought about.

'Aye well, I'm no' exactly "with-it" when it comes to pop music. My theory is that they got it right in the seventies and so there's no' any point in anything they've come up wi' since then.'

'Bloody hell, a dinnae half pity your daughters – living wi' the dad that time forgot.'

Though not exactly relaxed, Donnelly felt that Avril's current demeanour would not be seen as anything out of the ordinary to the unseen scrutiniser, perhaps now back from his sojourn in the loo. Not in this place anyway.

'It's a Dad's job. You know, to be out of touch. I bet yours is the same?'

'A wouldnae know – a've no' exactly seen much o' 'im in the last ten years.'

'Does he no' come then?'

'Naw – no' much. A wouldnae say he's disowned me but it's like visiting me is a duty – somethin' you have tae dae but really dinnae want tae. Like picking up your dog's shit after them.'

118

Donnelly was hit with a wave of paternally inspired sadness and sympathy. He felt his eyes pricking as he replied:

'His loss then – you seem like a clever girl ... a nice girl.'

'A nice girl that takes drugs, goes wi' men and kills thum. A don't blame 'im at a'.'

The two looked at each other – the oddest of couples, sharing a silence of understanding.

Donnelly was suddenly aware that the room, in fact the whole building, was unnaturally bright. 'So nothing could be missed?' he thought, 'or to illuminate the minds and souls of the inmates?' Remembering his purpose, he asked,

'A thought you said you didn't remember killing Paul Bannerman. How do you know you killed him if you don't remember it?'

This was a shot in the dark and he felt a vague unease about having asked the question. He liked the girl and he knew he shouldn't be playing psychological games with a vulnerable psychiatric patient. But Donnelly didn't operate a filter for the appropriateness of questioning.

Avril began to look anxious once more:

'No' you as well. A've had psychologists asking me that. Loads o' fuckin' psychologists. Look, a hud the knife in ma hand, a wis oot o' ma heid; who else d'ye think it wis? It's no' gonnae've been one o' they footballers is it? Why wid they kill thir teammate? Listen, a dinnae ken it wis me but a ken it wis me, if you know whit a mean? A'm a bad, bad person, a deserve a' thit's happened tae me.'

Great, tidal sobs began to convulse through her tiny frame. She looked utterly defeated and Donnelly felt like he wanted to pick up the poor wee creature and hold her till she found some peace.

He didn't though, of course. Wouldn't have known how.

'Listen, Avril, a don't mean to be crude, but do you make a habit o' killing footballers?'

Silence.

'No? A didn't think so. Why would you have done so this time then? Why would you believe that of yourself? A don't think you've got it in ye.'

The tears had passed and those large brown eyes flashed angrily as Avril looked straight through him. 'How the fuck do you know? You know nothin' about me, absolutely fuck-all. A wis a nice girl, gorgeous in fact, if a say so masel'. And clever. When this happened a'd completed a year o' university – first one in ma family tae go. Ma Mum and Dad had such great hopes for me. That's what makes this all the worse for them – ma Dad particularly. But a'd dropped oot. A don't need tae tell ye why.'

'Drugs?'

'Aye, drugs. A'd try anything once, but usually two or three times. Smoke crack cocaine two or three times and it's too late. A have, whit they call in here, "an addictive personality". A wish tae God a'd got addicted tae mountain climbin' or somethin'.'

Avril paused as if to consider how her life might have gone if that or some other adrenalin filled activity had come into her life before drugs had taken hold.

'The thing is, by the time this happened a wisnae a nice, clever girl. A wis a drug addict. And drug addicts are capable o' almost anythin'. A know 'cause a'd done maist o' it already.'

'But you hadnae killed anyone, Avril. It's a big jump.'

'No as big as ye think. A'd come close. A nearly stuck a knife in ma boyfriend once. Well boyfriend/dealer – bit o' both.'

'Well he probably deserved it – that's no' the same.'

'Aye it is the same, killing people's wrong, regardless o' who they are. My God, a'm the one in the mental hospital. A shouldnae be havin tae give lessons in morality tae you. Although you are a journalist, a suppose.'

Donnelly smiled as he looked at the face of the young girl seated before him. He had been wrong, she wasn't empty at all. There was a spark there which had somehow, against the odds, never been extinguished. She may have been defeated but, incredibly, she wasn't without hope. As the staff member arrived to tell them that their time was up, Donnelly reflected on the happy coincidence that had led to what was good for him also being good for Avril Gallacher. He was convinced that something happened that night that wasn't exactly as had been told – by one and all. And he knew that this could lead to a great story for him and ... what for Avril? He wasn't sure, but he knew one thing, regardless of the story, he wanted to see her again.

'Same time next week then?' he chanced his arm as he was led out of the room.

Her eyes were on the floor but she seemed thoughtful. Just as she looked sure to tell him never to return he noticed something, a movement in her eyes perhaps, or a twitch of her mouth. After what seemed like forever, she exhaled:

'Aw fuck it. Whitever. *Uncle* David.'

Chapter Twelve

The hubbub of conversation was gone; the commercial radio station switched off and the only light came from one solitary computer whose lonely buzz was all that disturbed the silence. Donnelly worked alone, late into the evening at the offices of the *Daily Standard*. He knew, however, that one other person was still in the building and he knew she would have to go through the main office and past his desk to leave.

Was it a coincidence that he found himself as one of the last people left in in the building, with one of the others, of course, being the delectable Steph? Of course not. He would claim so though, presenting his need to complete some relevant research and the current discomfort to be experienced at home as evidence in his defence. A jury in full possession of the facts, however, would not have to deliberate long before finding to the contrary. He may not have wanted to go home, but his usual venue for extra "research" was the Holyrood Tavern, half a mile down the road from the office.

Somewhere in his conflicted mind he knew that he was hoping for another post-work tryst with the object of his desire. Even as the word "tryst" popped into to his tabloid-infected mind, he felt a little embarrassed and pondered as to when a "tryst" became a "tryst". Was carnal intention alone enough to justify the term, even if from only one side, or did a romantic, perhaps sexual, relationship actually have to be in existence for a meeting to earn this particular sobriquet?

'Fuck,' he thought, 'I'm doing it again, this bizarre, immature reverie. What am I doing here? And "reverie"? Am I living in a "Mills and Boon"? Or imagining that I am?'

He knew though, that despite the dangers to his marriage and his family, he wanted something to happen. He would take the risk because the benefits outweighed those dangers. No, that wasn't it. If he actually weighed them up, they didn't. Of course they didn't. But at that moment, and lots of others like it since he had first met Steph, the cost/benefit analysis equation simply didn't work. What he wanted right here and now was more important than anything else. That fanciful equation required recalibration to deal with the strength of current desires.

'Oh my God, Jim, you're here late again?' She pointed out the obvious as she headed for the stairs, raincoat fully buttoned in preparation for the fight against the inclement Edinburgh elements.

Donnelly's heart beat quickened but he affected a calm demeanour, raising his eyebrows and pursing his lips in a kind of stoic, hard-done-by expression.

'What's up? Problem with your story or ... things not so good at home?'

It was only as the bait was being taken that Donnelly became fully aware that he had set it.

'Ach, it's aw right, hen, you just head off. You dinnae want to be delayed by me and ma trivial domestic issues.'

Donnelly experienced something approaching pure joy as he saw Steph unbutton her raincoat and walk the few metres to the nearest kettle before turning it on and settling down on a seat opposite him.

'I know that it takes a lot for tough old blokes like you to unburden yourself so if you're willing to talk I'm certainly willing to listen. And after all, what have I got to rush home to?' She paused briefly. 'Oh, wait a minute ... it's the last episode of CSI. Could we do this tomorrow?'

It only took about five seconds for Donnelly to realise that she was winding him up but that was long enough for him to feel it in the pit of his stomach. Hopefully he hadn't shown it though.

'Only kidding, that's what iPlayer was invented for, eh?'

'Eh, aye,' Donnelly replied.

'So, dish. What's up? Don't tell me, your wife's chucked you out 'cause you've been playing 'hide the salami' with that new cutie on reception?'

'Aye, that's it. You've nailed it. Nineteen year old girls just can't get enough o' ma trendy hair-cut and rippled torso. It gets tiring after a while though, I don't mind admitting.'

'You may not have a rippled torso – as far as I'm aware – but you do have a certain rumpled charm ...'

'Brilliant – less "rippled" and more "rumpled". Kind of like "Rumpled of the Bailey, ha"?

Steph looked confused.

'No seriously, I could see why a younger woman might find you attractive. You've got a kind of rough charisma about you and you have very ...' she took a while before settling on 'manly features.'

They both took a moment to sip from the coffee that Steph had prepared and in the, almost romantic, computer screen light, they shared a moment.

Another moment later, however, Steph became aware of

what she had just said and panicked as she realised it could have sounded like a come-on whilst Donnelly was thinking:

'Bloody hell, I think I'm in with a chance here, that sounded like a come-on.'

'What I meant ...' Steph began but gave way to Donnelly's simultaneous declaration:

'You know you're a very bonny woman, Steph?'

'What I meant, I was just, eh, thanks. I mean I was just ...'

Donnelly attempted a retreat:

'I mean to say that some of the guys in the office were just saying that. Not that I disagree. I mean I don't agree or disagree. No, that's not right, I do agree it's just I don't have an opinion, well ...'

Steph had regained her composure:

'Come on, I can take it. Am I attractive or not?'

Donnelly's demeanour changed and he looked right into her eyes as he said:

'Yes, of course you are – you're lovely, that's the problem.'

He was aware he had raised the stakes, but as poker was his second favourite "sport" after football, he had instinctively felt that it was the right thing to do.

Steph let his statement hang in the air for a moment whilst she decided whether it might be safest just to leave it alone completely. She couldn't resist though:

'What do you mean, "that's the problem"?'

'I know it might be silly, but I'm not gonna lie. I'm quite ... taken with you. You've brightened things up for me over the last few months and I'm glad.'

As declarations of love go, it was restrained, but it still had a profound effect on Steph. She'd guessed that he fancied her of course. She knew she had that effect - on older men particularly. Two drunken passes in consecutive years at Christmas parties from both her head teacher and the head of social subjects had demonstrated that. She put it down to her curvy figure reminding them of the crushes they had felt in their youth for movie stars of a previous generation. This felt different though. Donnelly looked really sincere.

As he told her of his daughter's misreading of the kiss she had seen them share and his wife's instinctive understanding of both what had actually happened and what he might have wanted to, she felt an outpouring of emotion towards him. She wasn't exactly sure what kind of emotion or "emotions" it was but she acted on instinct as she moved towards him and silenced his babbling with a very tender, if ambiguous, kiss.

*

It had been over five years since the wife of one of Stuart's ex-team-mates had provided Jo with the phone number of Eck McDougal. Whilst not a private investigator as such, he made a living finding things out for people, and in recent years had been fully employed by a succession of Glasgow WAGs who passed his phone number on much as most people would pass on the details of a competent plumber or decorator. There was no-one in Glasgow who knew more about the illicit affairs of Athletic or Glasgow Rovers footballers than Eck McDougal. And that included the journalists at the *Daily Record* who also purchased his services from time to time. For a number of years, Eck had been planning to write a book about the underworld of Scottish football, an exposé which would show the public the real truth behind the public image of "those smug bastards". He perhaps hadn't noticed that many of them had already done a decent job of that themselves. He was still, he reckoned, one big story away from having enough material to make it worthwhile. He lay back on the white leather armchair in his slightly dowdy, eccentrically furnished, Partick flat. One would be tempted to imagine that the flat housed a collector of eclectic tastes: there was a modern, red leather sofa here, a traditional teak sideboard unit there, and so on. And as for the ornaments, the dominant piece was a large, shiny ceramic tiger but many other, equally tasteless items jostled for the viewer's attention. Truth be told, however, that Eck had been "given" most of these "pieces" as reward for favours done. For friends. Or anyone really. He was the "go-to" man for information of all sorts. He traded in it 24/7. He got cash for the big jobs, of course, but would take items, in-kind, for wee bits of knowledge here and there. Anything, as long as it looked expensive. He, himself, was also adorned expensively, but with a commensurate lack of what might be considered good taste. His hair betrayed an interest in the music and style of the "Mod" era and his short, though thick set, frame was clad in Fred Perry and Sta Prest.

'This one sounds good,' he thought when he got the call from Jo.

Jo could have asked Eck to try and find out why her husband had given Mark Sinclair two thousand pounds. But then Eck may find out more than she was comfortable with him knowing and instinctively she felt that wouldn't be a good thing. She was sure her husband wouldn't be involved in anything unpleasant but 'perhaps,' she thought, 'he's made some mistake.' It wouldn't be the first time that she'd helped him deal with one of his mistakes.

She decided it would be best simply to get Eck to find out how she could "bump into" Mark Sinclair and she would take it from there.

*

So it was that Jo found herself nursing a cup of instant coffee in the unusually basic surroundings of the Cuppa Cafe in deepest Possil, waiting for Mark Sinclair to make his usual pre-bookies morning visit. She was aware of her own condescension as she found herself thinking: 'Well it's clean, at least.'

This was her third attempt at the meeting and she was feeling more than a little uncomfortable about the attention she was getting from some of the regulars who were beginning to debate the possible reasons as to why this expensively dressed, and more than a little attractive, creature had been moving amongst them. She winced at the loud throb from a pneumatic drill in operation on road works just outside the café and sat in increasing discomfort.

She was thrilled when, this time, Sinclair did appear and she was fully prepared to go through her pre-planned routine of feigning surprise, slight recognition and eventually offering a coffee and a cake for the non-plussed ex-footballer. She had her "visiting a client" alibi at the ready and they soon settled to apparently random chit-chat.

'I don't mean to be rude,' Jo asked the now-relaxed and quite chuffed Sinclair, 'but you're not looking so well, Mark. You're not ill or anything are you?'

'A'm fine. You've jist no' seen me fur a while. It's jist lack of training and ...' Mark smiled. Jo wasn't sure if it was a sly smile or a rueful one. Possibly both.

'... and a minor heroin addiction.'

He had almost whispered his last statement, and with the noise from the drill, she wasn't sure she'd heard him right.

'Did you say: "heroin"?'

'Aye. Are ye shocked, like?'

'No. Well, a wee bit. Not "shocked" as such, I mean … well anyway that kind've explains something. Stuart was a little coy about the reason for his recent, eh, gift to you. It'll have been for rehab I suppose? He's such a generous man, my Stuart'.

Sinclair couldn't resist a slight smirk at that last remark but managed what appeared to Jo to be a marginally sarcastic: 'Aye, very generous.'

'What, you don't think it was generous? Giving you two grand to help with your addiction. Seems pretty generous to me.'

'Aye well, it's no' quite as straightforward as that is it?'

'How not? It seems straightforward.'

Sinclair recovered his composure:

'Yeah. Yeah, you're right. Sometimes a talk crap. It is straightforward. And very generous, aye.'

Jo wasn't sure whether "shifty" was just Mark Sinclair's default setting but he was definitely not looking like a man you could trust. She reached over, touched him on the top of his hand and looked into his eyes. 'What's up, Mark?' she asked. 'What's wrong?'

The double whammy of the touch and those gorgeous

brown eyes had an almost hypnotising effect on him.

'It wis tae help me wi' ma addiction, it really wis. It's jist thit it wis also aboot, ye ken, solidarity, aboot aw fur one an' one fur aw, ye ken?'

'No, Mark, I really don't know. What do you mean?'

'Ye know, that night – whit happened tae Banns – and that lassie. It's made us aw closer than we wid be, ye ken?'

Jo continued to dig but having already employed the big artillery she eventually realised that she was going to get no further and made her excuses, paid the bill, and left, feeling no more knowledgeable but no less suspicious.

*

Davie hadn't planned to bump into Mel that night in the East Port bar. Things were going great with her and he certainly wasn't ready to risk her coming into contact with the likes of Andy Parks. Truth be told, he didn't want to have that much social contact with Andy and the others himself. He was, however, on a rare night out with his team mates when he spotted her on the other side of the room.

He avoided these nights out like the plague. Not only did he not particularly enjoy his team mates' company but he found it very hard not to drink alcohol when with them. He didn't want his problem to be known around the club for fear of the management finding out which could possibly lead to his job being put at risk. However, he sometimes ran out of excuses and he accepted that once every few months he'd have go out to keep up appearances.

Worried that his drinking could easily get out of control again he'd planned a range of strategies to avoid getting paralytic. He figured that he could buy non-alcoholic lager on *his* rounds; make his drinks last and go to the toilet when others were going to buy rounds so he'd "accidentally" be missed out. His plan lasted till about halfway through the first drink at which point he knew he'd need another ... and another.

By the time his eyes met Mel's over an extremely packed bar, hers may have been eager and welcoming, his, however, were red and extremely blurred.

'Hey, is that no' yir burd, Davie,' shouted Jim Drylaw over the noise of the music and chat.

'Aye, that's hir. She's wi' hir pals though so a'll jist sae hi and leave hur tae it.'

'Not at all,' said club captain, Andy Parks, 'we want tae meet this lassie, and she's wi' a couple o' fit burds that I fur one would like tae git tae know.'

Through alcohol impaired vision, Davie recognised his friend Rab's girlfriend Susan and Mel's flat mate Gail. He didn't want Mel or her friend to be exposed to his feral team mates but he was drunk enough to not realise just how drunk he really was. He therefore believed he could probably handle it. He had no choice anyway.

At Parks' insistence, the girls joined the guys who quickly put a few more tables together to accommodate them. Mel had heard about this crowd so wasn't too keen. Susan didn't mind, though she made it plain pretty quickly that she had a boyfriend and so was not up for any unwanted attention. Gail, however, was recently single and keen to meet some men, particularly those better toned than the Dunfermline average.

Mel immediately spotted Davie's inebriated state, but, though disappointed, she knew enough to realise that his journey to sobriety was going to be an uphill struggle. Davie, however, sincerely believed he was hiding it from her and that he was succeeding in his attempts to act normal, i.e. sober.

Two more drinks in and Mel decided to have a quiet word in Davie's ear, discouraging him from further imbibing. She may have been quiet but Davie was not, and his response brought their disagreement to the attention of Parks:

'Show some balls, Davie, ur you wan o' they blokes thit dis whit thir burd tells thim?'

Not only did Davie agree with his team captain, he graphically demonstrated this agreement by cupping said balls in a defiant gesture before heading to the bar for another round.

One more drink and Davie's confidence was turning to bravado. Though faintly disgusted, Mel decided to save Davie from himself by suggesting that she get them a taxi and see him safely home to his Mum and Dad's.

Egged on by his team mates he demonstrated, definitively, to Mel why he really shouldn't drink at all by letting her know that she was being tight-arsed and should fuck off home if she didn't want to have fun.

The last thing Mel heard as she left the bar, fighting back tears, and consoled by her friends, was Davie's voice, prominent in a chorus, led by Andy Parks, of:

'Bros before Ho's; Bro's before Ho's, Bro's before ...'

Chapter Thirteen

'You sufferin' wi' that hip again, Norm?' Donnelly felt compelled to ask as Norman Campbell lowered himself into his chair accompanied by a symphony of moans and groans.

'Well, I suffer every day, Jim. It's just a matter of degree. They ask me at the hospital to rate the pain from one to ten. "Never below a seven," a tell them, "frequently a nine or ten".'

'So where does that leave heart attacks, slipped discs and decapitation on the pain scale then?'

'Or child birth!' came a female voice from the other side of the room.

'Ah well,' Donnelly interjected, 'I don't really believe all that guff about child birth being more painful than a heart attack or whatever. I think it's one of the great female lies.'

'Oh, this should be fun,' replied columnist, Alison Wilkie, 'and what are the others, pray tell?'

'Well one of my favourites,' replied Donnelly, warming to his task, 'is what I call the "Great Marks & Spencer's Deception". Wherever you go in the country with your wife, or similar female equivalent, they want to drag you into Marks and Spark's for an hour and a half. You, reasonably, point out that they go into M & S twice a week back home and then it comes ... the big lie: "You see" they tell you, "Marks and Spencer's have slightly different stock in different parts of the country".'

Laughs and general noises of assent emanated from

male voices throughout the office drowning out Alison's protestations: 'That's true, really, it's true ...'

'Anyway, all I know is ma hip's bloody sore and I'll call it a ten if a like.'

Norman felt a bit stupid when no-one replied to his protestation and he felt compelled to speak again:

'So where you headed then, Jim, I see you've got your coat on?'

'My God, Norm, you should be the investigative journalist with those powers o' observation. I've got a meeting with Mark Sinclair; you mind he played for Athletic a few years back?'

'Aye, I remember him – you're still on your Paul Bannerman story then?'

'Aye, I'm gettin' there.'

'What's he doing now then?'

'Nothing, that's the great thing, on the dole, and from what I hear, on the smack. I think he could be the weak link in the chain on this one.'

'Where are you meeting 'im? No, don't tell me. In the pub, right?'

Donnelly smiled as he left: 'Where else?'

*

Sinclair was already settled in a remote corner of one of the Grassmarket's countless hostelries when Donnelly arrived. Keeping his head low, he had evaded the gaze of the bar staff to avoid having to buy a drink whilst he waited. Sinclair was quite clear about the purpose of this meeting as far as he was concerned, free drink and fifty quid "expenses".

'Hi, Mark, how're you doing? Drink?' was Donnelly's cheery opening gambit as he offered his hand. He noted the weak handshake as Sinclair replied, 'Aye, cheers, man, a'll hae a pint o' the guest lager, ta.'

'Aye, start as you mean to go on,' mumbled Donnelly as he smiled and headed for the bar.

Sinclair felt at home in licensed premises but this one was a bit too plush for his liking. It felt like it was designed for tourists rather than for actual, proper drinking. And Edinburgh always made him nervous, anyway. A Drumchapel boy, his view of the capital was confused. He knew it was posh, full of bankers and public school boys but his assumptions had been challenged by the Trainspotting phenomenon. The heroin boom in early eighties Edinburgh had given way to the AIDS epidemic later in the decade and had confounded many people's image of the city. Sinclair wasn't quite sure whether he was most worried about avoiding "upper class wankers" or "AIDS infected junkies". Best, he thought, just to avoid the city altogether. Unless, of course, he was being paid.

'There you go, ma man, one each. A thought a'd try the guest beer too. A think it's English mind but we'll cope, eh?'

They smiled as they supped their beer and enjoyed both the smooth flavour and the shared token anti-Englishness.

'So, you're no' playin' fiba' anymore, Mark?'

'Naw, ah'm jist, eh, ye ken, ah'm jist, eh ... naw.'

'A remember ye though, playing for Athletic. A'm a bit of a Hearts fan and a remember ye playin' pretty well against us on a few occasions; decent full back.'

'Aye, thanks, a've had some great games against Hearts over the years. They're no' a bad team considerin'.' Donnelly didn't want to know what he had meant by "considerin' ".

'So, how do you keep yirsel' busy then?'

'Oh, ye know, a bit o' this and a bit o' that, ye ken?'

Donnelly had a fair idea of what "this" and "that" might consist and so he simply nodded whilst planning his attack. A past master at this kind of interrogation, Donnelly usually had a strategy with regard to the asking of questions. Unlike the Scottish national football team, however, he also had a Plan B when required and could improvise when instinct told him what would be best.

'So, what really happened that night? How did Paul Bannerman actually die?'

Despite his questioning of Avril, he did not really entertain serious doubts about the important parts of the accepted version of events. But like an attacking midfielder who could get past a defender with just a sudden change of pace, Donnelly had decided to knock Sinclair off balance with such a direct, and slightly shocking, question.

'Whit d'ye mean "How did he really die"? Who's been sayin' different?'

Two short sentences, but something in Sinclair's animated response imparted a wealth of information as far as Donnelly was concerned. Going with the flow, he replied:

'Well, you know, as a journalist, a can't reveal my sources but let's just say, a'm not needing you to tell me much, but just to back up what a've already heard.'

Donnelly's inner smugness was immediately dealt a blow as Sinclair did the inevitable and simply called the journalist's bluff:

'Go on then, who's telt ye whit? Abody a'ready knows how he died.'

Hoping he was onto something, Donnelly had to think quickly:

'Well let's just say that John McDougal's spilt more than a few beans ("more than a few beans?!" thought Donnelly) and a now know a lot more about what really happened with Avril Gallagher. Also, a've spoken tae the lassie hersel'.'

This was essentially a fishing expedition on Donnelly's part but it was having an obvious effect on Sinclair. Already concerned at what he may have possibly revealed, Sinclair suddenly had another dire realisation, of a more pressing disaster:

'What' he thought, 'if this meeting ends before we even get past the first pint?'

'Anyway,' he announced, whilst quickly draining his drink, 'time fur another, eh?'

'Aye, of course,' Donnelly conceded, reasonably satisfied with the result so far. 'Two-nil ahead at half-time,' he thought, as he headed towards the bar.

Sinclair looked around at the mixture of American tourists, students, and well-heeled office workers enjoying the traditional, if reasonably classy pub grub. He wasn't sure which he hated most. After a moments thought he concluded that it was probably the students who were the most objectionable. Though slightly scruffy, their faces seemed plump and well-fed and their expressions seemed smug. It was as if they were saying:

'This is just a muck-about for a few years; I'll soon be able to buy and sell you.'

'Gie me the fifty quid! Go on, gie me thi fifty quid noo,' Sinclair demanded as Donnelly arrived back at the table. He wanted to ensure that if this meeting went badly, he wouldn't be leaving without his money. The discomfort he had been feeling whilst Donnelly was at the bar had got him more worked up and Donnelly immediately realised that he had to calm things down, to regroup a little before going on the attack again. Sinclair was definitely needing to be handled carefully.

'It must hold pretty bad memories for you, that night,' Donnelly began again, trying to appear concerned whilst fishing for the money in his wallet.

'Naw it disnae, there's nothin' tae feel bad aboot,' Sinclair replied before realising what he'd said and adding, 'a mean, of course it holds bad memories, of course it fuckin' does.'

Donnelly handed over the fifty quid. 'A can't help thinking about Avril, about how the lassie feels about it all. It ruined her life, of course. A went tae see her in Strathgyte. Weird place. It's all tarted up now, but still, a fuckin' weird place tae go.'

'Whit did she say?' asked Sinclair, concerned. And before Donnelly could answer, he added:

'Fuckin' cow killed wan o' ma mates, ah've nae sympathy'.

'A telt ye, she telt me what really happened,' Donnelly replied, fishing once more.

'And you believe hir, d'ye? A mental, murderin' hooker.'

'She was not a prostitute!' For the first time in the conversation Donnelly had lost his cool. There was something about that poor, beaten girl that pressed his paternal buttons. Somehow, despite it all, there was something about that girl.

138

'Whatever - she wis still a murderin' bitch.'

'Was she, Mark? And if she was, why? What made her do it?'

'Ye ken why, he caught hir thievin' so she killed 'im.'

'It disnae add up, Mark. A've met her, she's no' a murderer. And a can see you know that too. You've practically admitted it.' Donnelly took a conjectural leap. 'You've more or less told me that the truth isn't what people think it is. And when a tell the others what you've told me, when I speak to Stuart Robertson ...'

Mark Sinclair hadn't moved as fast since his football career had fizzled out. Before Donnelly had finished his sentence he'd stood up, thrust his upper body across the table and grabbed hold of Donnelly by one shoulder and one lapel. His wispy beard, yellow teeth and beery breath were up against the surprised, and slightly fearful face of the journalist.

'A've telt ye nuthin', Nuthin' right? 'Cause thirs nothin' tae tell.' His forehead thudded against Donnelly's, who could feel the other man's spittle on his own lips. 'Yir jist makin' stuff up oot yir heid. You say a've telt ye anythin' different and yir deid, got it?'

He thrust him back into his seat pausing to notice that Donnelly's pint had spilled and was now pouring onto the older man's trousers. His own was intact though. He drained the last third in one go and headed for the door, turning only to issue one last threat:

'A ken folk, ken? Folk that you widnae want tae meet. You better be careful, careful goin' tae yir car at night; careful leavin' the pub at the weekend. You jist better be fuckin' careful.'

If Donnelly had a pint for every threat he had received over his career, his liver would be in an even worse state than it was. Nonetheless, it was a chastened journalist who straightened himself up, took a look around to see who was watching and headed for the door.

*

'Davie, it's time fur training, son, yiv barely left yir room a' weekend. C'mon, ye dinnae want tae get in trouble wi' the club.' Agnes hadn't seen Davie when he'd arrived home in the early hours of Sunday morning but she'd heard the unmistakeable sound of heaving coming from the toilet as she and Tam had listened for clues as to his state after that ill-starred night out. Emerging only for food, and not often at that, they knew that something was obviously not right but they had not been treated to the full, gory details.

'Phone thim and tell thim a'm still sick. A'm no' goin in, right?' Davie was far too well practised a drunk to still be hung-over thirty two hours later, but having tried for most of Sunday to phone and text Mel with no reply he certainly was ailing.

'Are ye sure, son? Are ye sure?'

Davie pulled the covers up again and replied, 'Aye, I'm sure.'

*

'Christ, Jim, I know you're getting on a bit, but really, have you actually wet yourself?'

Steph was the last person he'd wanted to see as he'd attempted to quietly drift in and out of the office to collect some papers before heading home.

It was a downcast and sheepish Donnelly who answered her without meeting her eyes.

'Naw, of course not, I spilled my drink – well actually someone else spilled my drink. It was – och – it disnae matter, I'll tell you another time, I've got tae go.'

With that he sidled, sheepishly, out of the office leaving Steph perplexed.

A few minutes later Donnelly found himself sitting on a bench in Holyrood Park. Yes, he was still processing his meeting with Sinclair, but it wasn't that which had brought him down to his favourite "thinking bench". It was the brief encounter with Steph, and the memory of that kiss; that beautiful, though annoyingly inconclusive, kiss. It was even more memorable than that of the Glasgow variety which he had just suffered. They had quickly parted that night, embarrassed and flustered. But he had thought of little else since. He couldn't forget what he hoped was the promise of that kiss. Or the guilt.

Chapter Fourteen

'Right, boys, the main objective here is no' tae make fools o' oorsel's, right?'

Nervous laughter rippled round the rather plush Athletic changing room.

'They've got six ex-internationalists and three current internationalists, including two members of the current world cup holders; we've got one ... ehm ... current internationalist, Stu?'

'Aye, current internationalist - I played in the Finland friendly earlier this year,' Stuart Robertson responded to Graham Todd's gentle ribbing.

'Anyway, they've got Fernando Aguila and we've got Jim Forrester ...' After waiting for the laughter to die down, Todd added, with impeccable comic timing:

' Still defending right enough, but currently defending the honour of the lovely ladies of "Temptations" lapdancing bar on Lothian Road from the attentions of mental punters wi' hard-ons.'

About to go out onto the field to face a far superior side in front of nearly thirty thousand football fans, it was understandable that many of those gathered were feeling more than a little nervous, particularly given that some were not even full-time players anymore, or players at all for that matter. Athletic had drafted in a few of their current side to lower the average age a little and ensure that the likes of Mark Sinclair wouldn't have to spend too long on the field. Nevertheless, during the pre-match preparations, at least a quarter of the squad were missing at any given time, attending to the needs of their nervous bowels in the adjoining cubicles.

Davie Thomson had not left his room for four days before forcing himself, at his parent's desperate behest, to get dressed, packed and in the car to Glasgow. He was keeping quiet and trying to focus on his father's words over breakfast.

'This is something fur ye tae enjoy, no' tae worry aboot, son. It's jist a game o' fitba'.'

His Mum had added:

'Whitevur else is goin' on fur ye son, jist forget aboot it fur the day. Jist try tae enjoy it. Ye love fitba' and yir dad's right, that's a' it is, a game o' fitba'.'

'Jist a game o' fitba',' he repeated to himself like a mantra.

'Whit wis that, Davie?' asked Ally James.

'Eh, nothing, man, jist gettin' masel' psyched up, ken?'

'Aye, a'm scared shitless tae.'

The mood was decidedly different at half-time:

'Fuckin' hell, that wisnae too bad; twa-wan doon tae a team like that? No' bad at a'.'

Todd summed up the mood of the group, most of whom were caught between slightly manic elation and profound exhaustion. Added into the mix were a rich array of strains, knocks and bruises on which a small army of physios and assistants were quickly getting to work.

'Fuckin' hell, Andy, that was inspired. Why the fuck did you decide tae stop playin'?'

This was asked of Andy Stevenson, goalkeeper, by an incredulous Stuart Robertson. Stevenson had apparently lost his nerve not long after the Bannerman incident and now worked in IT in Newcastle. The sub keeper for the day had been told to expect plenty of game time on the assumption that Stevenson would make a few early howlers and have to be replaced. He'd been back playing Sunday league football, however, in the last year, with some of his mates from work. He was still terrified, but quietly confident, that he might do all right.

'Thanks, Stu; I'm actually quite enjoying myself, a must admit.'

'Well keep on enjoying yirsel', pal, because it wis two-one going on ten-one if we're honest, and you're the main reason why it wis jist the two.'

The mood was different again at full time:

'Christ, a feel like a've gone ten rounds wi' Mike Tyson,' was John McDougal's summing up of his personal state of fitness after ninety long minutes. There were no demurring voices.

'Five goals though - five wan. That's kind o' embarrassing.'

There was no response for about a minute till eventually Davie spoke, in a small voice:

'A nivir thought a'd hear masel' say this, but ye ken whit, a'd've taken five-wan bifore the start o' the game.'

A few moments further silence, then a number of voices:

'Aye, five-wan - no' bad considerin'.'

'Aye, a' can cope wi' that - a thought we wirnae too bad.'

'A'm happy enough wi' that tae be honest.'

Then ironic cheers of:

'Five-wan, five-wan, five-wan, five-wan!'

Their gallows humour, mixed with a genuine sense of limited pride soon gave way to grumbles born of aching limbs, swollen calves and a common belief among many, that they may never walk unaided again.

'Tell ye one thing,' Mark Sinclair predicted, 'we'll murder these guys at the bar later.'

'Aye,' added John McDougal, 'fuckin' amateurs.'

*

It was after the dinner, after the speeches, after the official drinks and even after the unofficial after official-drinks drinks (during which the ex-Athletic boys, as predicted, soundly beat their rivals in the alcohol-imbibing stakes) when this band of brothers came to embark on another sentimental discussion about their great, late departed pal: Paul Bannerman.

'A fuckin' gentleman.'

'Sound as a pound.'

'A bloody good midfielder, but.'

'Raise your glasses, gentlemen,' Stuart Robertson began, 'to a great man, and our friend: Paul Bannerman.'

And it was even later before the conversation inevitably turned to something, or someone, on all their minds: James Donnelly.

'I'll tell you what,' Robertson announced, after hearing the tales of those who had spoken to the journalist:

' I'm gonnae speak to him. A wisnae gonnae, but I think

it's time that James Donnelly encountered the famous StuRob charm. A'll put 'im straight'.

Mark Sinclair remained quiet throughout.

*

Jo had attended the match, and the reception, but afterwards, had discreetly withdrawn, with the other wives and girlfriends, in the manner of well-bred Edwardian ladies allowing the gentlemen space to smoke and discuss the issues of the day. Jo was fully aware of the sexism she encountered in Stuart's world but she viewed it with ironic detachment as if observing the patterns of children's play. Truth be told, she was quite happy to leave before the drinking became too serious, even competitive, it could be said.

She was sleeping, therefore, when Stuart arrived home, drunk, in the early hours of the evening. He didn't, however, sneak in quietly, wash, clean his teeth and slip silently into bed. No, he failed at the first hurdle, unable to open the front door with his work locker key; he rang the bell, unselfconsciously, and greeted Jo with a puppy-dog smile and a beery kiss.

A few years earlier, Jo might have weakened, faced with Stuart's boyish charm but having had to deal with this particular scenario once – or perhaps ten times – too often, she simply let him in, locked the door and went back to bed.

She had fallen asleep again by the time he made his way to bed wearing only a smile and an erection. His breath smelled no better, however, and his lustful advances were dismissed with little fanfare.

'Aw, go on, darlin', you know you want to ...'

'Aye, I know I want to go to sleep, now shut the fuck up and leave me alone.'

*

Although she hadn't seen him since that terrible night, Mel had accepted Davie's offer of four tickets to the match – for her Mum and Dad, and best friend, Susan. Mel didn't really want to see Davie but hadn't completely decided whether or not to cut her losses and leave him to his drinking and macho, boorish behaviour. She did like the idea, however, of taking her parents to the match as the guest of a player and with great seats and "hospitality" to boot. She justified this, by telling herself that they were still officially an item and that this was part of the process of helping her make up her mind.

For his part, Davie took it as a good sign that Mel had deigned to come to the event at all and he felt slightly more optimistic despite her refusing to see him. 'With a bit of luck,' he thought, 'she'll be impressed to see me playing on the same pitch as famous players from the telly.'

Mel believed herself to be a sensible girl, with her head firmly screwed on. Even she, however, could feel herself becoming seduced with the glamour of the occasion and Davie's place in it. He'd played well, too, and if pressed she would have to admit to a vaguely school-girlish crush on the version of Davie that she watched running, passing and tackling on the field of dreams.

Davie had also calculated, correctly, that getting Mel's parents to the match would have a positive effect. There's something instinctive about a parent's desire to see their child's social status enhanced and their appreciation of the invitation and subsequent enjoyment of the day had certainly brought them "on-side".

It was with all this in mind that Mel had agreed to meet with Davie for a walk in Dunfermline's Pittencrief Park on Sunday afternoon, the day after the big match.

Pittencrief Park held many significant memories for Davie. He remembered the play parks, maze and mini-zoo from family visits in his childhood. His parents were never exactly well-off and The Glen provided a regular, inexpensive, day out, the only cost being the obligatory ice-cream from the ever-present van. Later on, The Glen became a venue for teenage drinking, then eventually the geological feature from which the park takes its nickname provided quiet, covered areas in which to take girls and indulge in endless kissing accompanied by the occasional furtive grope.

'A can't help it, a still spend half my time in here looking out for peacocks,' admitted Mel, in reference to the birds which roamed freely in the park and which would occasionally please the punters by showing off their spectacular plumage. 'A always used to get such a thrill when I saw them when I was wee.'

'Yeah, it's a great place this isn't it – a spent tons o' time here when a was a bairn.'

A brief silence was broken by Davie:

'The most important thing to do here, of course, is to buy an ice-cream. What d'ye want? A ninety-nine?'

'Aye, go on – wi' strawberry sauce.'

Davie left Mel sitting on a park bench and practised his speech as he waited in the queue for ice-cream. It was a bright winter's day and, though not warm, it was just about still the weather for ice-cream, though some would have preferred a mug of hot chocolate. Davie felt uncharacteristically emboldened by the afterglow of yesterday's match and planned to come straight to the point. That was the great thing about Mel, he felt he could talk about anything with her – stuff that he couldn't talk to anyone else about.

'A'm no' like that ye ken – the guy, in the pub, that night, that's no' really me.'

'Wow, Davie, not even "Here's your ninety nine – d'you want sprinkles"? Or, "Did you enjoy the match?"'

'If a don't say what a need tae say a'll no' have thi guts tae say it at a'. A just want ye tae know ... what a mean is, a *need* ye tae know, that that isnae who a am.'

'But to some extent it is though, isn't it? The amount of times a've listened tae my female friends talking about guys and saying: "A know he disnae seem very nice when he's with other people but see when it's just him and me – he's really lovely". Or: "He only shows his sensitive side tae me". Or, worst of all: "A know he's a bit of a bad boy but a can change him". It drives me mental. If he's nice he'll be nice tae everyone; if he only has a sensitive side when he's wi' you maybe he's just trying to get intae your pants; and why pick a bad guy that you have tae make good? Why not just pick a good one? My point, Davie, is that a don't like the side of you that a saw that night and a don't want to be around that.'

'But that wis the drink. It's the drink that makes me like that. A'm trying ma best tae stop it. Bit ... bit ... it's ... hard.'

Davie spotted a peacock wandering into view to the right of, but slightly behind Mel. He wanted to tell her; he felt it would cheer her up, perhaps be seen by her as a good omen. He knew it wasn't the time, though.

'Naw, Davie, you've got to take responsibility for your own actions. You can't just blame the drink.'

Davie misunderstood:

'But, Mel, I thought you'd understand, it's no' that easy – the drink's hard tae beat.'

'Oh, for God's sake, Davie, d'ye really think that's why a don't want tae see you? Because you have a problem wi' drink? Give me more credit – a know it's hard – and a'd be willing to help you. It's no' the fact that you can't stop drinking – it's the part of you that comes out when you do. I'm no' prepared to put up wi' that.'

Davie felt the tears come just before Mel saw them. Never having cried in front of anyone but his parents, and not for over ten years at that, Davie was embarrassed beyond belief. But it wasn't tears of despair, it was tears of relief. Relief at what Mel had just said. If it wasn't the drinking that she couldn't cope with; if it was the macho crap that he had to spout when he was with his pals. Well he could kick that habit much, much more easily than he could kick the booze. If need be, he'd just never go out with them again. Mel was much more important. Truth be told, he didn't like most of his friends anyway.

Mel was aware of the irony inherent in her holding Davie in her arms and wiping away his tears. Was this exactly what she'd just been talking about, a man who would only show his sensitive side when he was with her?

But the combination of those rare, manly tears, and Davie's words convinced her that he was worth persevering with:

'A'm so sorry, Mel. A'll no' be like that again. Apart fae Rab, a dinnae like any o' thim onyway. A'll gie thim a' up fur you. Nae problem'

'Don't be daft. A'm no' asking you tae do that.'

150

'This is the real me though, well no' the tears mibbae, but this is the real me ... the only me.'

She watched his eyes widen as he seemed to look behind her. She followed that gaze and was treated to the wonderful, and nostalgic, sight of the peacock in full display. The beautiful "eyes" on its feathers seemed to meet hers and she, too, began to cry.

Those tears, and her embrace, told him all he needed to know.

Chapter Fifteen

Dinner in the Donnelly-Davidson household was rarely relaxing and never at a consistent time. Sometimes it had to be late because Fiona wouldn't finish ballet practise until seven, or early because Katy had to start football at half-past six. Add in Katy's band practise and drama club and Fiona's Thursday night Guides and the timing of every evening meal was a problem to be solved. And that's before considering Jacqui's shifts and Donnelly being Donnelly.

Then there was the difficulty of actually getting the girls to all these activities. They were old enough now to attend the local stuff themselves but some activities proved more challenging, logistically. Football training at Sighthill, for instance, too far away to be worth going home in-between but too lengthy to kill time reading the paper.

Jacqui felt a kind of vague unease at how fully programmed her children's lives had become. It felt like a kind of middle class disease, one that she associated with the kind of aspirational mothers that she both despised and feared she had become. But the girls, she reminded herself, had requested, or practically demanded to take part in all these activities themselves. The reason, she supposed, that her generation had spent more time amusing themselves was that only a fraction of the opportunities existed in her day. And right enough, amusing herself, usually meant hanging out at the park with the older boys who would give her cigarettes and try to take advantage in return.

Then there was the business of how to cater for a family

with two vegetarians (Katy and Fiona), one quasi-vegetarian (Jacqui, who had never managed to wean herself back off fish after craving it during both pregnancies) and one anti-vegetarian (Donnelly, obviously).

On this occasion, they were eating stir fry noodles and vegetables with soya "chunks" for protein, about which Donnelly still complained bitterly even though he had long-since gotten used to them and, if truth-be-told, occasionally included them in meals he cooked for himself. But only, "cause there's never any bloody chicken in this bloody house."

This meal also had the advantage of brevity of preparation time, always important when someone has just rushed in and someone else needed to be out in ten minutes.

The conversation went along familiar lines:

"How was school ... fine ... what do you mean fine ... just fine ... what did you do ... nothing ... what do you mean nothing" and so on.

On this occasion, the familiarity of the routine pleased Donnelly. That, and the relatively relaxed atmosphere helped him believe that his rehabilitation was complete and that he was once more accepted as a full member of the society that was his family. He knew he didn't deserve it though. It was a tale of two kisses, the one that had been observed had been innocent, but the one that they knew nothing about was, he hoped, not.

*

Donnelly was not easily star-struck, having met a fair few famous people in his time. Also, his natural cynicism led to him disliking most celebrities. Most people actually.

153

He would not have admitted it, therefore, but he was quite excited about meeting Stuart Robertson, Scotland's premier football personality. Robertson was certainly one of the country's most successful footballers, though, most would agree that these days that particular bar is not set very high. He was, however, even more impressive as a personality: bright, charismatic and very articulate, he was natural television material. This was not harmed by his, some would say, good-looks and many would say, cheeky smile.

People like Robertson generate a kind of gravitational pull which makes others want to move towards them, to spend time in their company. Women certainly fancy him, and men – well they kind of fancy him too, in a macho, non-gay way of course. Apart from the gay men who, mainly, fancy him as well.

Having turned down his request for a meeting on three occasions Donnelly was very pleasantly surprised when Robertson phoned him personally to suggest they meet. Of course, when meeting Robertson, the balance of power was different from Donnelly's previous meetings with the likes of John McDougal. It was for this reason that Donnelly found himself on the train from Edinburgh to Glasgow.

Scotland's two major cities are only fifty miles apart and it is estimated that twenty thousand people live in Edinburgh and commute each day to Glasgow whilst twenty five thousand go in the opposite direction. Those who have strong feelings about the cities' relative merits would no doubt make something of those statistics. Some might say that more are travelling to Edinburgh because it's better. Others would point out that if more are travelling east to the capital that's because more wish to reside in Glasgow, proving its attributes are superior. Glasgow's Miles Better or Edinburgh's Slightly Superior? Take your pick. Donnelly had no doubt where he stood in that particular debate: that Hearts resided in Edinburgh would be enough reason to favour the capital anyway, but on top of that he interpreted the clichéd notion that citizens from the west are more friendly as meaning that you're more likely to get accosted by drunks on Argyle Street on a Saturday night.

The fifty minute train journey was long enough for him to plan his strategy. He knew it had to be a little more sophisticated than that for some of the other meetings but, after all, though he was clearly brighter than the like of Mark Sinclair, Robertson was still a footballer and his brains were, therefore, mostly in his feet. Donnelly felt he could handle him.

Getting off at Queen Street Station, he made his way west along Sauchiehall Street to the cafe at the CCA or to give it its full title: the Centre for Contemporary Arts. Donnelly had been glad of Robertson's suggestion that they meet for morning coffee as opposed to lunch, as he was finding it hard to justify the expense account he was racking up on a story that never seemed to be finished. However, he had never been to this place before and it didn't sound like his sort of joint. Those two words "contemporary" and "arts" were deeply concerning to him. If it were not for his wife, Donnelly would purchase all adornments required for his walls from Ikea, though frankly, he'd prefer a signed print of Hearts legend: Dave Mackay.

The exhibitions put on at the CCA tend towards the more esoteric end of the art spectrum, showing work which Donnelly would describe, succinctly, as "crap". To be honest, Robertson was no keener on the art on display in the CCA but he was much more comfortable in the "arty" surroundings having been schooled by Jo about the world of speciality coffees and mezze. It was he who had chosen this place, rightly believing it to be out of the grizzled journalist's comfort zone.

Robertson was late and Donnelly early, leaving him with nearly twenty minutes to kill in these uncomfortable surroundings. He was relieved to find, however, that it wasn't just a cafe, but a cafe/bar. An overpriced bottle of imported lager soon found its way down his grateful throat allowing him to relax a little.

'Beer, great, I was afraid you'd be on one of those fancy coffees; think I'll have one too.' Robertson offered his hand and a warm smile before ordering a bottle of something Belgian. Eschewing the proffered olives with a disdainful wave, he sat down next to Donnelly.

'I'm the same, can't see the point of olives,' offered Donnelly. 'They're kind of like salty grapes.'

Robertson laughed. 'I have this theory that the test to see whether you've become a middle-class wanker is if you eat olives and go on skiing holidays. One's ok – I mean I can't go skiing because of insurance but I might when I stop playing – but if you do both, you've crossed a line.'

'Too true,' replied Donnelly, nodding his head vigorously.

'How's your beer?' Robertson asked as he settled into his seat.

'Pretty good,' replied Donnelly before regaling him with a funny story about buying beer on holiday in Egypt.

Robertson laughed appropriately and before Donnelly knew it he'd spent a pleasant half hour drinking beer and chatting about holidays, lager and, of course, football, with one of Scotland's most famous proponents of the game.

Both men knew that they'd eventually have to get round

to the topic they were actually there to discuss, though neither really wanted to. Though he wouldn't articulate it, Robertson instinctively behaved as the alpha male in most situations and he had come to be seen as such. It was he, therefore, who decided that the elephant in the room had begun to smell a little and could be ignored no longer:

'So, Jim, I guess we need tae talk about that terrible night. A night, don't forget, when a lost one o' ma best pals. You'll understand it's not easy for me, ye know, revisiting it but you seem a very persistent guy and, what with the anniversary and that, maybe it's time to lay it to rest. A mean that night, not the memory of Banns of course. That'll never leave us.'

'Aye, thanks, Stuart. I'm sorry if you've got the impression that I've been a wee bit pushy on this. It's just an instinctive journalist thing.'

'That's ok, so let's be upfront, all right?'

A nod from Donnelly.

'What a'm wondering is, what's your angle on this? It doesn't seem to be just a commemorative piece; you've been asking too many probing questions for that. A don't mean to be rude, but you've been upsettin' people a bit. Now you seem to be a nice guy so I don't think you'd do that if you didn't have a really good reason. What do you think there is to learn about that night that your readers need tae know?'

'Ehm, it's not so much, I mean, I don't really ... have a particular thing that I'm ... you know, trying to find out. It's just ...'

'You're just uneasy about it, eh? A can understand that. A mean a'm uneasy about it – I think we all are. A can't help wondering, if only a'd stayed longer; maybe if there'd been less drink about. And the girl, she didn't set out tae kill anyone that night. A have a certain amount of sympathy for her, though that might not be shared with all the guys. The lassie had issues, she wis stoned, she did somethin' stupid. Now she's doolally in a mental home. A mean; nobody came out of this ahead, particularly Banns of course.'

'I suppose that was my initial impetus,' Donnelly replied. 'It occurred to me that very few o' that team, with the honourable exception of yourself and maybe two others, went on to achieve much in the game, despite the potential that most of them had. The normal career trajectory includes a bit of a decline for the last few years before retiral but most of those guys went downhill immediately after that season. After that night.'

'Aye, you're right. A mean a suppose a was aware o' that on one level, but thinkin' about it, it's pretty bad, eh?'

Robertson seemed to find a place in the middle distance upon which to settle his gaze and Donnelly felt it appropriate to leave a few seconds silence. He prolonged this further when he saw what looked like a hint of a tear in the corner of the footballer's eye. It was Robertson who broke the silence.

'People don't like to think there's any sensitivity at all amongst footballers, and right enough, a've come across a few tough guys all right and a few that you wouldnae like tae meet on a dark night – mainly Rovers players, obviously.' He smiled. 'But, ye know, footballers are people too and ye can only imagine the effect that something like that has on folk. Think about Davie Thomson, he turned tae booze. Wi' Mark Sinclair it was drugs. Some, like Andy Stevenson, they just lost confidence a think – fatal for a goalie. Though did ye see the way he played last week? A think he could be on his way back. But you're right, it's tragic – the lost potential.'

Again, Donnelly left a few respectful seconds of silence before:

'I don't mean this in a bad way like, in fact it's a good thing, but it begs the question ...'

'StuRob!' A shout from across the bar interrupted Donnelly's flow. 'Make sure ye score on Saturday. Gaun yirsel', big man!'

Robertson wasn't really very big, but the issuer of this popular Glaswegian greeting only had two options available to him: "big" or "wee". "Gaun yirsel, medium size man" or "gaun yirsel, reasonably tall man" simply wouldn't do. It's not clear if there have been any academic studies on the matter but it would seem sensible that most would opt for the larger option unless the evidence was conclusively to the contrary.

Robertson waved and gave a thumbs-up to his well-wishers from across the bar.

'It's funny,' he told Donnelly, 'a few years ago a wouldn't get bothered in a place like this. It's not somewhere many football fans would come. But now it's all change, working class guys'll come into a posh bar, especially in Glasgow, and the whole, what dae they call it "gentrification" of football means that the intelligentsia think it's cool tae like the game. I mean even Steven Fry! He's on the board at Norwich ye know? Him and Delia. What's the world coming tae?'

'Aye, a heard Noam Chomsky was arrested for causing trouble at a Stenhousemuir match last Saturday,' replied Donnelly.

Robertson was a little bit sketchy as to the exact identity of Chomsky but laughed anyway. Truth be told, Donnelly wasn't entirely sure what he did either but he knew he was supposed to be really clever.

'Anyway,' Robertson replied, stretching the first syllable

to indicate a relatively imminent end to the meeting.

But Donnelly hadn't forgotten his question:

'What I was gonnae say earlier was: "How come, ye know, how come you've done so well?" You seem to have coped with the tragedy better than the others.'

'Yeah, a suppose a have. A'd like to say it's because I've got amazing inner strength but to be honest, a'm not sure a have. A've had my moments you know, very dark times. Still do occasionally. But a could sum up the reason in one word: "Jo". She's fuckin' amazing, that girl. I owe everything tae her, she keeps me going, keeps me right, and you can quote that in your paper if you like.'

Stuart allowed a little silence, for effect it seemed, then went on:

'A was young when it happened. And Toddy was our captain. But he, you know, had issues, and, even back then a was kind of the leader. And as time's gone on a've had to look after that group of boys. They look to me for support. And a'll always give it. Those boys and me have gone through a heck of a thing and a'll always be there for them.'

Donnelly smiled and Robertson continued:

'You know, a've enjoyed this, it's been quite cathartic, and a hope it's been useful for you too. You know how it is though, you can't balance a top level football career and a burgeoning media profile by spending all day in a bar can you?' He smiled a self-parodic smile. 'A'm gonnae have tae make a move.'

Robertson's expression of enjoyment made Donnelly realise that he had enjoyed himself too and remember that that was not what he was there for.

'Yeah I've got a train to catch too, but can I just ask you just one more thing? It'll only take a minute.'

'Quickly then, eh? A'm due at the BBC. In fact, a'm due at the BBC and then the training ground. And then, believe it or not, back at the BBC again.'

All of a sudden, there was silence as the coffee machine was temporarily switched off. The sort of silence which only happens when you weren't aware of how noisy it had previously been. The sort of silence which actually sounds like something. It added import to Donnelly's question:

'The thing is, I've spoken to a few of the lads, and to Avril as well. She's never remembered what she did to Paul Bannerman but the mist is just beginning to clear a little and I think that things are gonnae become clearer still. Next time I see her a think I'll know a lot more about what actually happened.'

In all the years Donnelly had watched Stuart Robertson being interviewed on the television he had never seen any sign of anything other than affability on those pleasant features. He saw something different now. His mouth stopped just short of a grimace whilst his eyes turned stony and steely.

'You comfortable wi' upsetting a mental patient, Jim? Givin' her false hope? Disturbing her presumably already fragile, mental equilibrium? And how did you get in there anyway? They're letting her speak tae journalists?'

'I ken what ye mean, Stuart. I did wonder, at first, if I was gonnae upset her. But, ye know, I think I might actually be able to help this girl. Make her see that she's no' who she thinks she is.'

'For fuck's sake, Jim, leave it tae the professionals; yir

no' a shrink, ye ken?'

Donnelly realised that he strayed onto dangerous ground and tried to find his way back to safer territory:

'Aye, you're probably right, Stuart, maybe a shouldnae go back.'

'Quite right, Jim. A'm glad you see what a mean.'

Robertson's face seemed to have gradually morphed back into its familiar genial guise. Donnelly wasn't quite finished though, and he risked one more enquiry:

'Some of the boys seem a bit nervy when they talk about her though; kind of like they're afraid to deviate from the party line. There's somethin' ... I don't know, there's just somethin'.'

'Jim, a can understand that journalistic nose must be twitching. Wouldn't it be incredible if there was more to this story than meets the eye? It would be the scoop of a lifetime for you, eh? A understand that, and a don't blame you but there's two things you need to think about - no, three things, actually. One, none of us really know exactly what happened – we'd gone by the time it all took place. Two, who else could've killed Banns? Who'd have wanted to? What possible motive is there? And three, yeah, if a'm honest there is a party line. We went through a traumatic event together. There's a bond between us that probably only soldiers in a war have. So we stick together – look after each other. Think about this, what if the police had not been convinced about Avril's guilt? What if they had thought, like you seem to, that there was more to this than meets the eye? If you were one of us, do you not think it would be important to make sure that everybody was singin' from the same hymn sheet? All of us were drunk, or stoned. What if someone had a poor memory of the night because of the booze and had said something that contradicted the others. You're damn right there's a party line. But that's not an indicator of some sort of guilt but a means of ensuring that the innocent are not implicated. Ridiculous to think we could be of course, but crazier things have happened.'

As he smiled goodbye to a waving Donnelly, Robertson was already on his smartphone, finding the contact details for Strathgyte.

*

As he reflected on the meeting on the train back to Edinburgh, Donnelly couldn't help feeling that he'd given it his best shot and still, somehow, come up short. Robertson's reaction to his suggestion that Avril was becoming clearer was interesting but understandable. And the point about the players having agreed a shared version of events made perfect sense. Robertson made perfect sense altogether, unfortunately. Donnelly's disappointment was, however, mixed with some degree of relief. Ok, the story was less explosive without any great new revelation but, deep down, he hadn't wanted to believe that any of those lads were implicated in the death of their pal. He'd have to concentrate on the emotional toll that the incident had taken on them all. And Robertson had made a good point:

'Nobody came out of this ahead, especially Banns.'

He would have to concentrate on how everyone was traumatised, even, or maybe especially, the girl.

Donnelly wasn't much of a texter. In fact, he hated mobile phones almost as much as he hated Hibs. Having, for years, vowed he'd be the last person in Scotland to own one, he'd finally relented, at the behest of his family. And his boss.

163

Now he carried a phone but stubbornly resisted using the vast majority of its functions.

He had fifty-five minutes to kill, though, and no newspaper. His phone, therefore, became a prop to help him avoid making conversation with the old lady opposite. Who better to text then, than Steph, just to see how she was. By the time he'd reached the capital, he found that he'd organised to meet her for a drink and a chat and he'd also let Jacqui know he was working late. 'God,' he thought, 'maybe that's why kids text so much, it's awfy easy to lie.'

Chapter Sixteen

'It's for you, Stuart, pick up the other phone. It's Mark Sinclair.'

Sinclair had hoped he wouldn't get Jo when he phoned Robertson's landline but as Robertson had been screening the calls to his mobile Sinclair felt he had to take that chance. He had been friendly but brisk when Jo had tried to engage him in conversation.

'I've got it, Jo; you can put the phone down.'

Jo waited a few seconds, put her hand over the mouthpiece and shouted:

'Yup, that's it.'

She'd long ago discovered that on the latest generation of phones there was no noise made when picking up or putting down a second handset.

'What's up, pal?' Stuart dreaded the reply.

'Nothin' really, a jist thought a'd tell ye a bit o' good news.'

'Great, what's the story?'

'Well, ye ken that money ye lent me? The good news is that a didnae spend it a' on drugs.'

'Well, that is good. A'm awfy pleased tae hear it. So, is that what ye phoned tae tell me?'

'Aye, a mean, naw, a phoned tae tell ye thit a invested some o' the money in something very useful; somethin' good for a' o' us.'

165

'O … kay … Mark, can ye just get tae the point; what have ye spent the money on?'

'Aye, aye, a'm gettin' there. Ye see, a wis thinkin' aboot oor wee problem. Aboot that cunt, Donnelly. And a suddenly thought: "a grand wid see him gettin' a wee fright – a wee warnin' tae keep his fuckin' nose oot o' things that dinnae concern 'im". A ken a few folk, ye ken, through ma … situation. A ken folk that arny very nice. Folk that'd frighten the life oot o' ye. Well that's exactly what they're gonnae do, frighten the life oot o' Donnelly.'

Robertson didn't know where to start. In response to the silence Sinclair began again:

'Yir welcome, pal. Consider oor problims solved.'

In two separate rooms both Robertson and Jo had very similar physical reactions to this news. Both slumped downwards; Jo from a standing to a sitting position and Robertson from sitting to practically lying on his chair.

'What the fuck did ye do that for?' was all Robertson could manage to say. 'What the fuckin' fuck?'

'What the fuck do you mean: "What the fuck?". It's fuckin' genius, they'll no' say who sent thim. They'll jist gie 'im a general warnin' tae keep his nose oot o' stuff, then he'll leave it alone, believe me.'

'Fuck, Mark, a met wi' the guy yesterday, put him right, smoothed it all over and now this. All this'll do is make 'im even more suspicious.'

'Jesus, Stu, a thought a wis doin' a good thing; a thought ye'd be happy. Thirs nae fuckin' pleasin' some folk.'

'Call them off, Mark, right?'

'A dae ken, Stu, it's no easy tae get in touch wi' thim. It

166

might be too late. It's whit he needs onyway.'

And with that the phone went down, closely followed by another, then another.

Both Jo and Stuart were left contemplating their next move but she acted on hers before he had a chance to.

'What's up, love?' she asked, as she entered the bedroom where he was still slumped on a chair. 'I heard a bit of swearing; has something happened?'

'Naw, nothing much, nothing at all really.'

'Nothing for me to worry my pretty little head about, eh? For fuck's sake, Stuart, don't patronise me – what's wrong?'

'It's nothin' really. Honest. It's just Sinclair, and that money I gave him. He's just gettin' intae bother, that's all.'

'What money was that, Stuart?' Jo affected surprise.

Sometimes when a situation is getting worse, an earlier worry becomes overtaken by events and doesn't seem such a big deal. Robertson would rather that Jo hadn't found out about the two thousand but it could be covered by an easy lie and perhaps one that could solve two birds with the proverbial:

'Sorry, love, I meant tae tell ye. A lent Sinclair a bit o' money – you know he's an addict? It was for rehab, but he's gone and spent it on more drugs. I feel terrible – I've actually bought drugs for 'im, ye know?'

'And he phoned you up to tell you that, did he? "Jist thought a'd let ye' ken, a've spent yir dough on gear, is that a' right, pal?"'

Robertson pulled on his stylish brown leather brogues as he spoke:

'No, of course not. I'd heard on the grapevine. I've been leaving messages for 'im and that was 'im gettin' back to me. He admitted it eventually.'

Jo considered breaking cover on this one, but years of experience had taught her the benefits of playing the long game:

'I'm sorry, love, I just hate to see you so upset.'

'That's no problem, darling ... eh ... I've just got to pop out for a wee while, I'll be back soon, ok?'

Robertson had his coat on and was out of the door almost before Jo could even reply:

'No, Stuart, it's not ok,' she said quietly, to no-one.

*

Donnelly glared at the screen of his phone for a few seconds whilst contemplating what had just happened. He had desperately wanted to give up and simply phone Steph but having embarked on what had turned out to be a fairly lengthy text conversation he felt that to do so would make him seem like the old fogey he was trying to avoid appearing to be. His biggest problem was that seconds after he had laboured over what seemed like a long contribution to the dialogue she had responded with something even longer. Getting the balance right between speed and accuracy – or inaccuracy – had proved very difficult.

After a very stressful three quarters of an hour Donnelly now relaxed back in his train seat, only to look out and realise he was passing Murrayfield Stadium and therefore only had five minutes before he would have to leave the train and carry out the arrangements which he had laboured so hard to put into place.

*

'Aw fuck, eh, Russell Grant, eh, Alex Salmond, eh, aw fuck, naw, that's better, that's better.'

'Oh my God, Davie, what was that about? Fat guys? Have you got a thing for fat guys?' Mel failed to stifle a giggle.

'Fuck, did a say that out loud?' Davie looked down at Mel's reddened face and resumed thrusting himself into her.

As Mel continued to giggle he looked crestfallen and slowed down:

'Naw, it's the opposite. A dinnae want tae come too quick. A want tae make it good fur you. It's jist tae calm me doon a bit, thinkin' o' naked fat men.'

It occurred to Mel that if done too often Davie's "turn off" technique could have the opposite effect. Like Pavlov's dogs he might start to make an association in his mind, an association between naked fat men and being close to orgasm. Mel thought all that but felt it best only to say:

'Ah, that's nice, Davie. Keep doing that. Yeah, jist that.'

After a few more minutes of positive noises from Mel, Davie allowed himself to climax, thrusting irregularly now, before lowering himself onto her and nuzzling his face into her neck.

'Aw, that wis great. Did ye come?' he asked, breathlessly.

'Couldn't ye tell,' she replied, 'that was wonderful.'

'Wis that a "yes?"'thought Davie. Women, he felt, have a wonderful array of apparently positive but ultimately non-committal answers to that question. 'A'll take it as a "yes", she certainly looks happy enough.'

'Mel,' he whispered, keeping his face buried deep in her neck, 'A, you know, a ...' he lowered his voice further so almost inaudible, 'A ... love ... you.'

'Pardon,' asked Mel. 'What was that? You *what* me?'

He raised his head slightly.

'A said ... whit a said was ... a ... '

He saw her smile and realised:

'You besom. You ...'

She shut him up with a kiss.

'I heard you, Davie. I heard you. And you know what? I think I'm starting to feel that way too.'

*

Whilst Stuart walked to the car, Jo walked to the living room. The difference was that he walked with agitation and purpose whilst she moved slowly with the air of one who had run out of ideas. He jumped into the Ferrari and drove without pausing to fasten his seatbelt. She fell onto the enveloping sofa and stared aimlessly at the perfectly painted ceiling and immaculately sculpted cornice.

Stuart only drove for about two minutes before parking at the side of the road and frantically punching at the buttons on his phone. Jo lay back and allowed the tears to flow.

'Fuck,' shouted Stuart. 'Answer the fucking phone, you junkie arsehole.' Repeated attempts came to naught. 'Fuck, fuck.'

'Fuck,' shouted Jo as she smashed her hand down onto a cushion. She'd caught her husband out in a flat lie – and one unconnected, it seemed, with infidelity:

'What the hell am I gonnae to do now? Fuck, fuck.'

*

Considering its position in the historic heart of Scotland's capital city, the back entrance to Waverley railway station is a relatively dark, and often quiet, place from which to emerge, even in the early evening. The walk down Calton Road and up Old Tolbooth Wynd can be an even more lonely, if picturesque, experience. Choose a foggy night and one might imagine oneself transported back many hundreds of years to a more dangerous period in the Old Town's bloody history. Thoughts of this occupied Donnelly as he made the – admittedly non-foggy – journey towards the Royal Mile and his assignation with the woman who put a spring in his step.

It was an occupational hazard that Donnelly made enemies from time to time. And more than once those enemies had resorted to physical means of retribution. The sound of footsteps from behind, therefore, made him feel a little uneasy. Who is not a little unnerved by the noise of brisk footsteps from behind in a dark place? A quick glance afforded him the briefest view of three young-looking men walking purposefully towards him. He was aware of feeling his heart beat much faster than usual and reminded himself that muggings are relatively rare in Edinburgh and there was really nothing for him to worry about.

Without realising, Donnelly had quickened his step but was aware that the young men were still bearing on him and talking quietly, but urgently. As he moved to the side to anticipate, hopefully, their passing, his heart rate almost went through the roof as one of them spoke:

'Hey, pal?' he called out in what to Donnelly's ears, was

almost certainly a menacing tone. 'Hey, pal?' he repeated.

Bracing himself, Donnelly half-turned to face three, admittedly, quite well dressed figures, backlit by a nearby street lamp. Unable to make out their faces he tentatively replied: 'Aye, whit is it?'

The words that emerged were spoken urgently and with some vehemence:

'Can you tell us how to get to the railway station?'

Donnelly felt a palpable sense of profound relief as he answered their question and watched them heading away, even more quickly than before, in the opposite direction.

'Stupid old bastard,' he thought, as he continued, with a lighter gait, to the pub where he hoped Steph would be waiting.

*

If anyone had been watching Steph and Donnelly for signs of intimacy when they met in Jenny Ha's, they would not have noticed anything too obvious. This was not the meeting of lovers or even long-standing friends. But if they'd looked a little more closely they might have observed a curious mixture of warmth, reserve and a little excitement. Donnelly had known for weeks that he was attracted to Steph and he had started to believe that his feelings were reciprocated. She knew she felt something: tenderness, admiration maybe? But why, she wondered, would she be remotely interested in this slightly crumpled, unprepossessing, middle-aged man. Yet Donnelly did have a charm of sorts. There was something indestructible about him, like he'd taken a thousand blows and was still, against all odds, standing. It gave him a faintly, and oddly, heroic air.

If the unknown observer had opted to hang around despite the unpromising start to the encounter, they would still have required both good vision and advanced skills of perception to notice the development of the relationship over two hours and five rounds of drinks. A small touch here and a lingering moment of eye-contact there would be the only reward gained for the effort they had put in. Yet the relationship was developing, if in slightly different directions. Donnelly was becoming more and more comfortable and relaxed in Steph's company whilst she, beginning to become aware of a faint stirring of something, was becoming distinctly nervous.

It was Steph, therefore, who pointed out that they both had work in the morning and should make a move towards home.

'Thanks, Steph, I really enjoy talking to you, you make me feel so relaxed,' Donnelly revealed as they exited the pub. He had already hailed a passing black cab as he finished his little speech.

'Away ye go, you old softie, I had a great time too. But my bed beckons.'

What took place next, happened so quickly and was so rich with import of one kind or another that Donnelly was completely unable to remember the sequence of events at a later date. However, in brief, vivid, episodes he recalled the following and assumed that they had happened in this order:

He leaned in to kiss her on the cheek but somehow felt emboldened to move towards her lips.

She looked surprised, possibly reluctant, but didn't quite stop him.

The taxi driver sounded his horn and she got in the car.

They both waved as the taxi drove away.

He felt an almighty, quick and hard blow to the back of his head and fell to the pavement.

There was a flurry of further blows to his crotch and ribs, presumably from kicks.

He heard a number of things said but remembered only this:

'That's a warnin', pal. Keep yir nose oot o' ithir folks business or ye'll git worse'.

He passed out, face down, and rolled into the gutter.

Chapter Seventeen

In the strange, apparently random, geography of Scottish football, professional clubs are not arranged in such a way which makes any sense at all with regard to catchment area. It can only be assumed that in the early days, many hundreds of clubs were set up and those which made it to the big time, and are still professional, did so for reasons other than geographical spread. Perhaps they achieved the kind of good results which promoted supporter loyalty or maybe they were run with 'sound fiscal policies' (before such jargon existed). Possibly they benefited from particularly tenacious management at crucial periods.

Looking at the situation now, with a dispassionate eye, one could argue that Fife, for instance, does not boast a population large enough to sustain four professional clubs. The sensible thing to do would be to merge Dunfermline with Cowden United and Raith Rovers with East Fife. A dispassionate eye, however, is rarely cast on Scottish football. Try telling the supporters of the above named teams that they should merge and see what kind of response you get. Particularly from those of Cowden and East Fife who would likely find their clubs swallowed up by their larger neighbours. No, the die is cast and all the clubs must simply fight to survive in increasingly harsh economic times.

It's much the same in the Falkirk area, dominated by Falkirk FC but also represented in the professional leagues by Stenhousemuir, just two miles to the north and East Stirlingshire, also from the north of the town but currently ground-sharing with 'The Muir'.

Donnelly could have met Derek Ramsay – player/coach of Stenhousemuir - in a Falkirk hostelry but he eagerly accepted Ramsay's invitation to meet at Ochilview Park. A student of Scottish football he was keen to see behind the scenes at this venerable stadium. He knew, for instance, that it had been the venue for the first floodlit football match in Scotland, way back in 1951.

He grimaced as he glanced at the modern spires on the ancient palace of Linlithgow, observed on his journey to Stenhousemuir from the motorway. It was not so much that he had a problem with the merging of modern and ancient architecture but rather that turning, even slightly to the left, provoked pain in two of the three ribs broken in the attack he had sustained two nights before. Unfortunately, the other rib caused excruciating pain when he turned to the right. This rather limited his options.

He drove for a worrying two or three minutes without even realising he was doing so as he experienced one of what had been very regular flashbacks to the shock and, though he wouldn't admit it, terror, of the attack.

He recalled the suddenness then the helplessness as it continued and the fear of how far it may go. Then there was embarrassment as the ambulance arrived and the assumption on the part of those tending to him that he was drunk and that his injuries were self-inflicted. The fact that he had no facial injuries would have contributed to this, and of course, his unwillingness to tell the medical staff what had actually happened. As a journalist, he always chose to regard discretion as the better part of valour. However, on attempting to move him, it soon became obvious that his injuries were not of the sort sustained just through a drunken fall off the pavement.

His embarrassment returned, however, when Jacqui came to collect him from the Edinburgh Royal Infirmary casualty department. Although naturally sympathetic, Jacqui had been there before, both physically and metaphorically. She was aware that previous beatings sustained by her husband had been by those pushed too far by his relentless journalistic pursuit and if not *deserved*, as such, were as near as damn it.

Then there was the patronising sympathy from his two, long-suffering, daughters, who had also been through all of this on more than one occasion.

Despite clearly being in the wrong, Donnelly still managed to sound his horn and swear at the driver whom he almost killed as a result of practically driving off the road whilst lost in his own world.

Having not visited Ochilview for a number of years, Donnelly was disappointed to be welcomed by Ramsay into a tidy modern office within the relatively new stand, rather than the ramshackle howf he was hoping for. Ramsay confounded expectations in very similar ways, articulate and thoughtful, he defied the stereotype of the verbally limited, cliché ridden Scottish footballer.

'Hi there, Mr Donnelly, welcome to the centre of Scottish football!' There was a pause before Ramsay continued, 'a mean geographically, of course. We're kind o' in the middle o' the country, football-wise.'

'Aye, I suppose so,' Donnelly replied, 'plenty o' history here as well though, eh? It's clubs like this that are the heart of Scottish football. And Hearts, as well, of course.'

'Aye, yir a Jambo, eh? Tricky season. Ye've no' had yir troubles tae seek recently. A mean ye've been no' too bad on the pitch but off it? The managerial merry-go-round eh?'

'Well, you know what it's like. As a supporter ye learn to roll with the punches, there's nothing else for it.'

'Absolutely. Nae choice. Ye've jist got tae hope that the good outweighs the bad.'

'Aye well I'm old enough tae remember a few glory days and so I'm able to take the long view. Who is it you grew up supporting, Derek? Can I call ye that? Call me Jim by the way.'

'Aye, Derek's fine. A'm Athletic through and through. Actually born within a long free kick o' the stadium, so a wis.'

'Well you've no' had tae roll wi' that many punches then.' Donnelly saw the mildly disgusted look on the other man's face and quickly added:

'As a supporter I mean. Obviously, as a player, it's not all gone completely smoothly. Particularly with regard to what I'm here to talk about. D'ye mind if I ask you a few questions about that now?'

'Aye, go ahead. A'll make some tea while we talk.'

Donnelly grimaced as he turned towards where Ramsay had gone to make the tea.

'Are you alright, Jim? Ye look really uncomfortable.'

'A'm no' bad, thanks fur askin'. A got a bit of a doin' the other day. A few cracked ribs.'

'Fuckin' hell. A've had a few o' those in ma time. It's no' a lot o' fun. What did ye do tae deserve that?'

'God knows, 'cause a don't. Someone must no' be happy at something a've wrote. Or maybe someone doesnae want me tae write something ... Anyway, you were captain at the time, Derek. A presume that means that you carried more of the emotional load. How did you cope wi' that?'

'Thanks, Jim. Thanks for acknowledging that. Not many people have realised the extent to which a had to shoulder so much of that. Well, me and Stuart. On behalf o' some of the daft wee laddies you get in a football team. They grew up pretty fast mind. But aye, we had tae help them through it; tae hold it all together; tae talk tae Bann's family; tae go tae functions; tae make speeches; tae relive it day after day after ...'

Ramsay's eyes had reddened and his speech slowed to a stop.

'Jist gie me a minute,' he almost whispered as he composed himself.

'Take all the time ye need, son. A'm really sorry tae drag this up again for ye. Take yir time.'

'Hud oan a second,' Ramsay replied, 'let me put this wee heater on. The heatin's on the blink and it's Baltic in here.'

As usual in situations like these, Donnelly's genuine humanity made him feel for the person he was interviewing but this was outweighed, considerably, by the excitement he felt at getting some good, emotional content for his story.

'Is tea ok?

'Aye, that's great, milk and one sugar. A cut down fae three! Quite proud o' myself I have tae admit. I still prefer the full fat milk though. That other stuff's like water. You were close, eh? You and Banns. Sorry, a'm sure a've no earned the right to call him that. It's just what you guys always call him. You and Paul, I'm told you were pretty close?'

Ramsay seemed to sink deep into the hard office chair,

almost slumped as he talked slowly and deliberately:

'A loved the boy. A'd never've said that then, of course. A can't believe a'm saying it now, to be honest. And to a journalist. But it has to be said. A also probably shouldn't say this but a went tae a counsellor for a few years after it happened. That's where a learned that it was ok tae say that – even when yir no' drunk! Tae admit that a man can love another man withoot being, ye ken, gay.'

Ramsay smiled indulgently to himself, and Donnelly had to ask:

'What's funny, Derek? Are ye rememberin' something?'

'Aye, it's jist this business aboot me going tae a counsellor. A jist remembered that ye'll know aboot that 'cause it wis in the papers at the time. That was when opposition fans started singing, "two Derek Ramsays, there's only two Derek Ramsays". Depression, schizophrenia: it's a' the same tae them, eh?'

'Aye, football crowd's can be funny sometimes but no' exactly subtle, or sophisticated. Or accurate. What was he like?'

'A'm no kiddin'. It sounds like the kind o' stuff ye jist say when someone's deid but he wis jist the loveliest boy going, so he wis. Jist a better human being than the vast majority of those still walking this earth. The good die young, eh? A suppose it wis that humanity that got him killed ...'

Donnelly's body may have gone to rack and ruin; his teeth may have come to resemble downtown Beirut and his lungs may have been one pack of Embassy away from giving up completely, but his instinct was still finely honed. It functions beautifully, like a well-oiled Maserati. There was something about Ramsay's face after his last comment.

Something subtle but distinct. Something which made Donnelly believe that maybe he'd said something he felt he shouldn't.

'How d'ye mean, "his humanity"? How wis that significant?'

Ramsay's response was reasonable:

'A mean that he let the girl stay. He hadnae fucked her, like. She wisnae his type. But she was a poor wee soul and he let her sleep it off in his flat. Most would have chucked her oot, or maybe called her a taxi. But he looked after her, so he did. That was his mistake.'

Donnelly took Ramsay through the whole night's events and received the same familiar story as he had heard from the other players. The details were so similar that he was once more struck by the almost rehearsed nature of the various accounts. Why were they so similar? The obvious answer to that of course is that they were, quite simply, true. And he remembered Stuart Robertson's words:

'You're damn right there's a party line. But that's not an indicator of some sort of guilt, but a means of ensuring that the innocent are not implicated.'

When they parted it was with a handshake of some warmth. If Ramsay avoided Donnelly's eye contact it seemed more to do with his embarrassment with regard to his earlier, emotional admission than anything untoward about his story.

Donnelly eased himself into his car and headed back along the M9 towards Edinburgh. He was pleased with the amount of emotional content he had gathered for his story. That was, after all, most likely to be at the hub of the piece in the long run. 'Most of those boys seem pretty decent,'

181

he thought to himself. 'They don't seem like they're lying. Well maybe about some details, but not about what actually happened.'

But there was something about Ramsay's expression that still bothered him. And then, of course, there was his excruciating rib cage, reminding him constantly, that someone, somewhere, doesn't want him to find out something about something. To Donnelly, that was like a red rag to a journalistic bull.

It was late enough in the afternoon for him to feel justified in not going back to the office and he thought he'd surprise whichever members of his family he found with his unexpected presence at the Craigentinny bungalow they called home. Even better if there was nobody home at all and he could fit in a quick episode from the Columbo box set he had been given for Christmas.

As he drove into his driveway he thought again about how much he loved it. Having spent years in a Comely Bank flat, driving round looking for a nearby – expensive – parking space and then walking through the rain with two babies in car seats, he never stopped enjoying the luxury of that little expanse of concrete. Ostensibly, they moved to secure a garden for their twin toddlers to play in but the driveway and getting newspapers delivered to the door were what Donnelly really appreciated.

Lost in his musing, Donnelly almost missed the skinny, black-clad teenage boy who slipped out of his front door and disappeared down the street and into the gloaming, like a bad spirit. He didn't, however, miss the loud sobs coming from the upstairs bedroom of Katy, the more adventurous of those, now much matured twin girls. Girls who no longer played on the trampoline or swings in the aforementioned back garden but instead appeared to have moved onto more mature pastimes.

Fearing the worst, Donnelly ran up the stairs and in his haste committed the worst crime a parent can possibly commit. He entered his teenage daughter's room without knocking.

Katy almost screamed, with the surprise of the appearance, unannounced, of her father in her bedroom and at this, of all moments. Donnelly watched the face of his distressed teenage daughter and, later, was able to describe to Jacqui, a series of distinct emotions. First was shock followed by anger at her father's intrusion. After this came embarrassment at her distraught and dishevelled state. Lastly came a face that Donnelly had never expected to see again; it was a picture of pain, need and almost gratitude – gratitude that her daddy was there, for her, when she needed him. This was the last emotion Donnelly saw on Katy's face before she threw her arms around him and sobbed deeply into his neck. All of this took place in just less than a minute and Donnelly instinctively knew he would have to give her a little while before he could ask her what had happened.

It was a very long minute. He practised what he could say: "What did the little bastard do? Who was that little shit and what was he up to? Tell me who the little fucker was and I'll kill him."

All the time the chances of getting out in the car and hunting him down were getting slimmer. Eventually, good sense prevailed and he went with:

'What's the matter, darling? I saw that boy. What happened to you?'

In between heavy sobs, Katy managed to tell him:

'That was Lewis ... he's my ... was my .... boy ... friend. We were just … you know ... cuddling and that and I let him ... I can't tell you what. But I let him do something and then he tried to do something else. And I ... I didn't let him do that. And he ... he ... tried to do it again. And I told him, "No!" and he stopped and he said I was a tease and he said I was chucked. And I said, "No, you're chucked," and he, well he swore at me and ran out.'

Donnelly internalised this information and quickly decided that a vigilante mission was probably not required – though he'd happily have punched the little bugger's lights out – and that consoling his beautiful little girl was of more immediate importance.

'You're such a smart girl, love. Quite right. Don't let any boy treat ye like that. You only do what you want tae do. And what *I* wouldn't mind you doing. Not that I want you tae do anything. I mean, I personally dinnae want ... I mean I realise you maybe do ... but ... anyway, what I mean is, don't let anyone force you into doing anything. You're well shot of the little shit.'

Donnelly soon realised the greater complexity of the situation when Katy started crying again and replied:

'But I don't want to be shot of him, Dad. I really like him.'

Donnelly swallowed his response and concentrated on cuddling his very needy daughter.

Chapter Eighteen

Jo Robertson may not have been a typical WAG but she was still a woman, and a woman, she felt, had needs. Needs which had to be satisfied. Needs which could only be indulged at the Kurt Geiger shop in Princes Square - Glasgow's poshest shopping mall.

'You pretend you're not into all the glamour, the fake tan and the blond hair but see when it comes to shoes, you make Cheryl Cole seem like Ann Widdecombe.'

This was the view of Jo's fellow lawyer, Beth Stevenson, who was, it has to be said, very sensibly shod.

'You should be more sympathetic,' Jo replied, 'with all those druggies you represent. It's an addiction. I'm afflicted by a cruel addiction to designer shoes. I'm more to be pitied than scolded to be honest. Anyway, it's practical, you can't do without shoes.'

'Yeah, but you can do without shoes with four inch heels and little satin bows, and at a hundred and forty pounds too.'

'Yeah, well it's not as if I wear most of them anyway. I do look at them quite a lot though. Think of me like a collector, a curator, if you like, of beautiful *objet d'art*.'

'Which is it: collector or addict? Are you to be admired or pitied?'

'Oh God, shut up and tell me if you like these ones. And bear in mind that I'll probably never wear them!'

Later, over lunch in Cranachan, she unloaded to Beth

about her suspicions. What those suspicions actually were, though, she wasn't entirely sure.

'I just know there's something wrong. He's a man. He's weak. I can get everything out of him eventually ... usually. I find things out, with or without the help of Eck, and I work on him till he eventually tells me himself. But this time he's giving away nothing. I've tried, you know, my usual way of getting round him. And I've tried sadness, anger – all the weapons at my disposal but he won't crack.'

'I don't suppose there's any point in me telling you what I think, is there?'

'Yes there is. I value your opinion. It's just that, well, let's be honest, you've never really liked him, have you?'

'No, that's not fair, and not true. It's just that, well, I suppose I don't like him quite as much as he likes himself.'

Beth screwed up her face with embarrassment.

'I'm sorry. That sounded rude. It's just that no-one needs that much charm. I just always wonder what it's covering up.'

'What, you can't just be nice for the sake of it?' Jo asked and then lowered her voice to avoid the ear of a waiter hovering at the next table. 'I know he overdoes the cheeky chappy thing a bit but he is genuinely, just, you know, nice.'

'Well, I've said this before and I don't mean to be harsh but the day I have to hire a private investigator to spy on my husband is the day that I'd consider whether I was in the right relationship.'

Jo looked upset and concentrated for a few moments on her warm salad of crayfish tails and greens.

'I'm sorry,' Beth continued, making a point of making

eye contact with a sympathetic look.

'He's not actually a private investigator,' Jo replied, aware that this was a weak response and subsequently adding, 'but I know what you mean. I would never have believed that I would be the sort of person who would put up with so much. It's an equation, I've just always balanced the good and the bad and felt that overall, it's been worth it. Maybe it's because of our job, you know, sometimes, getting a guilty person off; giving them a second chance.'

Before Beth could reply, Jo continued:

'I know, and a third and a fourth chance.'

Jo sipped her Sauvignon Blanc and avoided Beth's gaze.

Some idle chit chat followed before Jo admitted that she had made contact with Eck McDougal once again and that she was meeting him that very afternoon.

'This is more serious, Beth, there's something very worrying going on and this time it could be the last straw. This might be the end.'

Beth moved her chair over to Jo's and slipped her hand into that of her friend.

'Come on,' she said, to a disconsolate Jo, 'I think you need to look at some more foot wear.'

*

Steph reached out to touch the bruise on the side of Donnelly's face then immediately withdrew her hand and limited herself to sympathetic noises accompanied by an appropriate, concerned, expression.

'That looks really sore, Jim. Are you ok?'

'That's no' the worst of it. Three broken ribs. Two kicks, three broken ribs – that's a pretty high success ratio. It's nice when people are thorough in their work – professional, if you know what I mean.'

They talked as they walked, through Holyrood Park on a cold but bright day. They had left for lunch separately and arranged to meet in the park, both instinctively concerned that they now had something to hide.

'So, was it just random or do you think it was a planned attack?'

'Planned, I'm afraid. At the end of the beating I can vaguely remember a warning: "keep yir nose oot o' stuff," that kind o' thing.'

'I'm so sorry, Jim. I feel kind of culpable. We, you know, kissed, and then it just happened. Like the two things were connected.'

'What, have you got a jealous husband you haven't told me about?'

'No ... but, maybe you weren't paying attention because of it. You know, because of what had just happened and ...'

'And nothing. Don't be so silly. If someone was out to get me they'd get me. I'm no' exactly double oh seven.'

'Yes, but don't you see, something wrong was going on and then something bad happened. I'm not saying it was cause and effect but it's like the universe was letting us know that what we were doing was wrong.'

'The universe, Christ. It was two hoodlums wi' steel-capped boots.'

'I know, I know. It just made me think. I've been leading you on and I don't know why. You're married, you've got kids, it's just not right.'

'Don't you feel anything for me? I'm sure you do. You seem to.'

'I do. But I'm not sure what it is. Somewhere between friendship, admiration and ... sympathy I suppose.'

'Sympathy! Well that's flattering.'

'I said friendship and admiration as well. It's complicated. I don't know what it is but it's not right. It's got to stop.'

Donnelly stopped. He sat on a park bench and held his head in his hands like a chastised child.

Steph remained standing and when he looked up, the late afternoon sun was behind her, making her appear to him as a very shapely silhouette and preventing him from being able to read her expressions. As she sat, he moved in close to see her face and she, instinctively, jumped back. She saw the expression of hurt on his face and began again:

'I like you, Jim, but not in that way. And certainly not enough to justify breaking up a family. You must see I'm right?'

'Right! What's right got to do wi' it? I'm making a fool o' myself, I can see that. But I want to. It's all worth it because you're worth it.'

'Well that's very flattering but maybe it's up to me to save you from yourself. You've got so much to lose.'

Donnelly had never cried in front of a girl yet, except his wife, and in private, and he wasn't about to start now, even if he felt like it.

'Fuck it; it's no a big deal. Yir only a lassie. I just wanted a bit o' fun wi' a cute wee thing, it's no' like ma heart's broken for fuck's sake.'

'I know, Jim,' Steph replied, partly saddened and partly happy to let him off the hook. 'It'd take more than a "cute wee thing" to break Jim Donnelly's heart.'

They moved off again back towards work both looking anywhere but at each other. Steph asked:

'So, if it wasn't random, who did it?'

Donnelly affected a jaunty tone:

'Well, the suspect list is long, not counting all the wronged husbands of my former conquests, of course, there's quite a few criminals that I've helped to put away and, of course, every Hibs fan who's ever read one o' ma football reports.'

'Seriously though?'

'Seriously? I'd have to go with Mark Sinclair.' Donnelly answered Steph's quizzical look with:

'One of my footballers. He threatened me when we met. I didn't take him seriously at the time but I do now.'

'Did you go to the police?'

'No way, Josè. A don't want them getting in the way of this. I'm on the trail and it'll take more than a few broken ribs to put me off.'

Steph would normally have mocked Donnelly for this display of bravado but she understood where it was coming from and let it go.

'Every time I think I'm making too much of this story ... something happens to make me more suspicious.'

As they approached the office, Donnelly looked at his feet and said:

'You know, I'm feeling one of my migraines coming

on. D'ye think you could let work know that I've had to go home sick?'

'I didn't know that you ...' began Steph but tailed off before adding, 'Aye, Jim, of course, no problem.'

*

If Jo had known about Eck McDougal's ultimate aim of writing a book to lift the lid on the sleazy goings-on in Scottish top-flight football, she would never have organised to meet him in that nice little Italian cafe on Byres Road. She certainly would not have let him know as much about her suspicions and fears regarding the death of Paul Bannerman. Even without that knowledge, she would ordinarily have been more circumspect. She was getting desperate, however, and she couldn't go to the police. Eck had always been discreet in the past and she obviously was in need of (semi) professional help.

As they parted, he assured her:

'Dinnae you worry, hen, y'can rely on ma discretion.'

Jo didn't know whether to laugh or cry. She worried about that, and much more besides. And although she feared it, she wasn't to know that bringing another suspicious and tenacious character into the mess that surrounded her husband could only make things worse.

Chapter Nineteen

Donnelly felt less nervous this time as he went through the security checks at Strathgyte State Hospital. This time he knew that the object of his visit was expecting him rather than her mother's brother. His mood improved further when the nurse who led him to his meeting with Avril Jamieson mentioned that she'd been looking forward to the visit from her 'uncle'.

'She doesn't see many people,' the nurse explained, 'and your visit seemed to cheer her up the last time.'

'Hi, Uncle David,' Avril greeted Donnelly with a slight, but distinct, conspiratorial smile, as he was led to the seat next to hers.

'Hi, darlin', it's good tae see you,' he replied, playing along with the joke.

'What's yir name?' The mood changed the moment they were left alone. 'You nivir telt me.'

'Really, I'm sorry, that wis bad of me. I'm James, well Jim, if ye like.'

'Aye, Jim's more like it.'

'Oh aye, why's that?'

'Well, it's, ye ken, an old guy's name. And nothin' flashy, jist plain old Jim.'

'Ta very much, a'm a plain old guy, eh? Here's me thinking you saw me as exotic but naw: a plain old guy.'

'Well ye know whit a mean, straight doon the line. Well, mibbae no'. Connivin' wee bastard more like.'

'Aye, a know; and a'm sorry. It's jist ma job, ye know?'

'Aye, well yir only here 'cause a get so few visitors and there might be some entertainment tae be got oot o' you.'

'A hope yir no' lookin' for me to sing?'

'Christ, no, but it's either you or Jeremy bloody Kyle, and a can only take so much o' that. A'm drugged up like, on mair drugs noo then a wis before. Ironic eh? Same junkie – different pusher!'

Donnelly smiled.

'Anyway, let's get tae the chat. What's been goin' on, Unc? Have yi downloaded Tulisa's new single yet? A bangin' tune, eh?'

'Ok,' Donnelly replied with mock seriousness, 'let's go through this bit by bit: "Tulisa" – animal, vegetable or mineral? Is it a boy a girl or a band? "Single" I'm fine with; "download" just about. Now as for whether it's "banging" or not would depend on how we're defining "banging". I'm thinking that it's a good thing so overall, no, I haven't loaded Tulisa's new tune down yet but I'm pretty sure that it bangs along with the best of them.'

Having played his part in the game she had begun, Donnelly's heart melted at the fullest smile he had seen yet from the girl sat before him. That smile revealed the attractiveness of the face she must once have had and could have again. This, combined with her surprisingly good mood and cheeky demeanour, left Donnelly feeling happy but confused. He was becoming aware that what he felt was paternal regard for the girl could seem like something else. Could this banter be uncomfortably close to flirting? Not for her, he concluded, and felt it safe to continue:

'I'm gonnae bring some Pink Floyd CDs in for you next time I come; educate you a bit.'

'Pink Floyd, now, is that a boy or a girl? A girl I expect. Sounds like a babe. D'ye fancy her?'

'Naw, surely naw? Yiv no' heard of Pink Floyd? A cannae believe it. A'm shocked – shocked tae ma core.'

'Calm doon, auld man. Everybody's heard o' Pink Floyd. A've got thir first album on ma iPod. It's mental, like. But they went down hill after *Piper at the Gates of Dawn*. Syd was the man, it wis jist flabby dad-rock after.'

Donnelly knew that dad-rock must be meant as a criticism but he found it hard to argue against. Pretty much all the Floyd fans he knew were dads right enough. Or granddads.

Just like an uncle and his niece, and absolutely nothing like a journalist and a murderous mental patient, they chatted amiably for fifteen minutes about music, Donnelly's daughters and her day to day life in Scotland's most notorious prison hospital.

Eventually, Donnelly could put it off no longer:

'A'm sorry, Avril, but a have tae ask, can ye tell me about that night. I need to know the whole story of what ye remember about the night Paul Bannerman died?'

Avril's demeanour changed instantaneously.

'A dinnae want tae talk aboot it. Ye cannae make me talk aboot it.'

'A know, hen, and a know that ye won't want tae, but, well, ye know, it's what a came here for.'

'Aye, well ye pretend that yir interested in me, interested

in helping me, bit really ...'

During the ensuing silence Donnelly surveyed the room. In common with most of the rest of the place, it seemed to be dominated by light woods and primary coloured plastics. 'Somewhere in between a doctors' surgery and an IKEA inspired nursery,' he thought. 'Cheerful, right enough.'

'Listen, Avril, a am interested in you. I think yir a really great girl. And a find it hard to believe you could have done what they say. A'd like to help you. A don't know if a can but a want tae try. And you'll have tae help *me* wi' that.'

'Bullshit! Yir jist lookin' fur a story. And a'm no' tellin' ye nothin'.'

'A'm sorry then, hen, but I'll just have tae leave in that case. And there's no point in me coming back. If you want me to visit, then ye'll ...'

He was too embarrassed to finish the sentence but they both understood what he meant.

'Business as usual,' she said, and let it hang in the air.

'Pardon?'

'Men, only interested if a gie thim whit they want.'

She looked into his eyes and she saw shame.

He began again, quietly. 'It's a'right, lass, it's a'right. Let's just talk about somethin' else. D'ye get Sky movies in here? Seen anythin' decent lately?'

Her eyes reddened and she very quietly replied: 'Thanks, Jim.'

'It's awright, lass, a'm sorry.'

Avril could see a distant look in Donnelly's eyes. She

could tell he had clearly gone somewhere else; somewhere not too pleasant.

"Sup, auld man. Somethin's the matter. Whit's the script?'

'Eh, it's … well it's just … well ye know a told ye a've got two daughters? The thing is …'

He surveyed the ward, an old woman muttered to herself and gently rocked back and forward in the corner of his eye. A member of staff talked quietly to another agitated younger woman further down the room. 'It really is quite a calm place,' he thought, 'and … sort of warm. I bet it's not always like this.'

'Ach, it's nothing.'

'Go on, Jim, go on.'

'We're no' here to talk about me.'

'Aye, but remember you've got tae entertain me or it's "goodbye Uncle David".'

She was only partly joking but it wasn't that which convinced him to go on. He knew he really wanted to. And somehow it felt strangely ok to unload himself to a convicted murderer. In a mental hospital.

'A know they love me, a know that. But … the thing is, they don't respect me. A'm their Dad. Yir supposed to respect yir Dad but … they think what a do is … immoral.'

'And what dae you think?'

'Bloody hell, Avril, you been taking lessons fae these psychologists?'

She laughed:

'Aye, a suppose a have, without meanin' tae. Anyway, yir, em, "deflecting". Get back tae the point.'

'Yeah, a do. Sometimes. But it's about the "greater good" ye know? Trying to get to the truth. That is important, surely?'

'Yes it is, Jim, but don't call me Shirley!'

'You are fucking amazing! *Airplane*, funniest film ever!'

'Do *you* think you deserve thir respect?'

'Yeah. A do. Most o' the time.'

'Ye know what then, a bet they do respect ye. Most o' the time. And when they don't, mibbae thir right and mibbae thir no'. They're young; young folk dinnae always understand. They'll mibbae understand later.'

Donnelly looked into her eyes, what seemed like caverns, deep set into a pale grey rock face and he wondered at her youthful wisdom.

They fell silent. Donnelly found it strangely enjoyable. It was something shared; something both mildly euphoric and soporific at the same time. It was recognition of a common regard; genuine affection.

'Ye wir askin' about films. It wis funny recently, a hud the tv on and a few of us were jist settling down tae watch it when suddenly some of the staff decided it would be a good night fur a Scrabble tournament. Or Monopoly or somethin', a cannae mind. Anyway, a kent what wis goin' on and a'm sayin' "naw, let's settle down and watch the movie, somethin' tae take us oot o' ourselves, somethin' escapist". And nobody else is gettin' the joke, except Steve, one o' the nurses. Guess what the film was.'

'A've no idea.'

'*One Flew Over the Cuckoo's Nest*! "Escapist," get it? A knew why they werenae wantin' us tae watch it, like. It wis a great laugh.'

As Donnelly laughed, Avril's face suddenly became more serious, and in a softer voice:

'A kin remember where we met, where we went tae next and where a wis when a woke up. That's aboot it, but a'll try ma best.'

'Are ye sure, Avril? Really sure? Ye don't have tae.'

'A know. Bit now yir no' askin' me tae, a ken a can trust ye.'

'Ok, folks, that's about enough for the day, then. Avril's got her class in half an hour. Five more minutes, alright?'

The kindly young man immediately realised he'd interrupted something and in response to Avril's expression quickly changed his tune:

'Just take as long as you want then. I'll give you a shout when your class is gonnae start, Avril; see how you're doing then.'

'Thanks, Richard.'

She composed herself then began:

'I was wi' three other lassies, drinkin' at St Jude's – a new bar, just open, very fancy. Always a good chance o' meetin' footballers and the likes at those kinds of places. Mind, a'm a junkie by this time and footballers means money, means drugs. One o' the ithir girls wis oan the game but a wis managin' tae avoid that up till then though a probably wid've succumbed eventually. A wis jist aboot maintaining a wee bit o' dignity by gettin' off wi' rich guys and gettin' them tae fund me rather than actually chargin' thim fur it if ye

198

ken whit a mean. A'd broken up wi' a rich guy that worked in finance and a wis sort o' seein' a guy who dealt, really so a could get gear cheap. Anyway, we saw these Athletic players and latched ontae thim. They wernae complainin' like 'cause a' three of us were pretty good lookin' and they could probably tell we were game. That's "game", no "on thi game" – at least in ma case!'

Donnelly just sat and listened as all of this came flooding out of Avril, apparently happy enough to tell this part of the story anyway.

'A fancied that Stuart Robertson bit a knew he had a burd and wis less likely tae want tae go oot wi' me, although sometimes that can be useful. Tae go oot wi somebody like that gies the opportunity fur a wee bit o' subtle blackmail. Anyway thir wis a few nice lookin' guys so a wis prepared to be flexible. Beggars can't be choosers, a suppose. They asked us tae go on wi' thim tae a club. A cannae mind the name though a know it wis somewhere on Bath Street. A wis gettin' a lot o' attention fi a guy called McDougal, John a think, bit he wis a wee bit rough, like and so a wis makin' a play for Ally James. He wis fit and seemed nice enough so all the better. A snogged him in the club and after a few hours they asked us if we wanted tae go back tae someone's flat.'

Donnelly could see her start to concentrate.

'Now a know it wis Bannerman's flat 'cause o' what happened later but a couldnae'a telt ye that otherwise. A jist remember that it wis really posh. A mean a'd been in posh places before but this wis really nice.'

Avril paused and eventually Donnelly intervened:

'A know it's hard but what happened next, Avril?'

'That's it. That's all a remember.'

Donnelly was shocked at the suddenness and finality of her statement.

'Could I maybe ask ye a few questions?'

'Aye, go ahead but a remember nothin' else till a woke up.'

'Were there drugs at the party, Avril?'

'Well a know, we'd only been drinking at the club. No, maybe a line o' Charlie. Aye, a think that's right, at the club. Bit at the party ... a don't know. Ye know ah've told this story so often in therapy thit a can't remember what really happened and what is jist the accepted version o' events.'

'Did ye have sex with anyone?'

'Aye, more than one.' She suddenly looked panicked.

'But I thought ye couldn't remember anythin' at the party.'

'A'm sorry, Jim, a remember a few wee things, here and there. A've jist got so used tae sayin' a know nuthin' tae folk. It jist got easier that way.'

'Even tae the doctors?'

'At first, aye, but now, naw, but they've got that oath so they're safe.'

'There doesnae seem much point in hiding things now a suppose. It's no as if you could get intae any more trouble!'

Smiling, she continued:

'Awright, there *wis* drugs at the party, more Charlie, rocks as well.'

'You mean crack cocaine. Had you taken that before?'

'Aye, plenty o' times but a think this must've been *some* batch.'

'Why?'

'Because o' what happened and because a cannae remember ony o' it'.

'But you remember taking it. Who else took it?'

'Don't know.'

'And what else happened? What about the sex?'

'Don't know.'

'What do you mean you don't know? If you know you had sex you must know who you had it with?'

'A don't know!'

'But you must know.'

'I ... don't ... fucking ... know!'

She had started rocking and tears had begun to flow.

'Listen, I'm sorry. Maybe it's been too much for one day. Maybe I should go.'

Donnelly reached out with both hands, to stop the rocking, to stop the shaking, to stop the pain.

'All o' thim!' she blurted through sobs. 'Every fuckin' one o' thim. I fucked every fuckin' one o' thim.'

Donnelly held her and she cried into his chest, gradually calming to a low, constant sob.

'It's alright, darlin', it's alright.'

'A'm jist a hoor, Jim. A murderous fuckin' hoor.'

'No! No, yir not.'

201

'A fucked a football team! Then killed one o' thim. What wid you call that? Eh? No' exactly every Daddy's perfect wee girl.'

'But did ye kill 'im? And why did ye, ye know, "go" with all the players?'

'No more, Jim. A've had enough.'

Donnelly could see the nurse coming towards them, alerted once more, by the raised voices. Quickly, he replied:

'Alright, enough. Enough. I'm sorry, really, really sorry. I don't mean to hurt you.'

'Right, Avril, time for your class. I think it's time for you to go, Mr Sutherland.'

'Aye, a know,' and turning to Avril:

'A'm really sorry, Avril. A'd like to come again. Nothing to do with … you know. Just to see you. To talk.'

He held out his hand but she did not respond so he placed a business card on the table.

'Please, phone me, if you want a chat. Forget the story; just give me a ring, eh?'

He looked into her tired, red eyes and turned away. As he left the ward he could hear the nurse's voice:

'What story? What did he mean, Avril?'

Chapter Twenty

'Look who's jist walked in, guys! It's Davie Thomson: sportin' superstar! Back amongst the common men, eh, Davie? Are ye back tae show us whit ye learned fi' Fernando and the boys, eh?'

Andy Parks wasted no time in attempting to bring Davie back down to earth.

'Aye, thirs one or two wee tricks a can show ye if ye like, Parksy, when we git oan the field. It cannae help rubbin' off on yi, playin' against that standard o' player, like.'

'Oooh.' This from three or four of the players, sensing, and encouraging a bit of competitive banter.

'Whit wis the score again, Davie? Three? Four? Five wan? And you scored ...?'

'A scored as many as you in your last six matches, big man. And that wis against the likes o' Dumbarton. Onyway, a wisnae playin' as a striker as such; a wis playin' in "the hole".

There was a brief silence as almost everyone in the busy changing room contemplated the potential for comedic value in a response to Davie's comment but no-one could quite think of anything. Eventually, Jim Drylaw came in with his best effort:

'Aye, well, talking of which, ye fair ripped that Sergio Benitez a new one in the second half, eh?'

The ripple of laughter reflected communal relief as much as anything else.

'A do seem to remember a went past him once, right enough.'

'You couldnae go past 'im oan a motorbike ye sad, deluded, cunt,' Parks countered.

'Aye well, at least a wis oan the same pitch as 'im, eh?'

'A think ye did get past 'im once. He kinda slipped a bit and a'm sure ye got past 'im.'

This was said in a quiet voice from the far end of the changing room.

'And who the fuck asked you, ye fuckin' queer cunt. If you've got tae share a changing room wi' men then ye should know tae keep yir fuckin' mouth shut. Save it fur gie'in yir boyfriend a fuckin' blow job.'

'C'moan, Parksy, that's a bit much, like,' Mike Davidson ventured, 'ye don't need tae be so hard on him; the lad's entitled tae his opinion.'

'He's entitled tae fuck all!'

Brian McDermott stood up wearing just boots, socks and shorts, the reddening on his face spreading right down to his chest. When his voice eventually came, it came almost as a scream:

'I'm not fucking gay. Not ... fucking ... gay. A've got a girlfriend. A've got a fucking girlfriend. Will you fucking leave me alone?'

The high pitch of his voice and the tears building up in his eyes undermined his declaration in the eyes of his macho team mates and a few sniggers started to spread round the room.

'That wis quite a wee tantrum ye had thair, hen. Go on,

let it a' oot, hae a good greet. Ye'll feel better fur it.'

The quiet malevolence in Parks' tone silenced the changing room until eventually, Davie's voice was heard, slow and measured:

'Number one: the boy says he's no' a poof. He's ma team-mate and if he says he's no' a poof that's good enough fur me. Number two: and what if he wis? What if he was a shirt lifter; an arse bandit, whatever else ye want tae call it? Who the fuck cares? One in ten folk are gay, ye ken? One in ten. That means at least two in this squad. Who d'ye think they are then eh? Me? You?'

Even Parks didn't seem convinced with his own reply:

'Well a think that's obvious, eh, boys? Takes one tae know one, eh? You and McDermott, now we know, eh?'

But as he looked around for support he realised that half of the players had already sidled out of the room and the others were concentrating on the task at hand or simply staring at their feet.

*

Donnelly drove through that bleak hinterland with equally bleak thoughts. He had, unfortunately, had to leave before really having a chance to make things better with Avril. He didn't think he would ever forget the look on her face as she had told him about having had sex with all of the players. Self-disgust would be closest to it, mixed perhaps, with despair. He was hopeful, however, that when she calmed down, she would not be so angry with him. They had shared so much after all. 'Fuck, I really hope so', he thought as he drove. 'I really want to see that girl again.' He realised with a surge of pride that this was not about the story. Well at least, not completely, this was about helping that poor wee soul. He was surer than ever that more was to be discovered about that evening and he felt that he knew where else he needed to go. He had been turned down on at least three occasions but now it was time to use all of his journalistic guile to make sure he got some face to face time with Davie Thomson.

*

Although he had joined the race a few weeks behind Donnelly, Eck McDougal was catching up fast. This could be put down to him having both time on his hands and no scruples whatsoever. If Donnelly could be described (as Michael Foot of Norman Tebbit) as a "semi house-trained polecat" than McDougal was a rodent with no domestication whatsoever. And crucially, he cared little about which side of the law he found himself on at any given time. He also knew people who could gain him access to telephone conversations taking place on other people's mobile phones. It was through this method that he became privy to the following useful exchange:

Stuart Robertson: 'Hi, Derek, how it gaun, big man?'

Derek Ramsay: 'Aye, no' bad, Stu, what's up?'

Stuart Robertson: 'A wis jist phoning tae see how ye got on wi'that journo, Donnelly.'

Derek Ramsay: 'Awright actually, a thought he wis a fairly decent guy, fur a journalist, like. He ken's his fitba' a'right.'

Stuart Robertson: 'Aye he does, bit that's no really the point. Did ye keep tae the party line?'

Derek Ramsay: 'Of course a did, Stu, whit dae ye take me fur?'

Stuart Robertson: 'A'm no' meaning tae be insultin', Derek, it's just that these guys are smart, they've got a way o' getting things oot o' ye.'

Derek Ramsay: 'Well he got nothing oot o' me ...'

Stuart sensed hesitation in the other's voice.

Stuart Robertson: 'Nothin'?'

Derek Ramsay: 'Aye nothin'. There wis ... well there wis jist one, kind of, uncomfortable moment, like.'

Stuart Robertson: 'Aye?'

Derek Ramsay: 'A kind've suggested that it wis Paul's good nature that got 'im killed but a explained that a meant that Paul wis kind tae 'er, let her stay the night and that. A'm sure that did the trick.'

Stuart Robertson: 'A certainly hope so, Derek 'cause if he believes there was more tae Bann's death than meets the eye then he could make oot that we did somethin' wrong. And we didnae, no' really. We jist did what was needed.'

Derek Ramsay: 'Calm doon, Stu. It's all good. It wis jist a tiny wee thing and a smoothed it over. Nae need tae worry. It's all good.'

'More than meets the eye, eh?' thought McDougal, 'dinnae worry aboot Donnelly, it's Eck McDougal ye've got tae worry aboot, Robertson, ya smug bastard.'

*

Davie sat in his car trying to calm himself down before driving. He felt shaken but slightly elated. Most of all, he felt something that he hadn't felt for a long time and found hard to identify at first. It was only when he realised how much he wanted to share it with Mel that he realised what it was and how good it was to feel "pride".

Kassy's Kitchen on Cowdenbeath High Street may not be at the cutting edge of the culinary world but the size of its menu means that you could eat there everyday for a year without repeating the same home-cooked treat. It was macaroni and chips nine times out of ten, though, for Davie in this, his regular lunch-time haunt. Mel opted for the "special" of veggie lasagne and neither had eaten a bite before Davie had launched into the story of how he had stood up to Andy Parks and his bullying of the unfortunate Brian McDermott.

Mel's pride in Davie added to his own and resulted in a warm glow only increased by the ingestion of the finest macaroni cheese in West Fife. Davie was a professional footballer and even in Scotland this meant a certain effort had to be made to look after one's body. His concession to this was to rarely have a cake or a pudding for lunch. Today was different though and he wanted to celebrate the temporary suspension of his usual self-hatred and decided he needed to do this by devouring something sweet. Mel declined and Davie made his way to the counter whilst trying to remember what name was given to his favourite sweet treat in this particular establishment.

It was called a "Double Biscuit" in his house, straightforward and self-explanatory, but he knew it was known as an "Empire Biscuit" in some places and "German Biscuit" in others. He opted for "Empire" and enjoyed the biscuit very much, even though he had been corrected and had to accept "German".

Mel only had an hour for lunch and Davie had certainly not intended to unburden on this particular lunchtime, but over two hours later she had phoned into work with a semi-plausible excuse and they had moved from Kassy's to the nearby, and unimaginatively titled, "Central Park".

'If he continues to hassle you, call the police. I'm sure it's illegal for a journalist to phone someone six times in a fortnight ... or if it's not, it should be.'

'A know – ma Mum's already telt him that. But, ye know, a think a' want tae talk tae 'im.'

'But why would ye'? It's just dragging up the past, and it makes you sad, understandably, so why put yourself through that when you dinnae need tae? And you really dinnae need tae, ye know?'

'A know, It's jist ... it's jist ... oh, a dinnae ken, a dinnae ken whit it is.'

They sat, close together, on what was left of a park bench, barely aware of a slight drizzle. Davie stared straight ahead and found himself reading the graffiti on an old municipal shed. He wondered if the writer's rather crude feelings towards "Wendy Reid" were shared by the young lady herself.

'Is there something you want to tell him? About what happened?'

'Kind of.'

'But you don't know anything else, you told me. You were stoned.'

'A know. A wis. It's jist ...'

'Just what, Davie?'

'Jist nuthin'.'

The sounds of the nearby high street polluted the silence,

car horns and dodgy brakes, the occasional shout or laugh.

'If there's something you want to tell him, don't you think it would be better trying it out on me first?'

Silence again, broken by a siren, probably police, Davie thought.

'Thirs things that would be easier tae tell him than tae tell you. A mean, theoretically, like. If there wis anything tae tell, there wid be things that'd be easier tae tell him than you.'

'Davie, what is it? What is there to tell? What are you not telling me?'

'Nothin', Mel. Jist leave it, for Christ's sakes.'

'Ok, fine. Just go back to being that guy, the guy who keeps things to himself. The guy who cannae be honest. The guy you used to be before I fell in love with you.'

There was certainly one level on which Davie was annoyed by what he might not have recognised as emotional blackmail but which bruised him nonetheless. That level was somewhere way down below the basement, however. In the hierarchy of feelings it was miles beneath the rush of joy caused by Mel's clearest declaration yet; that she was actually in love with him.

'Fuck,' he thought.' Fuck, here goes'.

He looked into her eyes.

'Promise me somethin', Mel. Promise ye'll still love me when a tell ye this.'

Mel didn't know how to answer. How can you make such a promise? How can you know how you'll feel, or still feel, after any new piece of information?

'I love you, Davie. You need to tell me it all.' This was the best she could offer.

There was a considerable silence before he felt able to respond:

'See the lassie - Avril. A fucked her. A mean, we all fucked her. A know now it wis wrong bit we a' jist ... well we a' jist ... took turns.'

He paused, looked at Mel's blank expression and took another breath before:

'And, well, a mean, a don't really know if she wanted tae. She wis a junkie, like. She'd've gone wi anyone fur some gear. Bit, bit she jist kindae went quiet, blank, sort of ... catatonic, like ...'

Davie felt physically sick as he watched the expression of horror gradually populate the face of the person he loved. The woman who had, who was, saving him.

Slowly, and quietly, Mel began to speak:

'So ... you ... raped her.'

'Naw! She didnae say, "no" like. She didnae say …'

'Anything?'

A deep breath escaped from him, like he was winded.

'Aw fuck ... aw Christ, did a'? Aw fuck, a did, eh? A did. A fuckin' raped a girl. A fuckin raped someone. A'm sorry. A'm so sorry, Mel. A didnae really know. A knew it wis wrong, but ... a didnae really realise. A'm so sorry ... aw fuck.'

She wanted to hold him, or at least she wanted to be able to hold him. But, no, she couldn't. Couldn't bring herself to do so. She turned away from him, got up and moved towards a concrete rubbish bin, half-destroyed by vandals. She turned

211

to him with a look on her face that he would never want to see again, then turned away and retched, violently, into the bin.

Chapter Twenty-One

'They call it "restorative justice", Avril. Or "restorative practices" in other contexts. It's getting used in so many different ways, by so many kinds of professionals, that it's a little hard to pin down.'

'Well you're gonna have to try, Doctor Davies, 'cause a've no idea whit yir talkin' aboot so far.'

Avril and the psychiatrist both instinctively settled back in the upright, but fairly comfy, matching chairs in which they sat, a few feet apart. It was near the end of their regular session and all the clinical staff who worked with her, felt Avril to have progressed very well in recent weeks. The meetings with her uncle had apparently contributed to shifting a kind of log-jam in the young woman's mind and she seemed to be in much better condition, psychologically. Well enough to be ready to deal with another kind of external intervention? Possibly, it was thought.

This intervention had not been planned, however, but rather had presented itself and so had to be considered very carefully. The fact that it had presented itself in the form of a well-known, and well-loved, sporting celebrity should, of course, be of no significance whatsoever. Celebrity, however, provides a powerful magnet and perhaps the offer of a visit from Stuart Robertson was proving more seductive than it should to both male and female hospital staff alike. That Robertson knew, and appeared to understand, some of the basic principles of restorative practices, had also had a positive effect.

'It's used by guidance teachers in schools dealing with bullying, residential workers in similar ways; the probation service, police, social workers, the list goes on. It's not so much a treatment programme as a philosophical approach to criminal justice ...'

'Aye, and?'

Dr Davies raised both of his bony, liver spotted hands together in a kind of praying gesture. He was a kindly, if slightly uncomfortable, man whom Avril felt resembled a skeleton with only the scantest stretch of skin covering a perfunctory bony structure.

'It's based around the idea that crime is not an offence against the state but rather against individuals and communities and that to foster dialogue between victim and offender can provide some measure of satisfaction for the former and increase accountability and consequent desire for atonement in the latter. Do you see?'

'Ok, a think a'm gettin' ye. What yir sayin' is that the criminal meets the victim, says thir sorry and everyone feels a wee bit better, right?

'In its most basic form, well, yes.'

'One problem though, Doc.'

'And what would that be, Avril?'

'Ma victim's deid.'

Dr Davies allowed himself a slight smile at what he knew to be a statement of fact but also a characteristic attempt at "gallows humour" on Avril's part.

'Well yes indeed, Avril, but of course there's more than one victim of most crimes, one has to think of the families involved, friends and also others present during the offence.'

'Aye?'

'In this case, the individual we're considering you meeting, falls into two of those categories.'

'Uh huh?'

'He was a friend of Paul Bannerman and was present on the evening he lost his life.'

Avril immediately looked a little less amused.

'I'm talking about the footballer, Stuart Robertson.'

'Fuck me.'

'Quite. But he's requested a visit and we feel that as well as being useful for him it may allow you to build on the recent success you've been having in coming to terms with what you've done.'

'Oh, fucking fuck.'

'I know, it's a tough one, Avril, and we can't make you, of course. But if you're up for it, we think it might be worth a try.'

There was about a minute's silence before a small voice replied:

'Ok.'

'I beg your pardon?'

'Ok, fine, let's do it; bring it on, whatever.'

'Are you sure, Avril?'

'No, but, yes, if ye ken what a mean. A'm sure.'

*

'Oh, Davie, for God's sake, yiv gottae go tae yir work,

son. Ye cannae dae this again. Ye'll lose yir job.'

Davie didn't manage to catch all that his Dad had said, partly because he didn't want to hear him, but mainly because it had been said from the other side of a closed door. It wouldn't be true to say that his parents were despairing as they had been here many times before and were well practised. Still, they wearied of the rollercoaster ride brought on by living with an alcoholic.

'Go on, son; tell me whit's wrong this time.'

After ten minutes talking to a piece of painted wood, Tam's persistence finally paid off:

'A'm suspended. There, are ye satisfied? A couldnae go even if a wanted tae.'

'What fur, lad. What on earth fur?'

'Aye, well that's the only good bit. A wis a wee bit upset aboot somethin' and then a went tae training and Parks hacked me.'

'Aye, so? Whit's new – he's an animal.'

'So a got up and lamped him one, on the pus. Should've done it years ago.'

After a few moments silence Tam replied:

'How long?'

'Don't know. A think it'll depend on whether Billy's fit tae play on Saturday. If he's no', it'll no' be fur long.'

*

Stuart Robertson made an impact wherever he went, whether nightclub or psychiatric hospital. There was a palpable excitement to be experienced in the State Hospital, therefore, as he was shown from the reception to the small, pastel-shaded room where Avril sat in waiting, along with Doctor Davies.

'Hi,' Stuart offered tentatively, to both as he entered. He would have spoken in a different manner to each individual if given the chance but, as they sat together he did not know exactly how to differentiate his greeting.

Their reactions couldn't have been much more different. Dr Davies rose quickly from his seat to offer both a hand and a warm smile. Lastly, he also issued a cheery 'Hello there.' Avril barely nodded as she sat, hunched so greatly that she almost looked as though she was trying to turn herself inside out.

Davies set the scene, explained a little about what they were hoping to get out of the session and how he was planning to structure the meeting. He had been on a course and was thrilled to have the opportunity to put some of what he had learned into practise. He knew he had to ask "restorative questions" and that he needed to elicit "affective statements" from the participants.

Avril and Stuart, however, had two very different agendas.

Stuart wanted to find out whether Avril was of any risk to him or his team-mates and if she appeared to be so, remind her of what she had done.

Avril just wanted to try and understand why she hated this man so much.

Neither were remotely interested in "restorative approaches" of any kind.

The approach was serving Stuart's agenda, however. As Davies asked him what had happened; what he was thinking at the time; how it had made him feel, etc, he had every opportunity to reiterate what he hoped Avril believed to be the truth about that night. He described what had taken place during the evening. He was aware that he was talking about the party and the drugs in the presence of two people, one of whom was bound by the Hippocratic Oath and the other, a convicted murderer. He felt he could take the risk. He even talked about the sex: 'Perhaps they were not all perfect gentlemen,' was his gracious concession.

From time to time both men could see a hint of a spark or a glimmer of something crossing the face and momentarily energising the body of the young woman who otherwise sat, darkly impassive. Davies was aware that this had been particularly noticeable during Stuart's description of the sexual events of the evening.

Stuart's first-hand description ended with his own departure from the flat that night. This didn't however stop him from telling the next, conjectural, part of the story with as much authority as that of which he had first-hand knowledge.

His description was detailed and his statements were certainly "affective". They were also emotional and blunt but relatively kind:

'I lost one o' ma best friends, Avril – you took a friend from me. You couldn't have hurt me more. A thought a would hate you for ever. That a could never forgive you. But now, seeing you here. Seeing who you are, and what has become of you, a think … maybe, just maybe … a can.'

Davies was thrilled with how it was going. 'In so much as it's meant to help both parties,' he thought, 'it certainly seems to be doing Stuart some good, and, if not helping Avril, no damage done, anyway, so far …'

The first part had been relatively easy, though. Getting Stuart Robertson to talk was hardly a challenge. Avril, however, did not look like she was in the mood to play ball.

They paused whilst refreshments, which had not been requested, were delivered. Small talk was kept to a minimum so as not to lose momentum. Davies was very much hoping there would be an appropriate opportunity at the end to secure Robertson's autograph for his sport-mad son. Josh preferred rugby, but would still be impressed with Dad if he came home with StuRob's signature on a piece of notepaper.

Davies went through his pre-prepared questions with Avril, adding a few he felt were within the restorative category:

'What were you thinking at the time? Who else do you think has been affected? What needs to be done to make things right?'

Avril responded with the minimum she felt she could get away with to avoid castigation for not engaging with the process. The questions annoyed her, though, and she was working hard to avoid the sarcasm she thought they deserved, particularly the last, though she forced out a reply:

'A suppose at least if a can say sorry it might make Stuart and his pals feel a wee bit better.'

Although that is what she said, what she had wanted to say was:

'Fuck all. Fuck all can be done, it's too fucking late.'

Throughout the process, however, she could not bring herself to look Stuart Robertson in the face. Both men had also noticed this. Davies put it down to guilt, and Stuart also hoped, and more or less believed, that this was the case. Avril thought so too, at first. But as she was describing her feelings about the middle part of the evening and about the sex, the sex that she now realised had taken place with every single one of the footballers. The sex that she presumed (or possibly remembered?) having with Stuart himself, she realised that what she was feeling was hatred. Pure and unadulterated, like the crack cocaine they had smoked.

Having gone through the motions of answering the questions as she thought she should, the change in Avril's voice was obvious when she suddenly looked straight at Stuart for the first time and asked:

'Did you fuck me?'

There was no response.

'A think ye did, like. A'm pretty sure. But when did ye come – no pun intended. Were ye first? Near the beginnin'? Somewhere near the end, eh?'

Still no answer.

'Wis a still awake? Or wis a … unconscious? Did ye fuck me when a wisnae even aware ye were dain' it?

Stuart cleared his throat, preparing to respond in some way.

'Naw, you were near the start, eh? Yir too guid-mannered tae fuck somewan comatose. And yir no' the type tae go last at anyhin', let's be honest.'

Stuart looked shocked and very uncomfortable:

'A did say that we wernae perfect gentlemen. And as we're talking about "restorative practices" then I should say:

'A'm sorry", it wis poor, ye know … etiquette.'

'Etiquette! Etiquette, you bastard. Is that what it's called when you wait in a line tae hae sex wi' a lassie till she's unconscious? "Poor fuckin' etiquette"? There's another word fur it ye ken: "rape", that's whit it is. You raped me you fuckin' bastard. You fuckin' raped me.'

Stuart was already leaving the room, protected by the slight, but wiry figure of Doctor Davies as Avril had leaped from her chair and thrown herself towards the fleeing footballer.

'Aye, get tae fuck, rapist,' her words rushed along the corridor, faster than his feet could take him.

Stuart declined Davies' offer of another cup of tea and a chance to reflect on the meeting. He did have one thing he wanted to say to the medical practitioner, however:

'Can you tell me why you've allowed that poor, deluded wee lassie to receive visits from a journalist doing a story on Bannerman's murder?'

In response to the blank look of the doctor, he continued:

'Where do you think she's getting these wild notions from, eh? James Donnelly, that's who. James Donnelly, a muck-raking sleazebag from the *Daily Standard*.'

Chapter Twenty-Two

'There's a spark about her, Jacqui. I know that doesn't mean that she didn't do what they say she did but there's something about her – something … decent.'

'Does she remember what happened at all?'

'A bit, but not the crucial stuff. She remembers the earlier parts of the evening and some o' what happened later on but then she just … well, I'm not sure she wants to remember anything else. It obviously wasn't a pleasant experience, whether she did it or not. She seems to have just taken on what she's been told she did and she believes it.'

'But why would she do that, Jim? You've got to think about the psychological motivation. There's always some sense to be made out of people's motivation, some, at least, partly logical, causal relationship, even if the original premise is a bit warped.'

Donnelly swirled the remains of his regular evening single malt around his favourite whisky glass and considered his wife's proposition.

'She thinks she's bad.'

'What d'you mean?'

'Well, she was a promising young girl who let everyone down. Her parents, particularly her Dad, have more or less abandoned her. They'd already done so before the incident. She'd squandered that promise on drugs. Her Mum kept in touch, but her Dad didnae want to know.'

'Ah well, now we can see someone else's psychological motivation anyway.'

'What ye on about?'

'You, ye daft old man. Daddy to every waif and stray that comes your way – well the lassies anyway.'

'I think that might be a slight exaggeration, Jacqui, but yeah, I won't deny, I feel something paternal for this particular waif.'

Jacqui emptied her coffee, and after a satisfied sounding, 'Aah,' she continued:

'So, she's obviously a girl who hates herself. Have you checked out her arms? Self-harms, I'll bet, though it could be anywhere on her body. Everyone else thinks she's bad. She knows she's been bad, to some extent, so ...'

'Yeah, I know. She believes that she's capable of doing bad things so why not believe it when others tell her she did.'

'Yeah, Jim, but I think it goes even deeper. I think that not only does she believe it, she *wants* to believe it. She wants to be punished. She wants to suffer for the suffering she's caused other people, her family in particular.'

'She does seem to wallow in it a bit.'

'And not only that, I think she may well want to let them off the hook.'

'What?'

'Well, if you think about it. Her family have let her down but she won't want to think that. They're her Mum and Dad; she wants to think the best of them. If she justifies their behaviour by being deserving of it then that lets them off the hook. It puts it all on her. No wonder the poor girl's in such a state.'

'Ye know, sometimes, Jacqui, just occasionally, your psychobabble makes a certain amount of sense. What you're saying is certainly consistent with what she's said to me.'

'And you know what; and I hate to say this 'cause I'm not sure you should be going to see this girl, but nothing will help her more than a father figure who believes in her, who actually shows her some regard. More by accident than design, Jim, you could actually be helping this girl!'

'What girl?' asked Fiona, by way of announcing her and her sister's arrival in the living room.

'A girl that Dad's doing a story on, that's all, love.'

'Is this the mental one that disembowelled the football player?' Katy's contribution was to the point.

'My God, Katy, I don't know on how many levels that was inappropriate. For a start …'

'She's winding you up, Mum; you should know by now how Bellatrix can push your buttons.'

'Tell her to stop calling me that, Mum.'

'You stop dressing like that and I'll stop calling you it.'

'I don't …'

'Enough!' shouted Donnelly. 'Don't dress like that, Katy; don't call her that, Fiona; don't wind your Mum up, Katy; don't wind your sister up, Fiona. Is that everything? No, wait, how did you know about this story, Katy?'

'Oh, no' again, Dad. Why do you always seem to think that we're deaf? Or stupid. You talk about things to Mum, we hear – no mystery … and then, sometimes, I google.'

'Well don't. This isn't an appropriate story for you to be reading about.'

'Don't you want us to take an interest in your work, Dad,' Fiona countered.

'Not when it's inappropriate and not until you can be supportive. You always seem to slag me off.'

'Why do you think that is, Dad?' Katy asked. 'Could it be because you tend to stick your nose into other people's lives and make them worse.'

'Christ, Katy, do you realise just how insulting that is? I don't mind the jokes but do you think I like being told that what I do for a living is bad?'

At the sight of Katy's crumpled face, Fiona's occasional sisterly solidarity kicked in:

'She disnae really mean it, Dad. *We* dinnae really mean it. We know that you go after bad guys in your stories, most o' the time, it's just that it might not always be the best thing for people to have their business spread all over the papers.'

There was a pause and each of the female family members looked at the disappointed and resigned face of the man of the house. Quietly, he responded:

'I know … you're right.'

'What?' or variations thereof, came from all three.

'You're right, love. It's certainly not going to do her any good, me putting her story back in the papers; making her go through it again. But it's been worth it, I think I am doing a good thing here. I think I might actually be doing the girl some good. But the story? Naw, it's just no' worth it.'

'Wow,' said Fiona.

No-one else had any idea what to say.

*

It had taken Eck McDougal only a few hours to work out where the point of least resistance would be. For his methods, how intelligent or savvy the player was didn't matter. He needed to decide who would crumble the quickest when faced with two very tough guys, fully tooled up. He quickly dismissed Jim Forrester (too hard); Stuart Robertson (too high profile) and Mark Sinclair (too mental) and homed in on the man whom he thought the most fragile, the most soft. A couple of phone calls later and two of his very large friends were planning a friendly wee chat with Davie Thomson.

*

Donnelly had been avoiding Steph all week. This hadn't been difficult because she had been avoiding him too. But you can only stay away from your office for so long and so it was inevitable that their paths would eventually cross.

'Awright, hen?' Donnelly slipped into what was his natural, patronising mode when addressing women.

'Aye, you?' Steph was prepared to let it go.

'Ooh, you could cut the sexual tension with a knife.'

Suddenly there was tension of another sort as Norman Campbell, perpetually out of the loop, had, unwittingly, hit the nail on the head. Much to the delight of everyone else in the room. Except Donnelly and Steph.

The silence was broken by the emergence of editor, Bill Slater, who announced that he was ready for his scheduled meeting with Donnelly, who gratefully scurried off from the frying pan to the slightly warm plate.

'I need to see a wee bit progress, Jim,' Slater hitting right away with his hardest shot.

'Nae probs, pal. I've got loads of stuff tae tell ye. I've interviewed at least five of the players. And the girl twice.'

'That's good, Jim, but I meant progress in the way of something actually on paper. You know, like a draft or something.'

'That would be silly, Bill. I can't write a draft till I actually know what I'm gonnae say.'

'Yeah, well that's the problem. When's that gonnae happen?'

'Soon.'

'Soon?'

'Very soon.'

'It'll have to be, Jim.' Slater steeled himself, but still couldn't look Donnelly in the eye when he said:

'A week then, Jim, I need something in a week. And stop neglecting the rest of your work.'

'Awright, Bill, nae probs.'

Slater looked towards his computer, assuming that the conversation had ended with one of Donnelly's usual pointless promises. But he soon became aware that Donnelly was not leaving.

'Eh, is there something else, Jim?'

'Aye, kinda.'

'Go on then, spit it oot.'

'Well, it's just … eh; I've decided to give the story a different emphasis.'

227

'Go on.'

'Well, I want to make it less about what actually happened and more about the effect. You know, of the death of a friend. On the players.'

Bill Slater may have been an easy going kind of chap, but he hadn't achieved the position of Scottish editor of the *Daily Standard* without being sharp.

'So, you're just writing a nice wee descriptive piece. What went wrong? That kind of thing. No actual investigative journalism as such then?'

'No. I ... investigated and ... I ... well I didn't find anything. So, you know, best to keep it more about the psychological effects.'

Slater's already red and blotchy face went even redder and more blotchy as he became as close to angry as he ever got:

'Jim, this was all I thought you were going for in the first place, but you got us to announce the return of your great series, revisiting crimes of the past. You buried the first story - about that local politician. Now you're reducing this one to a piece of emotional fluff. I was lukewarm about the idea in the first place. But enough's enough. Either dig up something worthwhile or just drop it. It's no' worth it. And we'll just quietly drop the whole series with it. Right?'

'Aye, right.'

He sidled out of the office and straight outside for a consoling nicotine hit.

'Aaw,' an involuntary exclamation escaped Donnelly as he spotted Norman Campbell in what was his own usual smoking spot. He didn't feel like company. He nodded to

Norman before turning to go round the side of the building, into what was really a prohibitive breeze, at least as far as lighting a fag went. And then it happened again, but worse:

'Aaw.'

This was on discovering that Steph was coming from the direction he was headed and that he was to be the victim of an unwitting ambush.

'S'up, Jim,' Steph asked, his demeanour making his misery obvious.

'No nothin', hen, just the usual crap.'

Campbell came round the corner and joined in:

'Naw, Jim. You always look like a Tory politician on a CND march but this is different. Something's really bothering you.'

Donnelly could easily have resisted the entreaties of his old colleague but he was much less immune to the charm of the irresistible Steph. It was she, therefore, who dragged it out of him and was the cause of the subsequent three-way conversation about Donnelly's moral dilemma.

Though uncomfortable with this open discussion on his business, Donnelly gradually realised that it was proving worthwhile. He had a sudden picture in his head of Steph and Norman perched on his shoulders dressed as an angel and a devil in traditional cartoon style. Campbell, of course, was taking the devilish position, stressing the means justifying the end. Steph, of course, was angelic in her defence of personal morality and doing the "right thing". Truth be told, he'd sooner have imagined Steph in the devilish get up but that could wait till another time.

The debate flowed back and forth, often without his input,

as he absented himself, deep in thought, until he interrupted whoever was speaking at the time with this:

'Fuck it! Fuck the story; fuck the series. I'm doing the right thing. She's too important. That wee lassie matters much, much more than a few lines on a page.'

Chapter Twenty-Three

Jim Forrester knew it would get colder than this, as autumn began to give way to winter. Much colder. He was still glad, though, that he'd dressed warmly. That is to say that he'd chosen to wear the full uniform of his occupation, popularly known as "bouncer". The dark grey overcoat protected the smart suit from the rain and the leather gloves completed the impressive ensemble.

As the wind rushed down Lothian Road, assailing the exposed flesh of young women with more fake tan than sense, Forrester wondered about the parents of some of the girls whose long legs were on display:

'Would you let your daughter dress like that, Steve?' he asked of his relatively new colleague, on duty with him at the front door of Temptations lap dancing club.

'Naw, Jim, a wouldnae. Apart fae the cauld, they're askin' fur it once they gadgies get a few drinks in thim. Some braw sights tae be seen, but. They're like sweeties in a shop jist waitin' tae be gobbled up. And in a few hours some o' thim'll be sittin on the kerbs or lying on the pavements; skirts up aboot thir arses, too drunk tae notice. It's nae wonder thirs that much rape and stuff.'

Forrester wasn't immune to the charms of attractive young women, but after stopping playing football he had now worked at the club for a number of years. And as he worked inside the establishment as well as on the door, he saw plenty of attractive female flesh in all sorts of positions every night. He didn't need to see it on the street as well.

'It's nae excuse though, eh?'

'Whit?'

'Tae assault a lassie a mean. Jist cause she's wearing a short skirt and lying drunk on the pavement.'

'Whit the fuck are ye oan aboot?'

'A'm jist sayin' that men shouldnae use that as an excuse.'

'Fair does, Jim, a wouldnae dae it masel' but a can see why some wid – after a few drinks like. When yir inhibitions are lowered and it's a' oan display fur ye.'

'Sorry, gentlemen,' Forrester interjected, 'at least two of your party are hardly able tae stand. Yis cannae come in a'm afraid.'

This was directed at a group of five young men, well dressed and apparently affluent, though clearly leery, with some of the group having to help others maintain a vertical position.

Protests were made, along with much use of the word "fuck" in longer or shorter versions. Jim and Steve were always in control, however. Sober and experienced, they dealt comfortably with groups like this five or six times a night, five or six nights a week. This is not to say that it didn't occasionally get dangerous. A knife could be pulled or a sudden explosion of violence could catch even a hardened professional unawares. Most of the time, though, a polite approach combined with the look and build of a heavyweight boxer did the trick.

'A dinnae think they would've been any bother, Jim,' the younger man suggested.

'We'd've jist been giving ourselves a problem fur later

on. A guarantee we'd've been throwin' thae cunts oot in an 'oor's time.'

'Aye bit they'd have paid thir entry fee by then. And a couple o' ludicrously expensive rounds. The management are no' wantin' us tae ...'

'Fuck the management, it's ma job tae protect the lassies in thair and a'd rather no take the risk wi' thair safety.'

'Aye, whitever. Anyway, shift change in twenty minutes. We'll be inside.'

'Aye, thank Christ fur that.'

*

Tea was over in the Donnelly/Davidson household and the four family members would soon be drifting away from the dining room towards the next item on their busy itineraries. Fiona, however, was being ushered to the kitchen by her mother:

'A've done all my dishes for the week,' she protested. 'A only need to do three for my pocket money – this would be my fourth.'

'No, sweetheart,' Jacqui replied, 'the first one you're counting was on Sunday and was actually the last one of last week's 'cause you'd only done two last week.'

'But Sunday was a double, Mum – nobody'd done Saturday night.'

'I've told you before, there's no such thing as doubles. If you don't do one the night before you can't count the next one as a double.'

'But Saturday wasn't supposed to be mine ...'

The conversation was taking place in the kitchen by this point and Donnelly had zoned out, confused by the contractual complexities of the housework system employed in his own household. He saw Katy heading for her room and, no doubt, overly loud, angst inflected rock music. He was aware that he hadn't had a chance to talk to her about her boyfriend situation since the night the slim young man had slipped out of her bedroom.

'Katy, just a minute, before ye go, what's the story wi' what'sisname? The sleekit wee bugger that wis all over you the other night?'

'Dad, a've got homework, can we do this another time?'

'Homework? So ye say but you've always got that music blaring. How can you possibly be doin' homework?'

'No' again, dad; a've told ye, it helps me concentrate.'

'Anyway, about the boy, go on, give me the headlines.'

Katy moved from holding the door to sitting on the arm of the sofa, making it plain that she would give him a bit but that she wasn't up for a lengthy conversation.

'Right, quickly then, he said he was sorry; a thought about going back out wi' him; a found out that he'd done the same with Lydia Jamieson a few months ago; I told him to fu ... to leave me alone; a wis gutted for a while - the rest of the day really; Mark Robinson asked me out after school the next day; a said "yes" and a'm seeing him on Saturday. He's nicer anyway, and he's got a great ... eh ... personality! So, all good.'

Donnelly was unable to formulate a response by the time his daughter had left the room and sprinted up the stairs.

*

Forrester could sense when trouble was about to start:

'A'm keeping a close eye on that group over near the stage, can you keep an eye on the "private" dances, Steve?'

'Sure man, am a' o'er it.'

Within the next half hour, Forrester's suspicions had been proven correct when two of the offending group had, with the encouragement of alcohol and their noisy friends, climbed up onto the stage to join the girl currently featured, for a rather too close dance.

Forrester dealt with the trouble swiftly and reasonably professionally. Perhaps he had used a little more violence than was strictly required but he viewed this as an encouragement to the miscreants to behave themselves in future.

Unfortunately, his colleague had not lived up to his side of their agreement and had taken the chance to pop out for an unscheduled fag break.

Forrester realised this when he heard the scream from the private area. By the time he got there, the girl (Sheree to the punters, Elaine to him and her family) had pulled herself away from a very drunk businessman type and retreated to the corner of the room, legs kicking out at her attacker.

Forrester picked up the man and threw him over a table and into a heap on the other side of the room in less than a few seconds.

'He grabbed me, Jim. He grabbed my … my fucking crotch, the fucking bastard; tried tae put 'is fingers in me. Fucking … fuck!'

She was shouting through tears as one of the other girls wrapped her in a dressing gown and held her whilst she shook.

Forrester advanced on the now very frightened man, preparing to do him some serious damage.

'Yir not so fuckin' full of it now, eh? You fucking, arrogant business types. Ye think everything's yours for the takin'. Well it's no'. These lassies arnae yours tae dae what ye want wi. Thir jist doin' a fuckin' job. A'm gonnae fuckin' teach you a lesson. A'll fuckin' kill ye.'

As the man backed himself against the wall of the small room he begged for mercy and, to the surprise of everyone who had gathered, attracted by the commotion, he got it. At least for the time being.

Forrester was still angry but calm when he spoke to the policeman half an hour later. He knew that the management would not be pleased with him for having involved the police. He suspected, in fact, that he might be out of a job by the end of the night. The legality of private dances and what was and wasn't allowed, was sometimes liberally interpreted at the club. The management, therefore, preferred not to draw attention to the practise and were consequently very much in favour of summary justice in these cases, usually to be dispatched in the lane behind the club.

Just before taking aim at the man with his heavy boots, however, Forrester had realised how much he wanted one of those bastards to be nailed. 'How much better,' he thought, 'for the guy tae have tae go to court and his family and work to find out. And if he wriggles out of it, a'll find the bastard.'

*

As they relaxed, at opposite ends of what was a frankly enormous sofa, Stuart and Jo were not equally engaged in the American crime drama showing on the giant plasma screen. But although she was half-reading a magazine and only half watching the TV, Jo asked Stuart if they could turn over to another channel.

'Another young woman getting attacked. See these crime shows? Why is it always a young girl in her knickers getting chased and murdered? I'm just fed up seeing it. Night after night, programme after programme, like it's a sport or something.'

'Yeah, but they'll get their comeuppance in the end, these guys.'

'Aye, maybe, but just the same; it's wall to wall. Just turn it over, will you?'

'Aye, all right, all right.'

Aware of Jo's mood, he thought better of going onto Sky Sports and instead, settled on Celebrity Big Brother. After a few minutes of the usual inane sexual innuendo, Stuart asked, out of the blue:

'I've always been respectful of you, haven't I?'

'What? Yes, of course.'

'I mean, sexually, like?'

'What?'

'I'm never too … insistent or anything?'

'No, of course not. Or you'd get short thrift if you were.'

After a few moments silence she added:

'Sometimes I like you to be … you know, to an extent.'

Stuart contemplated the complexity resulting from Jo's last statement.

'What was that all about, Stu?'

'Nothing.'

'Nothing?'

'Aye, nothing.'

*

'Call. For you, Jim, A'll put it through. Disnae want to give his name.'

Donnelly looked up from his computer screen and prepared to pick up his phone, interest duly piqued.

'Hello, Jim Donnelly here, what can I do for ye?'

'A'm no sayin' who a am but a wis thair that night when Paul Bannerman died. Anyway, a've been thinkin' aboot this a lot recently, the things that men dae and what they shouldnae dae and … well, it's jist made me think. A jist wanted tae say this: Avril Gallacher, she wis mair victim than criminal. We did a bad thing tae that lassie. That's a'. A jist wanted ye tae know.'

Chapter Twenty-Four

'Hi there, Mr Sutherland, can I have a wee word?'

Donnelly replied, anxiously, in the affirmative and was taken into a small interview room by one of the senior psychiatric nurses from Avril's ward who then introduced himself as "Dom". Donnelly preferred, for obvious reasons, to go straight in and out to his meetings with Avril with as little contact as possible with hospital staff. He had no choice, however, but to agree to this request and he braced himself for searching questions.

They sat in a small bright but bland room and the young man with a number one cut and intense green eyes started to tell Donnelly about Avril's progress:

'It's been quite striking in the last three or four weeks. She's both much more buoyant and much more lucid. She's told us a lot more about what happened on that night as well. I can't tell you what she's said, of course, but I felt you should know because it's not impossible that she could disclose something to you. She's very fond of you, you know.'

Donnelly was able to respond with honesty:

'And I her, of course.'

'We actually think that her chats with you have been part of this positive turn of events. You've made her cheerier for sure but also, somehow, more confident. It's as if she hates herself just a wee bit less.'

Donnelly was quite overcome. He could only nod in acknowledgement.

'This is why I'm going to let you in even though you're a bare-faced, shameless liar who would risk the mental health of a young psychiatric patient in order to write some sensationalist crap for a dodgy tabloid. Mr ... Donnelly is it?'

At this point Donnelly realised why there were a number of other male nursing staff hovering around nearby, looking like they were anticipating trouble.

'Aye ... aye,' was all the journalist could manage.

Those intense green eyes seemed to be both threatening and judging Donnelly as he tried again to respond and this time managed only:

'Sorry.'

'Ok, Mr Donnelly, here's what I think's going on here. You came down in the first instance with ill-intent. I mean, you wouldn't see it that way, but to right-minded people that would be a fair description of what was going on.'

Donnelly began to respond but then thought better of it.

'Then you met her. Got to know her. Got on well with her. And, proving that no-one's all bad, she liked you. Then you wanted to help her, and though you probably haven't realised it yourself, she started to help you. By that I mean she's helped you find some part of yourself that you're tabloid-infected mind had forgotten was there. And it made you feel good. How'm I doing?'

Donnelly sighed.

'No' bad.'

'So you thought, "Maybe I can achieve both things here – help her and help my story. Do a good thing and end up ahead?"'

Donnelly finally felt he had something to contribute:

'Aye, you're right – all o' that was right. Very impressive in fact. You should go on TV with that shtick. There's only one thing ye've got wrong, I'm not trying to help myself any more. I've already decided, the story's finished. I'm just wanting to help.'

He meant what he said. Or at least he thought he did. But that call, from, he wasn't sure who. That call was creating doubts in his mind. Again.

Dom stood his intense stare down and smiled almost imperceptively.

'Good, 'cause if you do publish anything we'll have you up on criminal charges before you can say "News of the World", understood?'

'Crystal.'

'And of course the reason that we let you come today is that Avril very definitely wanted you to. So, to that end, keep on doing what you're doing and hopefully, between us all, we can get that girl out of here. Eventually.'

The first thing Donnelly noticed, as he was taken into the large day room where they met, was that she had dressed up a bit for the occasion. Taking some care over her appearance was obviously a good sign, as was the open smile she gave him as he approached.

Her hair and eyes were dark, the eyes accentuated with a little mascara, and her mouth seemed fuller. 'Probably the lipstick,' he thought. Still slim, she was getting slightly less painfully so. She was turning back into a very pretty girl indeed.

Donnelly was disappointed at the effect this was having

on him, but it wasn't the first time that his paternal instinct had had to co-exist with something else. Not, he thought with relief, in relation to his own daughters. 'But fuck, it's complicated; pretty young girls can make a man feel all sorts of things. Conflicting things.'

'Or perhaps it's just me,' he thought, with a rueful smile.

'Hey, Unc, good to see you, whasup?'

'Nothing. Why? Did you think something was the matter?'

'No, old man, I just meant it in a cool, happening kind of way, you know, what's up? what's the story, that kind of thing. Ok, not that cool.'

'Ok, well, there's not much up. I've just been, you know, hanging with my homos, yeah?'

'Well, a never thought you were that way inclined but a'm sure it feels good to have come out. Have ye told yir wife?'

'It's not homos is it? I mean, I know that means homosexual but I thought it maybe had a different meaning as well, you know, under the 'hood.'

Avril was almost beside herself with laughter now. Could he be serious? She wasn't sure.

'"In the 'hood" you plonker, "in the 'hood!"'

'You know, this is the main reason I come here, just to provide amusement for you. Mock the old guy, that's what it's all about eh? You wouldn't do that to black people. Or poofs for that matter. But it's ok to mock the old guy. That's ageist and … mannist. See, they don't even have a word for anti-man. Our pain goes unacknowledged.'

She moved to put a consoling, if ironic, arm around his shoulder and he recoiled as if embraced by a leper.

'Oh well, a'm obviously not looking as good as a hoped. A guess none of that matters if you're a convicted murderer and confirmed psychiatric case.'

She slumped back in her chair.

'No, lass, it's not that at all. You look great. I mean, seriously nice. And I've never thought you were a murderer anyway. It's just, well I'm a man of a certain age, and lovely young lasses like you are dangerous to old men like me. I could have a dicky heart apart from anything else. And also, well, I've apparently been rumbled. By the staff. I don't know how.'

'A do. It wis Stuart Robertson – he wis here.'

Donnelly's face betrayed his shock.

'It's all right, a told him he was a rapist and he fucked off sharpish.'

'What?'

'More to come on that, big man.'

Her smile showed that she was starting to relax and he felt able to move on and indulge in a little more small talk before tentatively beginning to ask more questions:

'So, big Dom just told me that you've been feeling a bit better lately and talking more about what happened that night. Have you started to remember more?'

'Aye, a have, a wee bit.'

'So what's the headlines? What's, you know, up?'

'You know, bits and bobs. A remembered a bit more

aboot the drugs, who a fucked and how.'

She paused, for dramatic effect, then:

'Oh, and a realised … a mean, a don't know but … eh … a didn't kill anybody!'

'What? What? That's marvellous. That's … bloody marvellous. Oh my God.'

'A thought that would make you happy. You know, for your story.'

'Fuck the story, that's just incredible. Avril, that's amazing. Bloody amazing.'

'You know what, old man, you're amazin'. You've made me feel so good aboot masel'. Like somebody actually cares about me. A mean somebody who's no' paid to do so. Thanks, Jim, thanks.'

Donnelly felt his eyes prick and indulged himself with a self-conscious hug with the happy looking young woman sitting next to him.

'So who did? Who did kill 'im?'

'Aah, a'm afraid it's no' that good. A wis passed oot, A've no idea, but as a say, a was passed oot and he was still alive at that point, so …'

'It wisnae you!'

'Aye,' she sighed, 'it wisnae me.'

'Do you feel able to tell me anything else?'

'Aye, but it's no' very nice.'

'Well it can wait, if yir no' up to it?'

He felt bad, aware that he was manipulating her, appearing to not need to know, in order to make her more likely to tell.

But he had deadlines. He had to come up with something soon. Except, he'd decided not to pursue the story after all. Probably.

'Fuck,' he thought. 'Fuck, this is good stuff.'

'It's a' right. The thing is, the thing a remembered is: A said a knew who a fucked but now a know … a *was* fucked. Over and over. Over and fuckin' over.'

Donnelly had rarely seen someone's demeanour change so quickly, from one extreme emotion to another.

'Yeah, a had sex wi' one o' thim, willingly. And another, after a wee bit persuasion. But the methods o' 'persuasion' became a little more forceful. A was pissed and drugged and hardly capable o' stoppin' thim and they just went on and on. One after the other like a wis nothin' but a piece of warm meat tae … tae pummel till they'd come. A tried tae stop thim. A did try tae stop thim. A shouted, and screamed, and twisted, and turned, but eventually, they were holding me down, hand over ma face, hand over ma fuckin' face. Hand over ma …'

Donnelly held her as she cried and cried. Two members of staff tentatively approached but retreated when they could see that Donnelly's contact was coming from a place of care and that Avril was clearly in need of what she was receiving.

'They raped me, Jim. All o' thim. Or most o' thim, at least. They fucked me till a was no longer a person, no longer a daughter, a girl friend, a friend. They took ma humanity and they fucked it. Until what little was left of me, what was left after all the booze, and drugs, and sex, was gone. Until a was gone. And then a passed out. They literally fucked me senseless.'

They'd moved slightly apart but Donnelly still held her

hands in his and looking straight into her eyes he spoke slowly, and carefully:

'A'll nail them, Avril. A'll fuckin' nail them. A'll fucking destroy those heartless, evil bastards. You watch, a'll ...'

'Shh, shh, you're getting' too loud, you're attractin' attention.'

Avril had already given a nod to an approaching member of staff to indicate that everything was ok, but she knew they could stop the meeting at any time if they felt it wasn't conducive to her mental state.

'Aye, a'm sorry. But a will. A will get them.'

He considered for a moment:

'If you want me to. A'd decided, Avril, to drop the story. For your sake. A don't want tae do anything that could cause you pain. A really care about you, ken? A really, really care.'

After a shared silence he began again:

'It's your choice, Avril, A'll leave it alone – A'll still come and see you like, but a'll drop the story. Or if you want; a'll go after them. And a'll get them. It doesn't matter what happened to Paul Bannerman ... well, you know what a mean ... a'm not bothered about that. But for what they did to you, a'll get them, a really will.'

Almost immediately she replied:

'Go on then, Jim, get thim; get thim for me.'

Chapter Twenty-Five

Tam and Agnes were beside themselves with worry. They hadn't seen Davie for thirty-six hours and they'd tried everyone he knew. He'd gone on benders before – plenty of them. But they'd always tracked him down to a pal's house, or a girlfriend's. On contacting Mel, they'd heard about the row – though not the content – and it was a given that drink would be the result of such an emotional stimulus for Davie, the recovering alcoholic.

Mel was finding it hard to negotiate the complex matrix of emotions she was feeling, but for the time-being, at least, anger and disgust were registering more fully than worry or fear.

The Thomsons lived in a modest private house – financed by Davie from his Athletic days – in a tidy wee street where nothing much happened. As a retired couple with not too much going on they had become expert in the subject in which many like them excel: who's coming and who's going in the rest of the street.

They wouldn't have been the only ones, therefore, who had noticed the unfamiliar dark grey Audi which had been spending quite a lot of time in the neighbourhood of late. It had also seemed particularly odd that they'd never quite gotten a clear look at the faces of the occupants, always turned away, or hidden by a newspaper. And they'd mainly come at night. After two or three visits, Tam had plucked up the courage to go and speak to whoever was to be found within the suspicious vehicle. At every attempt, however, they'd gently moved away only to return later on in the evening.

There was no real reason to connect the suspicious car with Davie's disappearance but on one level they had instinctively done so. Alongside the worry about Davie, the Audi had become something of an obsession:

'That's it, next time they're back, a'm phonin' the police. A'm no gonnae go oot 'cause they'll jist skedaddle. A'm jist gonnae phone the police right away.'

Tam's resolve was sure.

'We should phone thim aboot Davie, Tam.'

'No' yet, the police'll no be interested until at least forty-eight hours – we've been through this before. But this way we can raise both things at once.'

'A' right a suppose, but a'm no leavin' this windae.'

*

Donnelly always felt a slight elation when crossing the Forth Road Bridge. A keen student of history, and a supporter of Scottish nationalism, he loved to drive over the Forth and gaze at the real object of his affections: the original rail bridge. Beyond iconic, for Donnelly, it symbolised all that was good about his native land:

'Ingenuity, creativity and hard bloody work; that's what it took,' he thought, 'and if we could rediscover those attributes we really could "be a nation again".'

A loud blast from the horn of an enormous lorry took him out of his daydream and made him realise that he would not live to see an independent Scotland if he did not pay attention to the road.

He had long since come to the conclusion that Davie Thomson could potentially be the key to this story. 'Well, the other key,' he admitted, 'after Avril.' But having been thwarted in his attempts to contact Davie by his parents' declaration of ignorance as to his whereabouts, and with no response from the player's mobile phone (the number of which he had paid good money to learn) he had given up after deciding to drop the story. Now, back on the case, he decided that confronting him at his house was the only tactic left for him to employ. He was on his way, therefore, to Davie's parent's home in Dunfermline: Scotland's ancient capital, aware, unfortunately, that it was no longer a place where a king may be found "drinking the blude red wine".

*

A few hours earlier, however, it would have been hard for Davie to have pinpointed which of the myriad of sensations had won the battle to have first effect on his developing consciousness on that freezing morning.

It could have been the numbness in his extremities as the result of the extreme cold; or the foul smell of cold sick, deposited during the night onto his clothes and the car seat on which he lay. Perhaps it was the excruciating stiffness in his neck when he first adjusted his position in the back seat; or even the heavy throb from a head not unused to hangovers but suffering all the same. Most likely, however, his first sensation was that of the sharp, low winter's light on this bright frosty morning. A white haze rose from the grass and the hedgerows surrounding the car, as it lay, apparently abandoned, in a lonely country lane.

He quickly remembered why he was where he was (random, drunken driving) but had no idea *where* that place actually was.

Fifteen minutes later, having done what he could about the cold, the smell and the various, competing pains, he started the car engine and drove out of the lane, and then, at a guess, left. Two more guesses took him to a street with some nice looking houses and eventually a small parade of shops, one of which incorporated the word: "Auchterarder" in its title.

Although a bit unsure of exactly where that was, he guessed he was no more than half an hour from home and quickly found a road sign which gave him a clue as to which direction to take. So it was that Davie found himself drawing up outside his parent's house just as another vehicle also did so, and just before a third. The grey Audi gave way to allow Davie to park and he responded with a tired, but grateful wave.

'Tam, Tam, phone the police, thair's that car.'

'No don't, there's Davie!'

'Whit is it? Whit's happenin'?'

'A don't know; another car's just arrived. A man's goin' up tae Davie. Oh no!'

'Whit?'

Agnes shrieked:

'It's Davie. And the two men from that car. They've knocked doon the ither man.'

Tam didn't hear the rest as he ran out into the street.

'They've got him.' Agnes screamed. 'Oh my God. Oh God, they've got balaclavas on …'

Tam ran up the street in hopeless pursuit of the car. Almost immediately, however, he tripped over something large and soft in the street and found himself rolling over the pavement before impaling himself on next door's prickly hedge.

His squeal of pain was echoed by that from the "object" over which he had tripped. He shouted out:

'Who the hell are you?'

'Donnelly,' the man replied, 'Jim Donnelly from *The Standard*. What's going on?'

'He's been kidnapped. Ma son's been kidnapped. And as fur you, yir no' welcome, so get the hell oot o' here!'

One man limped to his car whilst the other limped to his house and his waiting wife:

'Phone the police, Agnes, quick!'

'A have done, Tam. Thir oan thir way.'

*

Davie lay, face down in the back seat of the car where he had been put and he felt the weight of one of the men on his back.

'A'm gonnae get aff ye and ye'll sit up nice and normal, right?'

Davie had never known fear like it. He was incapable of doing anything but responding in the affirmative and doing what he was told. He found himself sitting next to a burly, dark-dressed figure with a balaclava on his head. That was the scariest thing: the balaclava. Like a scene from a crime movie, Davie knew it showed they were up to no good. Then again, the fact that they'd bundled him into a car was also an indication of something untoward.

The driver wasn't wearing anything on his head but all

251

Davie could see from the back seat was a crew cut of what would probably have been mousy brown hair and a scar on the left, towards the crown of his head. Davie had almost instinctively noted this, stuck, as he was, in what felt like a scene from some TV drama.

'You fuckin' honk,' the man in the back told him.

'A've been sick.'

'Shut yir fuckin' gob, naebody asked ye.'

Davie was aware that the accents were from the west coast, Glasgow, probably.

The car stopped in a quiet country lane. The man in front put his balaclava on and Davie was told to get out of the car. A shudder went through Davie's body as he imagined what might happen. He lost control of his bowels and the smell of excrement joined the aroma of stale sick.

'Fuckin hell, the cunt's shit 'imsel''

'Occupational hazard, pal,' replied the man in the front.

Davie stumbled out of the car and fell onto the ground. He felt a sharp pain in his ribs and tried his best to obey an order to get into the boot of the car. With a little help, he managed and as Davie curled up inside the pitch black boot the car drove away and the sound of the engine was joined in a duet by the echoing sound of his sobs.

'Thank Christ a can get this balaclava aff. It itches like fuck.'

They must have driven for over an hour before Davie was aware of the car leaving the street and stopping.

When he was dragged out, it was into what appeared to be a fairly large lock-up containing little other than boxes and tools. He struggled to stand and thought he was going to be sick again when faced with two large and imposing figures both once again wearing balaclavas. One appeared overweight though very tall, the other was leaner though equally tall. He was the one who had been in the front.

Davie retched violently but could bring nothing more up.

'Fuck, let's make this quick,' the heavy one said, 'he's getting more disgustin' all the time.'

The thinner man picked up what appeared to be a metal bar and Davie collapsed from fear, just as the man was attempting to hit him in the stomach with the weapon. As a result of Davie's fall, the weapon connected with his forehead rather than his gut and he hit the stone floor with an echoing thud. Out cold.

'Fuckin' fuck,' the man shouted. 'This is a fuckin' disaster. You better wake up, you fuckin' cunt. If you fuckin' die, I'll, I'll … fuck, a don't know what a'll do.'

He paced around for a few moments before telling the larger man to watch over him and that he'd be back in ten minutes.

*

Once more, Davie woke to a combination of foul smells and excruciating pain. He became aware of a pool of blood on the floor next to him and he instinctively put his hand to his forehead to confirm that the blood was from a gash which he found there. In a strange way this realisation actually made him marginally calmer. He'd been hit on the head with a metal bar and survived. How much worse could it get? Unless they were planning to kill him. Once again he struggled to control his bowel and was glad he was already lying down.

'Right, yah cunt, this isnae too complicated. We ask you some questions; you tell us the answers, the truth, like, then you go hame tae yir ma' and da', right?'

'Aye, right,' Davie replied, from a slumped position on the floor of the lock-up, leaning against some boxes.

'Stand him up,' the leaner man ordered. 'A want tae be able tae knock 'im doon.'

The other man roughly pulled Davie to his feet whereupon Davie felt a numb, tingling feeling in his head, presumably as a result of the concussion and once again, he went out cold.

'Aw fur fucks sake! Fuckin' stupid cunt. He cannae fuckin' stay awake long enough fur us tae fuckin' scare 'im shitless. Aye, a ken, he's a'ready shitless.'

The heavy man followed the lead of his boss and allowed himself a very slight smile at what had just been said and at the ridiculousness of the situation.

'Ok, time fur some scran,' the leaner man announced. 'Go tae Greggs and get us some rolls on something, meat, like, some fudge donuts and Irn Bru. Naw, wait thair, no rolls fur me. Git me a steakbake and a sausage roll. Don't be long, a think he'll wake up soon.'

Both had no sooner bitten into their hot pastries when Davie started to moan and wake up, once again to the pain and the terror.

'Christ, noo he's interuptin' oor scran. This guys got nae fuckin' etiquette whitsoevur. And a'm fuckin tired pullin' this balaclava oan, aff and oan again. Fuck sake, jist lie thair you and think aboot things till a've finished ma lunch.'

Davie did a lot of thinking and none of it was very

encouraging. He thought about Paul Bannerman and about that night and for the first time he very clearly connected those events to the hopelessness of his life since, and particularly his drinking. He thought about Mel and relived, once again, the look of horror and of disgust on her face when he had told her about the girl. He didn't deserve her. He didn't deserve anything. He didn't deserve the love and support of his parents. He didn't deserve ... anything.

'Right, git 'im up, slowly this time.'

Davie was able to stand, with a little assistance at first, and then on his own.

'Right, concentrate, cunt and we'll git this done quick. How ... did ... Paul ... Bannerman ... die?'

Davie stared at the mouth of the man, his lips and teeth made ugly by the framing of the balaclava opening. Detritus from the man's meal was on display, both on his teeth and on the wool surrounding his mouth.

'The girl killed him.'

'Naw, that's no a'. Whit happened?'

'Ye ken the story, a'body kens the story. She tried tae rob 'im; he tried tae stop her; she stabbed 'im, end o' story. Aagh!'

A kick in the balls and Davie was slumped again.

'No fuckin' good enough. A'll say when the story's ended.'

Davie sat up.

'Thirs nothin' mair tae say.'

Davie's interrogator had picked up the metal bar again. He pulled it back and violently thrust it towards Davie's stomach, stopping just short, causing Davie to gasp and close his eyes in relief and despair.

'Try again.'

Davie stared blankly at his torturer and, emboldened by hopelessness and self-hate, slowly said it again:

'Thirs … nothin' … mair … tae … say.'

This time the metal bar did not stop and Davie hit the floor again but this time with a faint smile behind his grimace.

'A'm an Athletic fan ye ken. And in a' the games a saw ye play, thir wis nae hint o' bravery, nae evidence o' ony kind o' backbone. What the fuck's this aboot?'

Davie stared at him, defiant.

Wearily, the man began again:

'Ok, a suppose it's gonnae call fur this; over the last few days we've spent a fair bit time ootside yir Ma and Da's hoose. Seem like nice folk, eh? Quietly livin'oot thir days in the nice wee bungalow ye bought thim. Wouldn't it be jist the thing if those quiet wee lives were somehow ruined? Say if yir Mum had tae cope wi' lookin' aftir a husband that wis doolally. If he had an accident like. That'd be terrible, eh?'

'Fuckin' evil beasts. That's aw yis are, fuckin' evil beasts. Is there nothin' ye wouldnae stoop tae?'

'Ooh, that hurts. They say it's sticks an' stones that hurt ye, but it's the name callin' that gits me. Cuts me tae the quick, like. Let's no beat aboot the bush, tell us what we need tae know or there'll be an accident in Dunfermline, this afternoon, got it?'

Davie got it all right and those two random Glaswegian thugs became the first people outside of those who had been present, to hear something approaching the truth, something which, if told in a court of law would exonerate Avril Gallacher and leave a dozen football players facing a very uncertain future.

Chapter Twenty-Six

They looked, from behind, like one of those new "modern" families. A wee boy and his two daddies walking along Dumbarton Road and into the pub. There was no hand-holding though as "Wee" Eck sat down, flanked by two very large and imposing gentlemen, one well-built and the other wiry.

'Ya dancer! That's better thin a could possibly have imagined. Fuckitty fuck, that's good.'

'A think 'e's quite chuffed,' the thinner man smiled at his colleague before draining a pint in two large gulps.

'Tell ye whit, this is goin' in ma book, that's fur sure.'

'Yir book, eh? Are ye writin' a book?'

'Aye, did a no' tell ye, it's aw aboot …'

'He's winding ye up, ya daft cunt. We've heard plenty aboot this famous book. A'll believe it when a see it though.'

'Oh, you'll see it soon, my son, believe me.'

'We'll see. Onyway, that's us straight noo.'

This was the man's calculation of where they all were in the bartering system of favours that Eck employed.

'Yes, boys, all square for the moment. A pleasure doin' business with ye.'

The two large gentlemen left and Eck pondered. 'This is it,' he thought, 'the last story a need fur ma book. It's gonnae happen.' He fancied himself to have a bit of style as a writer – nothing too fancy, but strong, vivid prose, hard hitting and to the point. He'd done an extra-mural class at Glasgow University but left before the end, finding it a little too poncey and pseudo-intellectual. But he'd learned enough to be convinced that he had the necessary talent. How hard could it be, after all? If Jim Traynor and Chick Young could write for a paper ... And with material like this, he was sorted.

He'd already started putting down an account of the Paul Bannerman story for his, long-gestating, exposé of the dark side of Scottish football, when he met with Jo to tell her what he had learned from his two large and aggressive friends:

Jo wasted no time in deciding what she had to do ...

Don't come home bastard Received: 11.34:25 Today from Jo

What? Received: 13.44:57 Today from Stu

What's up? Received: 13.51:27 Today from Stu

Missed call Received: 13.56:12 Today from Stu

Missed call Received: 14.01:17 Today from Stu

Jo whats happening? Received: 14.12:27 Today from Stu

Jo pls tell me whats up Received: 14.33:19 Today from Stu

Don't wanna talk about it. Just stay away Received: 14.42:41 Today from Jo

Going crazy here. Need to know whats wrong Received: 17.10:55 Today from Stu

Please? Received: 17.16:12 Today from Stu

Missed call Received: 17.22:41 Today from Stu

Fucks sake Jo what? Received: 17.29:36 Today from Stu

Bannerman Received: 17.37:02 Today from Jo

What about? Received: 17.38:49 Today from Stu

I know Received: 17.41:11 Today from Jo

By the time of the last text, Stuart was already outside the beautiful West End townhouse he (formerly?) shared with his appalled wife.

His key no longer opened the heavy beechwood door.

Having anticipated the unpleasantness that was about to take place in the street outside the house, Jo had chosen not to be present to hear the banging and pleading which ensued.

*

Davie was facing similar difficulties in establishing communication with his significant other:

'Hi, you're through to Mel's phone and I'm obviously not able to answer. Your call's important to me, however, so please leave a message ...'

'Hi, Mel, it's me. Please answer the phone or phone me back. Please.'

'Hi, you're through to Mel's phone ...'

'Hi, Mel, please pick up the phone ...'

'Hi, you're through to Mel's phone ...'

'Mel, it's me – please phone me back...'

'Hi, you're through to Mel's phone ...'

'Mel, please, a'm sorry, a need tae talk tae ye.'

'Hi, you're through to Mel's phone ...'

'Mel, a know ye hate me. A hate me too. But a need tae talk tae ye. Pick up the phone, please.'

'Hi, you're through to Mel's phone ...'

'Mel, please, a'm in hospital. A've been beaten up. A wis kidnapped. It wis the worst experience o' ma life. Please, a need tae talk tae ye. Pick up the phone, phone me back. Please.'

'Hi, you're through to Mel's phone ...'

'Mel, please, a need ... '

'Hi, Davie.'

'Aw fuck. Thank God, it's you.'

'Aye, it's me. Where are ye?'

'The Queen Margaret.'

'What time's visiting?'

'Seven till eight.'

'I'll be there.'

*

Eck was putting off making a phone call. He had had a half-hearted attempt at a wank at Susanna Reid on breakfast TV, and was now feeling smug in response to the sad antics of that day's pathetic guests of Jeremy Kyle. 'They should listen to him,' he thought, 'Kyle speaks a lot o' fuckin' sense.'

He didn't want to phone James Donnelly but he was starting to feel a little less smug as he looked beyond the mock Louis XV sideboard, his eyes drawn to the red-highlighted bill on top of a pile of other similar envelopes. That they sat in the hands of a half-life sized metal sculpture of a butler didn't actually help at all.

He knew that there would be a long gap between the receipt of his magnum opus by the lucky publishing company of his choice, and its eventual publication. Then there was the small matter of finishing the bloody thing. He didn't want to give away such explosive material to 'another writer', though. Jo had told him about Donnelly's involvement however, and he knew that he would likely be prepared to pay top dollar for such explosive information.

'Nae choice then, Ecky boy,' he thought, 'nae fuckin' choice.'

*

'A feel a've reached a kind of watershed, Norm. Ye ken, like an important moment in my journalistic career, my ethical, what is it they say, "journey"?'

'Yir "ethical journey"? Are you havin' a laugh? Please, tell me yir kiddin'.

Donnelly actually felt the slight specks of beer as they landed on his face from the spluttering mouth of his old colleague. Norman Campbell was not disguising his broad smile either.

Campbell was already aware that something was skew whiff when Donnelly had offered to buy him lunch because he "had something he wanted to talk over". Well, truth be told, he hadn't actually volunteered to pay but Campbell had prised the offer out of him. And now, sitting comfortably in a quiet cranny in the nearby Bannerman's bar, Donnelly was spouting New Age crap at him over their matching burgers and "fries".

Donnelly had started the conversation true to form right enough. Firstly about the venue:

'Why'd'ye want to come here, its full o' fuckin' students?'

Then the beer:

'You promised me the Deuchars IPA and it's off. Fuckin' typical.'

Then lastly, the food:

'I'm having chips wi' ma burger, no' "fries". What does that even mean, eh, "Fries"? Fried what?'

'Potatoes, Jim.'

'Oh aye, but what's wrong wi' "chips"?

'You seem a bit tense, Jim, what's the matter?'

This had been Campbell's question before Donnelly had gone off on his "ethical journey" soliloquy.

'Fuck off. Ye ken what a mean. I can't think of another way tae put it.'

Campbell had reduced his full smile to a subdued smirk before replying:

'Go on then, Jim, what's it all aboot?'

'This story o' mine, about the footballers.'

'I thought ...'

'I know, I thought I'd dropped it as well. You're about two changes of mind behind. I've never changed my mind so often since I had to decide between ma honeymoon and a Hearts European away tie. And before you ask, it was obvious in the end: honeymoon in Düsseldorf. Took a bit of persuading, but.'

'So back to the point.'

'Aye, well I spoke to Avril, and I know she didnae do it. And she wants me to find out what really happened. And now, I've been offered certain information. By that I mean, *the* information.'

'How come? Who from?'

'Aye, well, there's the rub. The "who" is easy. Eck McDougal. He's a sleazy wee Weegie who digs up info about footballers and the like. The "how" is more complicated: basically, he got Davie Thomson abducted and beaten tae a pulp by some bad bastards. Boy's still in the hospital. And now he's offering to sell me the info they got from their "conversation" wi' the poor lad.'

'And the problem is?'

Donnelly picked up the inference in his old friend's tone:

'A ken. A source is a source. And it's no' gonnae matter to Davie Thomson now, but, well, a'm just feelin' … different about things at the moment.'

'How different?'

'A don't know. It's just. It's just, a've been feeling quite good about maself recently. I think I'm helping Avril. And my family, my kids, they're, well … they're sort of proud of me. And a like that feeling.'

'Hah!'

'What d'ye mean: "hah".'

'I'm just thinking that that's one of the many good reasons why I've not got a family. Kids make ye sentimental.'

'Fuck, Norm, a should've known you were the wrong person tae ask. I should've asked Steph.'

'Yeah, but it's obvious why ye didnae. You knew fine well that I wis exactly the *right* person to ask. Ye asked me because you wanted the answer that ye knew I'd give ye'. Ye wanted me tae tell you to stop being so fuckin' soft and get the information ye need. Apart from anything else, yir doing it for the girl, eh? For that poor wee lassie in the mental hospital. Ye asked me 'cause ye knew a'd give you the right answer.'

Donnelly wiped tomato relish from both chin and cheek before replying, through a mouthful of burger and bun:

'Aye, I know, yir right. On every count. And ye've told me exactly what a needed to hear. Thanks, Norm. A knew I could count on ye.'

*

'So, what's the damage then?'

Mel was cool and serious but genuinely concerned.

'Eh, three broken ribs; dislocated shoulder; extensive bruising.'

Davie paused, then:

'Broken heart; terminal self-hatred and missin' will-tae-live.'

The merest hint of a fraction of a smile briefly flitted over Mel's face and lifted Davie's spirits momentarily.

Mel took notice of the three visitors at the bed next door to Davie's and lowered her voice in the hope of him following suit:

'What happened then?'

He told the story and watched her face show signs of

worry, pity, compassion, disgust, and, maybe, just maybe, love.

'A cannae tell ye how bad it wis, Mel. And, and, it wis a' a deserved. It's ma punishment ... some o' ma punishment, for what a did. A know how bad it wis now. You've shown me. An' a'm no' that man noo. A'm better than that. No' great, bit better than that.'

She still looked stony-faced.

'And a'm jist so grateful thit yir here and that a've got somebody tae tell. It wis ... it wis ... oh Mel ...'

As he sobbed, she held his hand. She couldn't quite bring herself to hold the whole of him but she already knew that she probably would, eventually. This was not a bad man in front of her. This was, in fact, a very good man, if one on a journey. She'd always said she wouldn't be with someone who she would have to make into a decent person. But she could see that he'd done most of the heavy work already. All that was really required was a few decorative touches.

*

In the Donnelly-Davidson household, Jacqui found herself in the midst of a regular and unruly struggle; a fight, indeed, for the possession of the TV remote control with her husband, James Donnelly. She won the fight too, but only after employing a combination of tickling and trickery. After Donnelly's entreaties, however, she agreed to leave the TV turned off to let him tell her what was on his mind.

'I'm going ahead wi' ma story, Jacqui, and before ye say anything, I've got a very good reason.'

Jacqui swallowed her criticism and simply asked:

'What?'

'Well, for one, I know what really happened that night
…'

'Uh uh?'

'I can't tell ye about that the now … well, I don't really
want to … just now … I found out by … well … you'll find
out. I'm just uncomfortable.'

'Well, if even you're uncomfortable, I think you can
guarantee that it's wrong.'

'No, Jacqui, this is more important. I've realised
something: this story o' mine, it's not about murder. I mean:
it is partly, but that's no' the story I want tae tell. It's not Paul
Bannerman's story I'm really interested in, poor bastard,
it's Avril Gallacher's. It's not about murder … it's about …
rape.'

An almost imperceptible smile played over Jacqui's lips
as she listened to her husband speak. He seemed different.
Like he'd been changed by this story. And by the girl.

'It's about men. And the way they treat women. It's about
attitudes, and arrogance, and … and … misogyny … and
violence.'

'I got a call the other day, from one of the players who
was there that night. He wouldn't leave his name but I'm
pretty sure I know who it was. It was Big Jim Forrester, now
working as a bouncer at a strip club. He sees it up close
there, the way that men treat lassies. A man like that, hard
as fuck, but he sees what's going on. I could tell from two
minutes of conversation, he's kind've ashamed tae be a man.
And so am I.'

Jacqui noticed a change come over Donnelly's face as

a look of righteous zeal, and enjoyment of his own oratory gave way to a more pained expression. He almost exhaled the words;

'I'm sorry, Jacqui.'

She raised her eyebrows.

'About Steph, the lassie at ma work. Nothin' happened but I did kind've betray you, in ma mind at least. And … and one kiss. I'm sorry.'

Jacqui held the head of her errant spouse into her chest before replying:

'I know, Jim. I know you are. And I forgive you. But don't place yourself alongside those other men. You may be a weak old bastard, and a bit Neanderthal in your attitudes at times, but you're not like that. And you know what's right and what's wrong. Like most men, you know where the line is.'

'But there's too many on the other side of that line, Jacqui.'

'That's true, Jim, but it's them that should be feeling ashamed, not the likes of you.'

They hugged silently for a few moments before Jacqui spoke again.

'Well ok, you could do with feeling a wee bit ashamed sometimes.'

Chapter Twenty-Seven

Stuart Robertson was well used to putting on his best face for media appearances. He could flash that cheeky smile and turn on that legendary charm whenever it was required. Disinclined to go into football management, he was well aware that charisma and a way with words were going to earn him a good living in years to come, just as skills with a football had done in those gone by.

He was grateful, however, that tonight's interview was on the radio, making it a little easier to cope with, considering that he was not only emotionally vulnerable but was, technically, homeless.

However, the programme had been billed as an "in-depth interview with one of Scotland's favourite sports stars" and was to involve a phone-in section for the public to ask questions. The interviewer, he knew, was none too incisive, but who knew what the fans might come up with? Although, the calls would be screened, it was nonetheless, harder to control these kinds of things. He was also painfully aware that he had already agreed to answer questions about Paul Bannerman and, given what he had just discovered, that worried him very much.

He was a professional though, and that famous smile was displayed, in succession, to the doorman at Pacific Quay (BBC Scotland HQ), the researcher who was charged with looking after him; and lastly, to Bob Manning, his genial host.

*

Jim Donnelly settled himself down in the upstairs study which doubled as a garden shed/den for this most manly of men, for which read: "most adolescent". As well as his computer and a TV, he had an easy chair and a kettle (with a secret stock of choccy biccies and of whisky for when required). It was the whisky that was needed tonight as he prepared to listen to Stuart Robertson being given an easy time by that "wet haddock", Bob Manning. Donnelly was armed and dangerous, however, he had a telephone at the ready.

*

'Welcome to Radio Scotland's "People in Profile". My guest tonight is one of Scotland's favourite sport's stars; a man known as much for his cheeky chat as his silky football; a man once described by Sir Alex Ferguson as "a good footballer and an equally good bloke". Of course I'm talking about Stuart Robertson. How ye doing, Stuart?'

'No' bad, Bob. No' bad at all.'

'We'll be touching on many things tonight as I try to get to the bottom of what makes StuRob tick. I'll be asking about your lovely wife, Jo and, of course, the impact that the tragic death of Paul Bannerman had on your life, but let's start at the beginning: when did you first kick a ball, Stuart? And when did you first realise that you were blooming good at it?'

*

Having enjoyed a kiss on the cheek from Mel before she left, Davie felt much better until he realised that it was time to listen to Stuart Robertson on the radio. He didn't really want to but knew he couldn't help himself. He lay back on his hospital bed, slipped in his earphones, closed his eyes and prepared to learn more than he needed to about the motivation behind the great StuRob.

*

Donnelly had already sworn at the radio on roughly five occasions by the time Jacqui came to ask him what the problem was. He managed to fob her off and poured himself another dram as he prepared himself for the phone-in portion of the StuRob spectacular.

*

Jo settled back into her elegant, Scandinavian style, faux-leather sofa and drained the first glass from a full bottle of red before bracing herself to endure her husband's faux-sincere charm. It had occurred to her by now, however, that perhaps she couldn't entirely trust the sleazy McDougal and she was listening for clues to her husband's state of mind. She listened with teary eyes through his declarations of love for his 'wonderful wife, beautiful both on the outside and the inside'. And she listened with a steely concentration as he talked about Paul Bannerman, 'team-mate and very good friend'.

'If he's bullshitting then he's doing a very, very good job of it,' she thought and then smiled at her own naivety:

'If bullshitting was a sport,' she mused, 'he'd have won more caps than he did for football.'

*

'So, listeners, I've delved as far as I can on your behalf and now the time has come for you to take over. We already

271

have some calls stacked up but there's still plenty of time to call. You know the number, so pick up that phone and you could have the chance to ask your question directly to the man himself. So, our first caller, Graham in Perth. What do you want to know?'

'Oh, hi, Stu, a know yir intae music; can ye tell us who yir favourite bands are?'

'Hi, Graham, how ye doin'? Well, a love a bit of R'n'B and rap, 'specially Beyonce and Jay Z but a suppose my all time favourites are Coldplay - best rock band ever.'

*

'Aye, if ye discount at least fifty great bands from the sixties and seventies, like.' Donnelly spluttered at the radio.

*

'Here's Kieran with a question about your Scotland career, Stuart.'

A young voice came on the line:

'Hi, Stu, it's amazin' tae be talkin' tae ye.'

'Nae probs, wee man, shoot!'

'Aye thanks, eh, ye only won thirty-four caps. D'ye no' think that someone o' your talent should have had more?'

'Well a'm no' finished yet but that's not for me tae say, pal. A jist play ma best and hope tae dae the people of Scotland proud when a get the chance. It's true, though, that others have said a should've played more often. It wis Denis Law that said we'd've qualified for the world cup in 2006 if I'd had more game time. No' for me tae say though.'

272

'Well, don't then, ya egotistical bastard,' Davie replied.

'Are you alright, Mr Thomson,' a young nurse enquired of Davie thus making him aware that whilst listening on headphones, he had been talking out loud to the amusement of the whole ward for the last five minutes.

*

Donnelly could take no more, and fortified by three whiskies, he decided it was time for Raymond from Edinburgh to make a call to Radio Scotland.

*

'Here's Danny from Motherwell with a question about the many great players you've played with.

'Eh, hi, Stu, a jist wanted tae ken who wis the best player yiv played wi' in yir career?'

'Well, that's a tough one, Danny, a've played with so many greats but a'd have tae say that one player stands out and that is the wonderful Jonas Steenberg, what a talent, eh?'

'Aye, he wis amazin', thanks, Stu.'

'Nae probs, pal.'

*

Jo had almost emptied the bottle of wine by her side and was beginning to wonder if she'd made a mistake. He was a smarmy bastard right enough, but not someone who could have been involved in something like this. Surely? How could she have been so stupid? You get to know somebody over the years and you'd know if you were living with a monster. You'd just know.

*

'Next up is Donald from Glasgow. He wants to ask about some of your great Champion's League matches.'

'Go ahead, Don, happy to answer your question.'

'A bet yir no' ya cunt. A jist called tae say that yir a useless Athletic basta ...'

'Moving swiftly on, the next call is from Raymond, from Edinburgh. He wants to ask you about that great Scottish Cup final of 2003.'

'Oh no, first a Rovers supporter and now ... you're not a Jambo are ye, Raymondo?'

'Aye, a'm a Jambo, Stu, but a still think you're a great guy.'

'Well that's a relief, what did you want tae say, Ray?'

'Heart's outplayed yis on that day but ye's still won. Hand on heart, d'ye no' think yir goal wis offside?'

'Well, Ray, I'd have tae disagree with the first part of what ye said but a suppose we all look at things from our own perspective, eh? As regards the goal, a suppose the simplest answer, in the words of the great King Kenny would be: "Mibbaes, aye, mibbaes, naw". It wis close, I'll gie ye that. Over the course o' ma career a must've had hundreds o' off-sides given against me that were wrong and the same the other way. They even themselves out, ye know?'

'Thanks, Stu, a'll take that as a "yes" then!' Could a maybe ask one more quick question, Bob?'

'Aye, seeing as how ye've made us all laugh, go ahead, Ray.'

'Thanks, Bob. It's jist ye were talking about Paul Bannerman earlier on and a just wondered, d'you ever feel guilty about his death?'

Unseen figures wearing headphones who had just settled down after the call from the Rovers supporter suddenly started to pay close attention to the on-air conversation. Whispered exchanges took place and hurried strategies were agreed. No need to panic was the general opinion and Stuart Robertson eased their stress a little further with his reply.

'Of course a do, Ray. There isn't a day that goes by when a don't wonder if there was anything I, or any of us, could have done. If a'd had a few less drinks or if a'd decided to stay the night rather than going home to my lovely wife then maybe … just maybe Paul would still be alive. Yes, Ray, a do feel guilty but a know, deep down, that it was wasn't my fault, it was just bad luck that none of us were able to help stop those tragic events.'

'Yeah, but that's not quite what I meant, Stu. What a really meant was: do you feel guilty about the poor girl who has been held in Strathgyte for the last ten years when her only crime was to go back to a flat with the wrong group of footballers? The poor girl who was wrongly accused, and wrongly convicted, of Paul Bannerman's murder. Do you feel guilty about that, Stu?'

'Hold on, Ray, that's completely out of order,' Bob Manning quickly attempted to re-establish some control over the situation. 'We're going to have to move onto our next …'

'No, let's hear him, Bob. Let's hear what he's got tae say.'

The unseen figures, poised to cut the caller off, stiffened, and remained poised. Heartbeats raced as technicians, producers and managers realised that with Robertson's permission, the programme was moving in a very interesting direction. One which could generate acres of news coverage.

Around the country, radio volumes were turned up, conversations suspended and the breaths of Jo Robertson, Davie Thomson and many thousands of others, were held.

Simultaneously, police switchboards began to light up with callers advising them to turn on their radios to hear what was being discussed on Radio Scotland.

'Your name's no' Ray, is it pal? A recognise your voice. You're that journalist, eh? Donnelly, isn't it? We've already spoken about this. What's goin' on? What do you think you know?'

As Donnelly spoke upstairs, he was unaware that his wife was listening in his living room downstairs. Having heard so much from him about Stuart Robertson over the last few weeks, she was keen to judge the man for herself. Donnelly's daughters, Katy and Fiona had both also gravitated to the living room and had become aware of the broadcast when they'd heard their father's name being mentioned.

'Aye, you're right, Stuart, Jim Donnelly here, *Daily Standard*. I've spoken to the poor wee lassie, Avril Gallacher, on a number of occasions recently, as well as half of your team at the time. And yourself, of course. And I've built up a very different picture of what happened that night.'

*

Avril Gallacher had started listening to the broadcast by this time, against her own better judgement, thirty miles south-east of Pacific Quay, at the State Hospital in Strathgyte. Avril was hanging on every word and had barely stifled a cheer at the name and voice of her friend: James Donnelly.

*

'Go on then, what do you think happened then, Jim.' Robertson was banking on Donnelly fighting shy of coming right out with what he had discovered. He wasn't sure about the law on slander but felt that the journalist wouldn't want to take the risk.

He was right.

Donnelly was going to have to box clever:

'You and I both know how he died, Stuart. And we both know that Avril was unconscious when it happened.'

'You don't know anything, Donnelly. Just the ramblings o' a mental patient who wants tae get out of prison. You should be ashamed o' yourself for coming on here and sullying the memory of Paul Bannerman with your unsubstantiated nonsense. A court of law found that girl guilty and that's the last word on the subject.'

'Stuart, Stuart, have ye' no' had enough o' all the lies. Would you not like to honour his memory with the truth? And as for the girl, shame on you. She did believe it you know? Until recently she believed that she'd done what you said she'd done. She's lived for ten years with the belief that she murdered someone and deserved all that's come of it. But now she knows. And I've got other evidence, sworn statements from three members of that team, including Davie Thomson. They were there and they've told me the truth. Now it's your turn. Come on, Stuart, do the right thing.'

'Oh fuck,' Davie said, out loud. 'A didnae … a didnae … a … but,' he thought, 'a should've done, and for aw Stu knows, a could've done.' He began to cry.

By now, more phone calls had been made and Tam and Agnes Thomson were sitting staring at their radio like families of old in pre-television days. Mel had also been alerted and had accessed the radio function on her phone. Most of Donnelly's colleagues, too, had tuned in, including a very admiring Steph.

*

'Bullshit!' Stuart replied, and in response to a frantic look from the genial Bob, quickly added, 'sorry about that, but the listeners will understand the strength of my feeling.'

'Up to you, Stuart, but I'll be going straight to a police station after this conversation to present them with my evidence. Best to come clean, eh? Go on, do the right thing.'

Across the country, televisions were being switched off and old trannies rediscovered. Some remembered that they could access radio programmes through their freeview systems and others, in desperation, had left their houses and entered their cars to make sure they could hear a radio.

As Donnelly had been speaking, Stuart had been aware of a series of vibrations coming from his trouser pocket and he'd scanned the many calls that had been coming in. Only one was of interest to him.

Please, Stuart. Please. Tell the truth, whatever it is
Received: 20.17:12 Today from Jo

'A don't believe you, Donnelly. They would never. They

know what happened. They know the girl did it. They know …'

Silence is usually the mortal enemy of the radio station. If a broadcast goes silent it doesn't exist. It dies. And Bob Manning was not the sort of broadcaster to let that happen. Normally. Even he, on this occasion, realised the value of letting Stuart's last comment hang in the air. On the airwaves.

Stu was, once more, scanning emails. He ignored all but one:

'Go on, Stu, it's time to do it' Received: 20.19.26 Today from Davie T

The silence was becoming unbearable and Bob Manning began to fear that his audience would believe they had been cut off.

'Well, Stuart, anything else to say?'

It was not the voice of a cheeky chappy who replied,

'We didnae mean it.'

*

Davie Thomson had two distinct reactions: shock and relief.

*

That relief was shared with Stuart. He knew that it was time. Time to take the massive weight of guilt of his shoulders and replace it with responsibility.

He continued, quietly, slowly and carefully.

'The lassie wis stoned. So were most of us. We had sex wi' her.'

Donnelly was getting bolder:

'Sorry; "you had sex with her". All of you? All of you had sex with the same incapacitated girl?'

'A think all of us. Most o' us anyway. She ... well, she ... passed out and we thought. Well, we thought she might no' recover. From whatever drugs she'd been taking.'

'You're saying you gang-raped a girl and thought you'd killed her?'

'No! No! It wisnae rape! She wis up fur it. It wis the drugs. We thought she'd OD'd.'

'For God's sake, Stuart, one man has sex wi' an incapacitated lassie and it might just be arguable whether she was able to consent. But then another. And another. And another? Did each man secure her consent? And then she became unconscious. Was it while someone was having sex with her? Did he then stop? Did, God forbid, anyone have sex with her after?'

*

Across the country, parents had covered the ears of young children or sent them out of the room. Frantic messages were being sent to the radio station headquarters from the police authorities telling them that this was now police territory and that the trial by radio phone-in now had to stop. At each level this message was held onto just a little longer than it should have been. No-one at the station wanted the broadcast to end before the confession was complete.

*

Jacqui Davidson had never been more proud of her

husband. 'How,' she mused, 'had this unreconstructed dinosaur turned into such a fighter for women's rights?'

*

'A don't know. A don't know.'

'And when was your turn, Stuart? Were you first, near the start, at the end?'

The question remained unanswered.

'So, go on, Stuart, how did he die? How did your good pal die?'

'We, we talked aboot it. Remember we were all drunk, or stoned. And we thought that mibbae folk would think we'd done something wrong and … and we decided no' tae phone the police.'

'Or an ambulance? For the girl that you thought might be about to die?'

Pause.

'Aye.'

'And what if she woke up?'

'We'd just say she was lying. She'd wanted tae have sex wi' us and that she had just overdosed.'

'And Paul Bannerman?'

'He wisnae stoned. And he was saying that we'd done it tae her. We'd … put her in that state. He wanted tae phone the police right away. He wanted us tae come clean. Our careers, our lives would have been up in smoke. All because o' one … one …'

'Stupid wee hoor? Is that what you were gonnae say, eh?'

'No, a wouldnae say that.'

The person who had taken the call from the police had hesitated as long as possible. So had their manager. The show's producer had also waited a few minutes before passing on the message to Bob Manning that he had to wind the show up, right now. Manning knew that they could just take him off the air whenever they wanted to but he tried to signal that he was winding things up – just a few more minutes.

'Go on,' said Donnelly, 'finish the story off. Put us, and yourself, out of our misery.'

'There was a fight. Paul had the phone. Folk were grabbin' 'im. A don't know where the knife came from … We just all knew that we were fighting for our lives. We couldn't let it happen. It was just people having sex but folk would twist it. Like you did. "Gang rape" you said. We couldnae let that happen. And remember we were off our heads. So, there was a fight and … and … Paul got stabbed. So we ... we just cleaned the knife and put it in Avril's hand. A mean, we thought she was probably gonnae die anyway. Better it seemed like her than ... Then we did phone the police but we knew he was dead. And the rest, well, the rest you know.'

Bob Manning took the opportunity to say,

'Well, folks, not what we expected when we started the programme but it's time now to wrap things up …'

'Wait, wait, wait, just one last question: "Paul got stabbed" you say. But actually, *someone* stabbed him. Who did it, Stuart?'

Breaths were held across the country, both amongst those who knew the truth and those who didn't. All, however, were desperate to know what Stuart Robertson would say.

He took a breath. "Time to do the right thing," he thought. "Time to be the man I should be". In a quiet but clear voice he replied,

'A did.'

Chapter Twenty-Eight

As the police arrived at Pacific Quay, Jo was at home packing clothes for her husband. Somehow, despite his actions, and her disgust, she still felt a duty of care for the man with whom she had shared her life for the last eleven years. When the phone call from the police came, she was ready for it and was soon on her way to the station where he would be held until a brief appearance in court the next day.

*

Donnelly was emotionally drained and slowly made his way downstairs to rejoin his family. At some point on the way down, however, the stair in the modest, semi-detached Gilmerton home became a grand marble staircase and the tiny hall became an impressive classical vestibule. Or at least that's what it felt like to him as he found himself feted by his family in a way he had never known before. Usually the butt of family jokes, or the target of teenage frustration and anger, it was obvious that all now agreed that he had done something very, very good.

Although he was touched at this surprising turn of events, there was one part of him just a tiny bit irked. The prevailing feeling from his family seemed to be that he had 'come good' whereas he felt that this was just him doing what he always did, searching for the truth. Only this time, the truth happened to coincide with what they thought of as "good". 'Well,' he conceded to himself, 'what we all think of as "good".'

Donnelly felt his children were a little young to have a fully considered understanding of morality in the world. He knew, however, that Jacqui had a more discerning opinion about the variability of "truth" and its relationship at any given time to the concept of "doing good".'

*

Nursing staff who had known Avril Gallacher for many years were grateful to receive warm hugs from the young woman who may well have, understandably, held a grudge against them for not doubting the established version of the "truth" which they had been given and, unthinkingly, believed.

*

Sitting at home, having turned off his radio, Dr Davies was already giving thought to her situation. She clearly did not belong in a hospital prison, being guilty of no crime. Coupled with her improving mental health of recent weeks, a case could certainly be made that she might soon not belong in an institution of any kind. These things had to be handled slowly and carefully, of course, but he was minded to start the process that would lead to her eventual emancipation.

*

'I'm sorry, Stuart,' Jo said to her husband in the short time they were given together at the police station.

'Why, Jo? Why are you sorry? I'm the piece of shit that should be sorry, that *is* sorry.'

'I'm just sorry for you. Whatever you've done, I know you're not all bad. You're capable of good, in lots of ways. I know that. But …'

She found it hard to believe she was looking at her own husband in these harsh and judgemental surroundings. Surrounded by hard and unforgiving metal and stone.

'Does that mean …'

'No, No, Stuart, it doesn't. It doesn't mean I'll stay with you. You know I'm well aware about the girls. All the girls you've fucked over the years. And I let it all go. Why? Because, I always felt that there were two sides to the equation. And there were enough positives on one side to balance out the negatives on the other. But I know now that I shouldn't have put up with it. No-one should. And now the balance is on the other side. And it's just not worth it. If I thought you could change … but really, deep down, I just don't know if you can.'

'A can. Really. A have. What happened, it was … complicated. It wasn't just me. But a've … a've accepted responsibility. You know? A was the leader, not just on that night, but generally. They looked up to me. And now a've … taken responsibility. Taken the rap. Maybe a can save them from …'

'But you did it, Stuart, you killed him.'

'It's no' that simple.'

'You either stabbed him or you didn't, Stuart?'

'A … well a …'

'Listen, I know you're sorry about what happened to Banns. But more than that, it's what you did to the girl. I don't believe you can really admit to yourself what you did. Maybe you will. I'll support you though. After all those years. And all we've shared. I don't think you deserve to be abandoned. But … not as your wife.'

By the time Mel had reached the hospital the next morning, Davie was already sitting by the side of his bed, dressed, packed, and ready to go. But, despite this, there was a cold, empty look in the eyes of the man that she was about to deliver home to his parents.

They sat, her hand on his, for a few moments before she felt it appropriate to talk.

'I suppose you'll have to expect a visit before too long. You'll have to go home and get some stuff ready.'

'A'm no' waiting for thim. A'll go get my stuff and go straight tae the polis.'

She craned her head to try to make contact with those blank eyes:

'I love you, Davie, and it's too late for me to unlove you. What I'm trying to say is that I'm with you now and I'm gonnae support you, I'm gonnae keep on loving you. Christ, that's some crap old song, isn't it, "Keep on Loving You"? Whatever. I will, you know. I will.'

'No! You won't. A cannae let you do that. A don't deserve it.'

'Tough, pal, ye've no choice; I decide who I love, and who I support. So you'll just have tae put up wi' it.'

There was little more conversation on the ten minute drive from the Queen Margaret Hospital to Agnes and Tam's home in Dunfermline. Davie accepted the unconditional love, physically expressed, by his long-suffering parents but he gave little back.

'Do you think I'll be able to tae get a phone call? To

Stuart Robertson in the jail?' he asked no-one in particular.

'I think you'll have to phone the jail and ask if he wants tae phone you and then wait for that,' replied Tam, who, unfortunately had some experience of this due to his other son's current habitation situation.

They heard Davie go on the phone as he went to his room to pack a bag then they waited, and waited, for him to reappear. Two attempts, one by Mel and one by his Mum, failed to get him to emerge from his room.

'A'm no movin' till a've spoken tae 'im.'

'But why, Davie?'

'A cannae tell ye. A'll tell ye later.'

The three shared some very uncomfortable conversation until Mel resolved to try one more time before leaving. As she made her way along the hall to his room she heard his phone ring and could not resist listening at his door to hear what she could of the conversation.

Unfortunately, Davie's emotional state led to him mumbling more and talking even more quietly than usual. She could only make out tiny snippets:

'… it's no fair … you cannae … a will … aye, a will …'

A look of resolve had replaced that of blankness in Davie's eyes when he finally emerged from his bedroom with his bag and moved to hug his Mum and Dad before heading towards Mel's car.

'Sorry, Mum, Dad,' was all he said before they drove off.

'Thirs somethin' a need tae tell ye, Mel,' he said as his parents offered one last wave to their departing son. 'Before we get tae the station.'

It was dull and grey, with a slight frosty mist as they walked, hand in hand from the car to the double doors of the police station in Glasgow. Davie had chosen not to go to the local station feeling the need to go back to the scene of the crime.

After a few formalities, Davie hugged his girlfriend gratefully, before moving through to an interview room. He whispered to her: 'Don't love me.'

Once again, she told him: 'Too late, pal, too late.'

'A'm no' worth it.'

'Yeah, you are. People can change. You're not that man anymore. People can change. And you have. You're a better man. And you know what you did wrong.'

Davie sat opposite a kindly-looking, ruddy faced, middle-aged man in a sergeant's uniform and began to talk:

'This is whit ye need tae know: Stuart Robertson wis, as always, the man runnin' the show the night Paul Bannerman died. He wis the man wi' the plan.'

He hesitated, took a deep breath, and continued:

'But he wisnae the man wi' the knife. That wis me. A'd like tae gie masel' up fur the murder o' Paul Bannerman. A killed 'im.'

Some other books from Ringwood Publishing

All titles are available from the Ringwood website (including
first edition signed copies) and from usual outlets.
Also available in Kindle, Kobo and Nook.
www.ringwoodpublishing.com

Ringwood Publishing, 7 Kirklee Quadrant, Glasgow, G12 0TS
mail@ringwoodpublishing.com
0141 357-6872

The Herbal Detective

Charles Gray

Strange things have started to happen in
the small town of Holy Cross. Black cats,
sneaking suspicions and wine-powered
ecstasy lay their grip on the clueless inhabitants and local news strongly suspects
witches are behind it all.

Meanwhile, poor Rosie McLeod is simply
trying to deal with day to day catastrophes
including lapsang souchong tea, carpet
slippers and the impending doom of old
age. With the innocent brewing of some
herbs the frontiers between innocence and
guilt, logic and magic, start to shift and events come thick and fast.

ISBN: 978-1-901514-26-1   £9.99

Scotball
Stephen O'Donnell

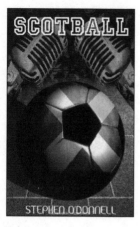

Peter Fitzpatrick returns home to Kirkintilloch with his Czech wife after five years in Prague. Resuming his previous career in banking and financial service, he feels unfulfilled. His application to host a television programme discussing the hot topics relating to Scottish football eventually finds favour. 'The Scottish Football Debate', or 'Scotball' is born.

Scotball is a searing examination of the current state of Scottish football and the various social, political and economic forces that combine to strangle its integrity and potential.

ISBN: 978-1-901514-13-1   £9.99

Paradise Road
Stephen O'Donnell

Paradise Road is the story of Kevin McGarry, who through a combination of injury and disillusionment is forced to abandon any thoughts of playing football professionally. Instead he settles for following his favourite team, Glasgow Celtic, whilst trying to eke out a living as a joiner. It considers the role of young working-class men in our post-industrial society.

ISBN: 978-1-901514-07-0   £9.99

Cold Roses

Gordon Johnston

There is a monster walking the streets of Glasgow.

DI Adam Ralston is no stranger to the dark side of human nature, but when a young art gallery worker is discovered, brutally raped, her throat slit, and a single red rose laid upon her corpse, he is thrown into a bloody maelstrom of violence and suspicion unlike anything he has known before.

Ralston must also battle his own personal demons and hold his family together as tries to track down the killer - a killer who leaves no clues, who grows bolder and who seems to be able to strike at will.

ISBN: 978-1-901514-23-0   £9.99

Cold Shot
Steve Christie

Cold Shot is the second in a Scottish detective series, following the career of Detective Inspector Ronnie
Buchanan as he uncovers the secrets and stories behind gruesome homicides in Scotland. This book, set in and around present day Aberdeen, is a fast paced roar through a twisting and dramatic serial murder plot that constantly challenges the reader's perception of hero and villain.

ISBN: 978-1-901514-24-7   £9.99

The Italian Connection

John Keeman

"My last memory was of walking down a sandy road in an Italian village along with three other soldiers..." In George Giles' mind, he is a twenty-seven year old soldier preparing to return home after Germany's surrender during World War II. But his body tells a different story; he is the serial killer Peter Hunter, who until recently was detained at Broadamoor for the criminally insane. Unlike Hunter, George has never killed, nor does he know of the 21st Century.

Faced with a London much changed from his memories, George seeks answers from the past and tries to uncover how he is connected to Hunter.

ISBN: 978-1-901514-20-9   £9.99

A Subtle Sadness

Sandy Jamieson

A Subtle Sadness follows the life of Frank Hunter and is an exploration of Scottish Identity and the impact on it of politics, football, religion, sex and alcohol.

It covers a century of Scottish social, cultural and political highlights culminating in Glasgow's emergence in 1990 as European City of Culture.

It is not a political polemic but it puts the current social, cultural and political debates in a recent historical context.

ISBN: 978-1-901514-04-9   £9.99

Yellow Submarine

Sandy Jamieson

Yellow Submarine explains how a small football club from a town of just 50,000 inhabitants became a major force not just in Spain but in Europe.

The success of Villarreal offers supporters a model of how they too might live the dream, without having to rely on billionaire benefactors.

ISBN: 978-1-901514-02-5   £11.99

Celtic Submari

Sandy Jamieson

An invasion of Villareal by 10,000 Celtic supporters in 2004 created a set of circumstances that has led to a lasting friendship between supporters of Villarreal and Celtic. This friendship is unique in football and offers the wider football world a model of camaraderie and togetherness that shows how football can be a force for good.

ISBN: 978-1-901514-03-2   £9.99